AWAKEN

MONARCH RISING: BOOK ONE

SYLVANA CANDELA

~ With Love and Light ~

from

Sylvana Candela

MONARCH RISING
BOOK ONE

AWAKEN

GREED IS THE ROOT OF ALL EVIL

SYLVANA CANDELA

This is a work of fiction.

ISBN (softcover): 978-1-7376706-0-5
ISBN (ebook): 978-1-7376706-1-2

Cover design by Sweet 15 Designs
Interior design by Wendy C. Garfinkle
Edited by Leanne Sype

www.sylvanacandela.com
www.peacefulworldpublishing.com

PEACEFUL WORLD PUBLISHING
SHERWOOD, OREGON

This book is lovingly dedicated to all children throughout the world. May you always find love and light in whatever lies ahead, and the courage, strength and wisdom to make this world a better place, for the future generations to come.

Table of Contents

Prologue

Who is this Beast?
His father is Lust; his mother is Fear,
His insatiable desire is for Power.
He stalks the lonely; smells their sorrow,
Lurks in shadows, devouring Light.
Who is this Beast,
Of ancient times? Always haunting,
Always taking, always needing more and more.
The more he takes, the bigger he grows,
The more destruction left behind.
Who is this Beast?
What is his name? His fury never ending,
He rages on and on; into the night,
Into the soul of humankind.
Reveal yourself, Oh horrid Beast!
Very well . . .
My name is Greed.

Introduction

GREED HAS GROWN. The lust for power and control has become the driving force of the Council who now rule One World of planet Earth. The Council consists of three rulers; one for each of the three Continental Territories of One World. They are Panamerica, ruled by PA; Euroslavica, ruled by ES; and Sinopacifica, ruled by SPA. The Council rulers are unknown and unseen; their identities are well hidden by their protectors, the Lords. The Lords rule over the Masters and together the government of One World is referred to as the Upper Crust (UC). The rest of the population is composed of the people (or servants), and unbeknownst to the people, the UC refer to them as slaves.

Over time, greed and cataclysmic global events, have greatly reduced the population. Big cities have almost entirely disappeared, and people now live primarily in small towns and villages.

The basic rights of the people have been gradually removed over the years: the right of free speech, to bear arms, own property, get legally married, congregate in a house of worship, own anything of intrinsic value – including all forms of currency, receive a formal education beyond age 12, and work at a job for a salary. Housing is provided by the UC in exchange for servitude, and the people are given a meager number of points per week to use for food and basic necessities. Homelessness and poverty are rampant for most people all over One World.

PA, ES and SPA's ultimate fear is to lose power over the people. After all, people far outnumber the rulers, and there is bubbling fear within the UC that the people may realize their innate power, rise up and one day overthrow them. Thus, the objective of the UC is to pare down the populace through worldwide genocide and replace the people with artificial intelligence. AI is far more efficient and will not be subject to rebelliousness. To keep the people oppressed and oblivious to their true powers, the UC must maintain vigilant control over the people while covertly reducing the population . . . into extinction.

PART 1
DARK CLOUDS

Chapter 1 – Flight

TWO INCOMING SIGNALS ALERT ES AND SPA. Each is receiving a message from PA to accept his transmission. The Universal Translator activates, and the Council members begin to communicate with each other, each in his own language: PA in English, ES in Russian and SPA in Chinese.

PA: "Greetings, my Kinsmen."

ES: "Greetings to you, my Brethren."

SPA: "Greetings, fellow Highest Ones."

PA: "An urgent matter has recently come to my attention that we need to act upon immediately.

ES: "Is it the matter concerning the Ebola outbreak? My Lords of Euroslavica have also brought this to my attention."

PA: "Yes, Brother ES, that is the matter at hand."

SPA: "And I have been informed about the Ebola outbreak as well, fellow Highest Ones. A rather interesting situation, is it not?"

The other two agree that the deadly outbreak is in fact intriguing.

PA: "This may be the opportunity we have been waiting for, Brothers. The one we spoke about when the last outbreak hit."

ES: "My thoughts are already with you, PA. And I am ready to take action."

SPA: "Remember how it failed the last time, though. We do not want the same mistake to happen. The slaves almost caught on and it caused several uprisings."

ES: "This is true, Brother SPA, although the commandos were able to snuff out the insurrectionists."

PA: "I concur, Brother ES, and our mind-control methods were swift and effective as well."

SPA: "Yes, yes, this is all very true. However, we might need something slightly different this time."

PA: "Yes, SPA. I concur. In fact, my Lords and I have come up with an idea which we feel has great possibilities at being most effective . . . and deadly."

ES: "What is it, PA? Do tell us, Brother!"

SPA: "Yes, yes! Do tell us!"

PA: "We let the slaves know that this is a new, more deadly strain, and that they will need a new and improved neutralizer to save them. But what they don't know is that we will be mixing in the same old effective neutralizer with something else.

"While some will actually be receiving the real neutralizer as a deception to the real agenda and will, therefore, survive, the others will receive something else—a bioweapon made of live Ebola. This will give us a great opportunity to drastically reduce the population over a very short span of time."

SPA: "That is truly excellent, Brother PA!"

ES: "Yes, yes! Truly excellent!"

PA: "Yes, yes, it is. We think it will be effective in carrying out our goals. I propose we get our Lords and Masters moving on this immediately."

ES: "I concur, Brother PA."

SPA: "And I concur as well, my Brethren."

PA: "Very well, then. It is done."

ES and SPA: "So it is, and so it shall be."

The transmission terminates.

* * *

Mimi finishes her journal entry before heading down to the boardwalk to see her sweetie one last time. She writes:

The news today was not good. But before I do anything, I must see my darling Ryan and let him know what is happening and what I am about to do. It breaks my heart to share this with him; although, I know he will understand. Please give me the strength and courage, Lord, to face this day and do what I must in the struggle that lies ahead. Your faithful servant, Mimi.

From the oceanfront boardwalk of Amber Beach, in Southern California, Mimi stares out at the golden sunlight sparkling over waves that crash to the shore. Her soul is heavy as she moves her gaze to search for the one who lives in her heart. Mimi spots her gentle man picking up trash around the picnic area. As Ryan finishes his work to head home for the day, Mimi sprints to catch up with him before he leaves, so she can deliver the news.

Ryan is a warm-hearted man in his early forties. His sandy brown hair tends to be unruly in the ocean breeze yet accentuates his hazel-green eyes that are always expressive. Since Ryan is a soft-spoken man of few words, those eyes often speak more than the words through his lips. His soul speaks directly from his heart. He delights in his job of keeping the beautiful Amber Beach spotless.

Ryan ties up the plastic garbage bag and places it in the dumpster behind the restroom. He catches a glimpse of Mimi, a youthful, energetic woman of fifty-going-on-twenty-five quickly coming toward him. Her long blond hair is blowing in the breeze, bouncing in stride with her anxious pace. Ryan smiles when he sees Mimi, although he detects a sense of foreboding in her hurried step. He closes and locks down the lid of the trash bin as Mimi approaches.

"Hi there!" Mimi calls out to Ryan when she reaches the edge of the picnic area.

Trying not to seem too fearful Mimi slows down; although, she has lost all control of the beating fury in her heart. Her eyes meet Ryan's and the couple moves toward each other in sync, their gazes locked. Before Mimi opens her mouth to speak again, she orders herself to breathe.

Ryan smiles tenderly at Mimi and speaks first. "Hey there!" he whispers to her.

Panting, heart pounding, and out of breath (her self-command was all but futile), Mimi nods at Ryan, forces a smile and lets out a barely audible, "Hi, Ryan, have you heard the news today about the virus?"

Ryan's smiling eyes turn to confusion, and Mimi knows that he has not heard the latest update.

Mimi explains, "According to the Council, this virus is not the average, every day, run-of-the-mill Ebola; you know, the one that we have a neutralizer for? Apparently—" Mimi pauses and closes her eyes for a moment. When she opens them, she looks intensely into Ryan's face and whispers, "It is a new strain. Oh sure, the Council reassures us that all is well, that the neutralizer we have now will work just fine, that we are not to worry about a thing, blah, blah, blah . . ."

Ryan lowers his eyes for a moment digesting what he has just heard. Returning his gaze back to Mimi's intense brown eyes, he murmurs tenderly, "I'm sorry."

Tears begin to well up in Mimi's eyes, and she spills out the rest of the information. "It's even worse than that, my friend. Our communication system is now on Emergency Use Only. So much for *'we are not to worry about a thing'* eh? Oh, Ryan!" Mimi sobs, "I'm so worried about my daughter and her family up in Oregon. I tried to reach them as soon as I heard the news, but personal communications were already shut down, and my little granddaughter, Elli, is only three years old."

Ryan folds his arms around Mimi pulling her close into his chest and they hold each other for a few moments. But for the two companions, moments feel like an eternity; indeed, *their* eternity is at stake as Mimi shares her plans.

"I hope you will understand what I have to do—what I *must do* now," she begins. Ryan's hazel-green eyes are only inches from Mimi's upturned nose so she can see the sadness growing in him as she reveals the rest. "I must go to Oregon and be with Elli, and I must leave right away, dear friend, first thing tomorrow morning before we are all sent to the Shelters like the last time."

Trying to say more, Mimi is overcome with emotion at the thought of how much she is going to miss Ryan. She knows it is going to be dangerous for her to make this journey, and she hopes Ryan will be reasonably safe sticking to his usual routine at Amber Beach.

"Sweet Ryan, I'm so sorry. I have to go," says Mimi.

Ryan gently touches her lips with his finger as if to say, *'It's okay. You need say no more; I understand.'* He presses his lips softly against hers.

Wiping her tears away, Ryan looks mournfully at Mimi and once again says, "I'm sorry."

Saying one last goodbye to Ryan, a sudden thought occurs to her. "Ryan, please promise me that no matter what happens, you will do your best to keep your distance from people. And if you are ever told to go to a Shelter, PLEASE DO NOT GO! Just have a few things packed and be ready to lock yourself into the boardwalk restroom here, and do not let anyone know where you are. After a while, you can leave here but only travel by night. Try to find others who are also on their own, toughing it out on the outside. But DO NOT TRUST ANY OF THE OVERSEERS. And if you can, come and find me. I am headed for Salena, Oregon, just north of the California border. Please promise me this, Ryan."

"Okay, Mimi. I promise."

Mimi walks away and heads back toward her beachfront dwelling. At the edge of the picnic area, she suddenly stops and turns around one more time knowing that she may never see her beloved Ryan again. She catches Ryan's eye only a short distance from her. Mimi points to her heart and then points to Ryan; she forms the words l love you with her lips, pointing to herself, patting her heart, and pointing to Ryan with each word.

Ryan flashes an ear-to-ear grin while repeating the same motions and words with his own lips, pointing at Mimi and patting his heart, expressing his love for her in return.

Looking up to the heavens, Mimi says a simple prayer as she watches her love disappear from sight. "Please, Lord, please watch over my Ryan."

* * *

Back at her dwelling, Mimi is fixing herself a meal and getting prepared for the next morning's journey. She knows she will have to travel light, taking only what she can fit into the sidecar of her autobike. Although people are generally allowed to move around and go about their business during a state of emergency, they must still be on the alert to receive instructions from the Council and ready to follow orders at a moment's notice. The hand-held electronic communication device everyone possesses, referred to as My Buddy, is issued by the Upper Crust and all notifications to the people are transmitted by the Overseers through My Buddy.

The Buddy System was originally conceived by the Council and set up and organized by the Lords. The system is now maintained by the Masters who write the scripts for the Overseers. Every minute part of the Buddy Communication System has been planned and implemented from top to bottom of the hierarchy in order to be a most effective form of population *discipline*. After all, that is what children need most from their "loving parents," as the people are constantly reminded through the Buddy Communication System.

My Buddy allows everyone to communicate with each other and to be entertained by various programs, except, of course, during times of emergencies. It is what Mimi and all of the world's population tune into every day when they check in to see what news and instructions they are being given by their "loving leaders."

Mimi checks My Buddy to hear the latest news about the Ebola outbreak.

Listening to the news, she hears the reassurance that the neutralizer for the new Ebola strain is forthcoming, and that

"Everyone is to hunker down and restrict your activities for the time being."

The Overseer announces:

"There will be no need to go outside much other than to your places of servitude and to obtain food from your local Centers. Any other activities should be limited until we have the neutralizer ready. And that should happen very soon, Dear Ones."

There is no mention of the sick or those who are dying of Ebola because it is considered too frightening for the people to hear. Only hopeful and positive messages are allowed to be spoken of and transmitted at all times, but especially during times of an emergency.

Suddenly, Mimi is gripped by a fear that she may be too late and unable to safely leave the area. "Oh Elli! My precious little darling! Gramma is coming! Gramma is coming!"

Mimi realizes that the opening of the Shelters is imminent and she must leave at once. Her immediate plan is to pack camping gear, leave before dawn, and work her way slowly up the west coast. But she must get some sleep first. During the night, Mimi has a vivid dream:

In a field of wild California Poppies somewhere along the California coast, the sun is bright and there is a fragrant breeze flowing through the field of Golden Poppies. Mimi turns her face upward toward the sun and feels its strength as it enters her body. The Poppies beckon to her as she drops to her knees and caresses them. From the middle of the field, she notices a little sprite emerging from the golden landscape. It is a childlike figure dancing happily in the flowers, coming toward Mimi. As the creature approaches, there is a familiarity to her and Mimi recognizes that the fairy-child is none other than her darling little Elli!

"Hi Gramma!" Elli sings out with a joyous sparkle in her little voice.

"Oh my! Hello my precious baby! Gramma is SOOO happy to see you!"

Elli and Mimi dance together in the middle of the Poppy field. They laugh and sing and twirl, filling Mimi's soul with renewed strength and hope.

Just as Mimi begins to awaken from this beautiful reverie, she hears Elli calling out to her, "Don't cry Gramma, everything is gonna be okay. Elli loves you; Elli is just fine! Don't cry Gramma . . ."

The dream fades and Mimi awakens with a sense of dread.

* * *

In the darkness of early morning, Mimi prepares to leave. Her rations of dehydrated food along with toiletries, some light-weight articles of clothing, and camping gear are all packed and ready to go. She turns on My Buddy to see what news and instructions there are for the day.

"Good morning, Dear Children, and what a beautiful morning it is, indeed! This is your Overseer, bringing you the highlights of the day ahead. Your instructions will follow, making it a truly wonderful day, indeed! First you should know that the Council has everything under control with Ebola and that you, their precious children, have nothing to fear."

A musical pause interrupts the announcement with a nursery rhyme jingle.

"My, that was fun! Ha ha! Yes, indeed! Remember to eat all of your fruits and veggies that the Council has so lovingly provided to you at your local Center Market. This will keep you all nice and strong against the Ebola virus. Yes, indeed! To keep you in good spirits, we are going to show you a variety of funny programs today, because as you all know, a happy heart is a healthy heart! Indeed, it is! Ha ha! One last thing, Dear Ones, here are your instructions for today: in case you do start to take ill, the Shelters will be opening up shortly. Be sure to stop by and receive your good medicine. The neutralizers will be here very soon, and they will protect you against the new strain. So, for now Dears, watch the funny programs, ha ha! Eat your fruits and veggies and stay happy! This is your Overseer, signing off for now, indeed!

Mimi turns off My Buddy and looks down at the device. "SCHMUCK!" she mutters.

Stepping outside, Mimi feels trepidatious about the uncertainty of her journey ahead. However, there is another unfamiliar feeling awakening within her that feels calm. A voice whispers in her heart one word: *Freedom.*

I wonder what freedom is? she thinks to herself.

* * *

Mimi's first stop is at The Center, an all-in-one shopping plaza where people go for all of their daily needs. There is a Market for food and all of one's basic needs; a Coffeehouse to sit, relax, and socialize with others; and a Rest Stop for those who do not have indoor living accommodations. The Rest Stop provides people with a shower and a place to roll out their sleeping bags at night, especially during inclement weather.

In spite of the Council's promise to keep everyone housed, the promise is, of course, dependent on having a place to be of service. The UC believes homeless people have disobeyed their Overseers, and that is how they have come to be in their predicament. The Overseers constantly remind everyone:

"If you follow the rules and do as you are told, you will easily find a place to serve a Master. The Master will be very happy to keep you in his servitude."

However, the reality is there are nowhere near enough places of servitude for everyone.

Mimi is steeped in thought about all of this as she looks at the Rest Stop and the people sleeping on the floor in the pre-dawn hours. The tiny flame of freedom that lit inside of her turns up a notch as she reflects, *I used to look down on these people, or at best just feel sorry for them. Now I'm not so sure.*

Inside the Center Market, Mimi grabs a couple of sandwiches and some fruit and veggies for the day. She scans her points card and prepares to leave. Looking around she catches sight of the Center Overseer, the only human who actually serves at the Center as everything else is automated. His function is more about security; that is, to make sure that everyone behaves and no one causes any trouble. If there is a problem or any "suspicious activity," the Center Overseer will report the incident immediately.

Mimi had the misfortune on more than one occasion to witness such a scene, and she knows how effective public humiliation is in helping to keep everyone in line. While watching him, she wonders if he can read her mind and know what her plans are. Although leaving the area is not exactly forbidden, at least not yet, during the current phase of the Ebola outbreak, Mimi knows that she has very little time before the situation could change, and with potentially serious consequences to herself. Without another thought she leaves The Center and heads north.

* * *

In a little coastal California community called Floraville, Doctor Penny is coming in from her gardening. She has been tending to her Marigolds, Lilies and Sunflowers, which are the centerpieces of her wildflower garden and the delight of her spirit. It is getting near dinner time and Dr. Penny, or Doc as the people of Floraville refer to her, begins to cook a scrumptious soup from the vegetables she grows in her backyard. Doc normally has a few people over for dinner, especially those who are without a dwelling to live in. But since the Ebola outbreak, she has been specifically told by her local Security Overseer to temporarily cease and desist from such activities. So, tonight there will be plenty of leftovers at Doc's empty table; a table that is normally graciously attended by those who are in need, and who provide much needed company and good conversation for Doc.

As the sun goes down in Floraville, Doc prepares a table for one, saying a prayer for those who are not present this evening and thanking the Lord for the bounty of her garden. Doc eats mindfully, cherishing every morsel. She feels the sacred healing properties of the food as it supports her body with wonderful nutrients. She is sad that she cannot share this meal with anyone else this evening. After dinner, Doc solemnly clears the table, washes the dishes, and puts the leftovers away for the next day. She sits down in her cozy chair with My Buddy and listens to the day's news and instructions:

Hey there, Good Children! Good evening! And a good day it was, indeed! I just know that you all had a wonderful time today listening to the humorous programming provided to you by your most kind progenitors of the Council. That did make me laugh out loud a whole lot today! Ha ha! Yes, indeed! Since you have all been so good about hunkering down and restricting your activities today, you are all being rewarded with extra points on your food cards! Yes, indeedee-doo!

For more good news, Children, the new Ebola neutralizers are expected to be ready and delivered to you any day now. Since we know you will all be in a rush to get neutralized, we are opening up the Shelters tomorrow. WOO HOO! So those of you who feel like you are most at risk, just come on down to your local Center, and the Overseer there will direct you to the nearest available Shelter. Yes, indeed! We know that you are all honest, Dear Ones, so you will only come tomorrow if you feel you are truly a high-risk person.

And now, a little good-night music and lullabies to finish off your day and cuddle you into dreamland. Ha ha! Yes, indeed. Good night and sleep tight.

Soft music begins to play as Doc turns off My Buddy. She contemplates what she has just heard, and a dark feeling begins to creep into her gut. After sitting a while with the deepening feeling that something is not quite right about all this news of Ebola, there is a startling knock on her front door.

Doc rises from her chair and goes over to the door. "Hello?" she calls through the door cautiously. "Who is there?"

"I'm sorry to bother you this time of the evening, ma'am, but I was sent here by some of your friends from the Coffeehouse at the Floraville Center," says a woman from the other side of the door.

"Yes?" Doc is a bit worried as she opens the door enough to peek at the stranger with long blond hair and a weary expression in her big brown eyes.

"Hi. My name is Mimi."

Chapter 2 – Refuge

MIMI AND DOC STAND IN THE DOORWAY looking at each other, both women uncertain of what to expect from the other. Doc breaks the silence.

"Won't you come in, Mimi?"

"Thank you, Ma'am," Mimi says as she steps into Doc's inviting cottage. It was a long day for Mimi. Her tired mind and body are grateful to be invited into a safe place.

"Are you hungry?" Doc asks Mimi.

"Oh yes, Ma'am. I certainly am!" Mimi says with a chuckle.

Doc laughs, too, and the two women begin to warm up to each other.

"Why don't you come into the kitchen and I will give you a bowl of soup. It has fresh vegetables that I grow in my own garden. And please call me Penny."

"Okay. Thank you." Mimi says. "The people I met at the Coffeehouse said they call you Doc."

"Well yes," Doc said smiling, "But I am not a real doctor."

"Oh?"

"Yes. Come on and have some soup. I will tell you my story."

"Okay, Doc – Penny!" They both chuckle. "And thank you so much for the dinner. I can't tell you how much your kindness means to me," Mimi says.

"I'm happy to be blessed with your company, too, Mimi," says Doc.

The two women sit at the table like old friends who have known each other forever. Though feeling ravenous, Mimi tries to eat her soup in a ladylike fashion, resisting the urge to wolf it down.

"Where are you from?" asks Doc.

Trying to slow down her eating a bit more so she can answer Doc's questions, Mimi manages to munch, slurp, and chomp out the words, "Amber Beach."

"Oh, I'm sorry to interrupt your meal with a Q and A session. Why don't I just tell you about myself first while you eat?"

Mimi mumbles with a full mouth and nods in the affirmative as Doc begins.

"I grew up right here in Floraville on this land when it was a fully functioning farm. My parents started out as farmhands here and eventually became the Overseers for the Master's property."

Mimi gulps and looks at Doc in awe.

"Oh no," Doc continues, "My folks were good people. Not all Overseers are bullies you know," she says, with a warm smile. "Especially farm folks and stewards of the land."

Mimi looks at Doc apologetically. "Oh yes, I'm sorry. It must be a wonderful thing to grow up surrounded by all of this," she says.

Doc nods. "Yes, it was, and I guess I got my passion for gardening from my folks and their farming way of life."

Doc continues on a somewhat sadder note, "But now there is not much need for our food because the population around here seems to be much lower than it used to be. But the Master still lets me stay in exchange for whatever food I can produce, with occasional help from people passing through, and whatever is actually needed in the Market."

"Oh, I see" says Mimi sympathetically.

She knows that the farming people as well as the Stewards (folks who work with the land but aren't necessarily farmers) are among the most highly respected of all the people, not only here in Panamerica, but also in Euroslavica and Sinopacifica. The Overseers of the farmland are even given a cottage to live in, such as the one that Doc inhabits. It is fair to say that Doc has Mimi's full attention at this point.

"When I turned 12 and finished school, I started to help out on the farm. I tended the plants and spoke to them as if they were my children, and, of course, I harvested the crops when they were ready."

Mimi's interest piques, especially in light of her recent dream about Elli and the Poppies.

"I think the fruit and vegetables grew bigger and better because I gave them so much love," Doc continues with a grin. "Anyway, that was a long time ago. My parents are now gone, and I am still here in this house. I had a Man once," she says wistfully, "but he is gone now too. He died during the last viral outbreak."

Looking aside quietly for a moment, Doc adds, "We had no children."

"I'm sorry, Doc," Mimi says softly.

"Yes, well—" Doc sighs, "That was well over ten years ago. Now I like to feed those who have no place to call home. It is a way for me to give back from the abundance that has been given to me, and I learn so much about life from these wonderful people as well."

"I know what you mean, Doc. I have had quite rousing conversations with them myself! Yes, indeed. Ha ha!"

They both laugh out loud at the irony of Mimi's reference to My Buddy's infantile language.

"So how did you get to be called Doc?" Mimi asks.

"Well, I know this sounds strange, but the more I got to talking to plants, the more it seemed that I could hear them talking back to *me*. Pretty soon they were giving me all kinds of messages about themselves, like which plants were good for certain human ailments. Before long, people would come to me when they weren't feeling well to find out what plants to take to help them feel better. And that, my friend, is how I came to be called Doc, she finishes with a twinkle in her eye.

"For me, it is healing simply to talk to plants and listen as they talk back to me."

"Wow! No Kidding?" Mimi is intrigued, and having finished Doc's magnificent soup, she pushes the bowl aside and takes out of her pocket something that she has been carrying around for the past couple of hours.

"I don't mean to interrupt you, Doc, but I've just got to tell you what happened to me this afternoon." Mimi takes the handful of flowers she is holding and puts them down on the table in front of Doc. "This morning I left my dwelling in Amber Beach. It was hard to leave, Doc, I mean besides the fact of now becoming homeless since I cannot make my seashell crafts for the Beach Master anymore."

Now Doc is the one who is interested. "Oh my! That sounds very interesting. What exactly do you make with seashells, if you don't mind my asking you?"

"Oh, not at all," Mimi says as she takes the seashell necklace she is wearing off of her neck and hands it to Doc. "Apparently, the Lords', Ladies' and Masters' wives like these very much, as well as other jewelry items that we craftspeople make."

"Why this is just lovely, Mimi," Doc says, holding the necklace delicately in her hands.

"Thank you, Doc." Mimi continues, "But my servitude and home is not all I left behind in Amber Beach."

Doc already knows what's coming as she asks Mimi, "Oh, so what's his name then?"

"Ryan," says Mimi, shaking her head and giggling. "It was hard to leave him, Doc. But I had to. Since we are unable to communicate with our families now through My Buddy, I don't know what is happening with my daughter, her husband and my little granddaughter, Elli. They are in Salena, Oregon, and that's where I am headed. I am worried about them."

"Yes," says Doc. "A lot of folks are doing the same thing, and that is when I lost the last few farmhands that I had here. I'm sure it must be terrible not knowing what's happening to your loved ones."

"Yes, it is, Doc. In fact, as I was starting to tell you, I had a dream the night before about my granddaughter Elli, and today, well, you just wouldn't believe what happened. There I was just a little bit south of Floraville, when off to the side of the road I saw them."

"What did you see?" asked Doc who is now totally taken in with Mimi's story.

"These!" declares Mimi with astonishment as she holds up the flowers she has placed on the table. "Can you imagine? Last night I dreamed about these things and dancing with Elli in a field full of them, and this afternoon I ride by the very place. So naturally I just had to stop and pick a bunch of them. It is just blowing me away, Doc. Do you know what they are called? And what do you suppose it all means?"

Doc smiles joyously at Mimi as she takes the little flowers gently into her hands. "These are called Golden Poppies, Mimi, and you have had a vision relating to them."

"I have?" Mimi cocks an eyebrow and sits up straighter in her chair.

"Yep! And as far as what it all means, I will ask the Poppies," says Doc.

"Wait. *What?*" asks Mimi, leaning forward and drawing her eyebrows together forming a wrinkle over the bridge of her nose.

Enjoying Mimi's reaction, and having an uninitiated spectator, Doc begins her process of communing with the flowers and holds the Golden Poppies against her chest. She closes her eyes and relaxes, feeling the loving energy of the little flowers entering her soul. Her heart begins to fill with pleasure as she feels a delightful life force flowing into her from the Poppies. Doc's breathing slows down as she attunes herself to the energy of the flowers. She becomes one with their energy, merging her life force with theirs.

Mimi is wide-eyed and still, captivated by the transformation of Doc's energy into one of rapture.

In her mind's eye, Doc can see the Golden Poppies laughing with pleasure. She laughs along with them and then speaks to them in her mind.

How beautiful you all are, little beings of the Creator! Doc can hear the flowers giggling as they respond to her; their joy is infectious.

Hee, hee, hee! You are beautiful too, Lady of Light!

Doc replies in her mind, *Thank you, sweet cherubs! I am honored to be in your presence.*

Clearly the honor is ours, Gracious Lady. What can we do for you? the Poppies ask.

First, would you kindly share with me the messages you possess? Also, why is it that you have chosen to come to Mimi at this time?

The flowers respond as they speak to Doc's heart; *We are here to light up the human soul with its highest vibration of love-energy, Lady of Light. You and Mimi are to become a strong beacon of love for others to follow. Wherever you see fear, doubt and darkness in the days to come, you may bring Light to those who need it most. For this you are needed, and for this you have both been chosen.*

Doc bows her head slowly into her cupped hands that are filled with the Golden Poppies. As she raises her head back up tenderly kissing the little flowers, she whispers softly, "Thank you. Thank you. Bless you, dear friends. Thank you."

Mimi is transfixed at what she is witnessing but uncertain about what she just saw. She is fascinated, nonetheless, and cannot wait to hear from Doc.

"Uh. Oh-*KAY?* Mind telling me what just happened, Doc?"

"Of course," says Doc, with a grin and a chuckle.

"I was holding the Golden Poppies against my chest and breathing in their energy while communicating my desire to know what messages they hold for us. I also asked them why they have come to you at this time."

"I see," says Mimi, although she really does not see at all. "So, what did they tell you?"

As Doc reveals the vision that she received from the flowers, Mimi suddenly becomes aware of a knowingness within her guts about the energy from the flowers.

"Why does this sound familiar?" she asks Doc. "As if I understand all of this already. I mean, I know that in my head none of it makes any sense at all. In fact, it just sounds plain weird. Yet, when you share the Golden Poppies' words with me, my guts are going, *yes, I know.*"

"You will come to understand it more in time. But for now, heed the messages of the flower spirits and simply learn to trust their guidance," Doc replies.

"Ok." This is about as much as Mimi can absorb for one evening anyway.

"Now there is something that I must ask of you, Mimi. As things are rapidly unfolding with Ebola, and considering the message that we both just received from the Golden Poppies, I am feeling called to leave here tomorrow and go with you to Salena. I also sense that we will be meeting up with others along the way and that we will be guided and protected as we go."

Doc lays her hands out across the table and with a gaze that is searching Mimi's face implores her, "May I come with you, Sister?"

Grabbing Doc's hands Mimi smiles at her and says, "Funny. I was hoping you would ask."

* * *

As Mimi prepares for bed that night, she takes out her journal and writes:

Thank you, Lord, for this comfortable sofa that I am about to fall asleep on tonight. Thank you for my new friend, Doc. Thank you for the wonderful meal that she has provided and the awesome food that we will be taking along with us tomorrow. And thank you for the message from the Golden Poppies. May I learn more about your precious beings of nature and hear the messages that they carry. Please guide our way and show us a safe pathway for our journey ahead. Please keep Elli safe and also her mama — my daughter Lydia, and her husband Sam. Please take care of Ryan and keep him out of harm's way. And please show me how I may be of service to you. Your faithful servant, Mimi.

Finishing her journal entry for the night, Mimi tucks her pad and pen inside her pouch. She and Doc will be heading out in the morning, and they will have a long day ahead of them, hopefully staying out of the Overseers' way. Although travel has not been restricted yet, rules are tightening up, and Mimi is determined to cross the California/Oregon border sooner than later, as she fears the borders may shut down altogether. The border crossings are more heavily guarded during any kind of emergency. And although they will be taking all the back roads possible, there are places where open exposure is almost unavoidable.

* * *

Just north of Floraville, while Mimi is getting ready to turn in for the night, an incoming message is pulsating on a Master's Communication Device. It is the device belonging to Master Howard, founder of the Howard Pharmaceuticals. He accepts the incoming message as his screen activates and the face of his Overlord appears.

"Good evening, Master Howard. My apologies for disturbing you at this late hour."

"That is quite alright, My Lord. What can I do for you?" asks Master Howard.

"Word has come down from the Council that there is something we will be needing from you."

The Overlord hesitates for a moment and then continues.

"It is regarding the research and development your company has been doing for the past several years."

"Yes, My Lord?"

"As I recall, it is under a code name since the project is top secret. Do you know what I am talking about Master Howard, Sir?"

Thinking about it for a moment, Master Howard really isn't too sure since there are many clandestine operations of questionable nature going on in his company.

The Overlord breaks the silence and says to the Master:

"Correct me if I'm wrong, but I believe it is called Project Snake Bite?"

"AAAHHH! YES!" Master Howard shouts out loud filled with excitement. "Project Snake Bite. Yes, indeed!" Snake Bite is the company's code name for bioweapons.

"Well then," says the Overlord, his tone impatient as he is eager to terminate the conversation and go to bed. "Are you ready to roll it out? That is, to coincide with the outbreak of the Ebola virus."

"Yes, of course. Yes indeed, yes indeed! We at Howard Pharmaceuticals are absolutely ready, My Lord. Have been for some time. Just waiting for the word from The Highest."

"Well, now you've got it," says the Overlord, "So get to it!"

"Immediately, My Lord! Immediately!" says Master Howard.

"Good man. And good night!"

The Overlord terminates the transmission.

"YEEE HAAA!" Master Howard screams wildly, racing up the stairs to his bedroom where his wife is waiting for him.

"Henrietta, my cherry blossom, get ready for me. I'm just a chargin' rhinoceros! Woo Hoo!"

* * *

Mimi hears Doc in the other room getting ready for bed as she gradually drifts off into an uneasy sleep.

The sun is setting over the Pacific Ocean and the colors in the sky are a spectacular splash of orange, red, violet, magenta and blue. Dancing with the colors of the setting sun, the ocean is enjoying its last brilliant display before the onset of nightfall . . . and darkness. Mimi turns around to see a shower of light from the sunset lighting up a massive field of Indian Paintbrush wildflowers. The colors of the flowers are the same as the colors of the sunset, and all of them sing together in a chorus of angelic voices. Her heart begins to sing with the angels, and the Indian Paintbrush flowers suddenly grow taller and even more beautiful, taking on what seems to be near human form.

Mimi is filled with longing as one of the flowers is definitely turning into a man. She starts running toward him as he grows taller and more defined, taking on the appearance of one whom she loves deeply. The wildflower morphs into Mimi's beloved Ryan, and he opens his arms as she rushes into his embrace. As they hold each other close, Ryan lifts Mimi up and twirls her around.

The sun is going down quickly now, and in the fading twilight Mimi catches a glimpse of Ryan's face. He looks at her with a sad, tender smile while blood pours out of his eyes. Mimi pulls back and screams in horror as Ryan softly calls out to her with his arms outstretched. "Don't cry Mimi. Ryan is just fine. Everything is gonna be okay. Ryan loves you. Don't cry . . . don't cry . . .

The dream fades as Mimi sees Ryan covered in blood. She wakes up crying out, "Please, dear Lord, protect Ryan. Keep him from harm's way. I love him so much, Lord. Please take care of him."

Chapter 3 – Shelters

THE NEXT MORNING, MIMI AND DOC load up their autobike sidecars with fresh fruit and vegetables, leftover soup, dehydrated food, toiletries, some light articles of clothing, and camping gear, including Doc's four-person tent. Heading toward the Floraville Center, Doc wants to gather a few more items from the Center Market and see her friends; the ones who sent Mimi to her. As they pull up and park their autobikes, Doc feels something is amiss.

"Be careful," she tells Mimi. "My guts are telling me that something has changed here."

"Mine too," Mimi says to Doc.

The women stare at each other.

"Are you starting to get the hang of this energy thing, Mimi?" Doc inquires with a wry smile.

"Maybe," says Mimi, still unsure but giving her friend a hopeful smile in return.

The two women enter the Floraville Center with caution. The Center Overseer spots them as soon as they walk inside and approaches them with a brusque stride.

"Haven't you two heard the news and instructions this morning?" he asks Mimi and Doc, through pursed lips.

They look at each other with apprehension and then at the Center Overseer shaking their heads.

"Uh, no. We haven't. Must've forgot . . ." says Mimi.

They were both too distracted with preparations for the day's journey that neither one of them thought to tune into My Buddy.

"The neutralizers are here and ready to go," says the Overseer, giving Mimi and Doc their instructions for the day. "Everyone is to go on over to the nearest Shelter and get neutralized. First come first served, you know! I'm sorry you gals will just have to be patient since you don't seem to be among the old, weak or infirmed. They will of course be first in line. But still, you should get on over there immediately since there may be some left over for the rest of you."

The Overseer forces a smile at them and nudges them out of the door. He hands them a card with instructions, which includes the location of the nearest, newly built Shelter. As they leave Doc spots her friends who are also being quickly shuffled out of The Center. Jerry and Linda and their little toddler Suzie are with their friends Blake and Maureen. All five of them seem confused.

"Hey there!" Doc calls out to them giving them a wave. They all stop as Mimi and Doc make their way over to the group of friends.

"Hey, Doc!" Jerry says.

"Hey, Jerry. Hey everyone!" Doc greets her friends. "What happened?"

Jerry answers, "About half an hour ago we were awakened by the Center Overseer and told that we all had to pack up quickly and go to the nearby Shelter to get the new Ebola neutralizer. He said that it was announced on My Buddy, but that he also received specific instructions directly from his Master at the same time. That's what feels so eerie and weird about the whole thing, Doc. I mean it all feels so sudden and rushed."

Linda is holding little Suzie tightly against her chest with the worried look of a mother who is concerned about her child's safety; Blake and Maureen are holding each other with the same look in their eyes.

"We all just have a bad feeling about this," says Jerry, "And if there was some other place for us all to go right now, we would rather go there instead of the Shelter. I just feel like I need some time to think about what's going on."

"Yes, I understand what you are saying," says Doc. "And I do know of a safe place that you all can go, where you can have some quiet time to consider what is happening and what you're going to do.

"I have a dear friend whom I grew up with. She was also the daughter of a farming family and has been left pretty much in the same situation as I am. Except hers is a more remote location, you know, out in the boonies. She does not get visitors very often, since her family is all grown up and moved to other parts. She is more of a recluse now. Plus, there isn't much to do out in the boonies if you follow my drift."

Everyone nods; they all get the drift.

"She is only a couple of hours from here," continues Doc, "and I'm sure that she will let you stay with her for a while. I know because she and I used to talk about such things as a what-if scenario. I can write a letter of introduction for you to take to her. What do you all think?"

Linda and Maureen express their gratitude together. "Bless you Doc, bless you. How can we ever repay you for your kindness?"

With a smile, Doc tells her friends, "Just get yourselves to safety quickly!"

Doc realizes she doesn't have materials with which to write the letter. "Good grief, I will have to figure out a way of going back into the Center Market and see if the Center Overseer will let me get some paper and a pen," says Doc.

"No, you won't," says Mimi producing her journal and pen. "Just tear a sheet out of this."

"Oh, thank you! I didn't know that you journaled, Mimi."

"I guess there is a lot that we are going to learn about each other, Doc!" Mimi says with an impish grin.

Doc dashes off a quick letter and hands it to Jerry. "Oh, and my friend's name is Judy. Here are the directions to her farming community. Now go, all of you. Take care, and may the Lord be with you."

The group of friends hug each other and say good-bye.

Doc turns to Mimi, "Do you want to go to Judy's house too? I know that you really want to get to Salena, but if you feel like you want to hang out for a while and have a place to rest and think, we can do that too."

"No," says Mimi, "but thanks for the offer. However, there is something that I am suddenly feeling called to do. I had a frightening dream last night about Ryan that I was planning to share with you later, but with all of this happening I feel like I must do something else first, if it is alright with you."

"Sure Mimi. What is it?"

Looking at the instruction card that the Center Overseer just gave them, Mimi says, "I feel the need to go to the nearby Shelter and check out what's going on."

Doc closes her eyes and puts her hands on her chest for a moment. Then she looks at Mimi and nods, "Yes, you are right. We must do that. I hear the word 'witness' speaking softly inside of my heart."

"Witness," Mimi repeats the word. "Yes." She also closes her eyes and pauses for a moment. Looking at Doc she asks, "Witness to what, I wonder?"

Doc takes the Golden Poppies out of her pocket and hands half of them to Mimi. "That is what we shall find out, my friend. And these little flowers will help us to do just that. They will give us the courage to go into what feels like a dark situation."

Smiling, Mimi takes the bundle of flowers into her own hands and caresses their gentle petals before the two women head for the nearby Shelter.

* * *

The Autobike Park is only a short distance away, but it is looming up ahead as an ominous foreboding of what lies just beyond. As they draw closer, Mimi notices how many autobikes are parked there. In fact, she cannot recall ever having seen so many of them congregated together in one park. The sight makes her stop riding for a moment as the feeling of uneasiness grows inside of her.

Doc notices that Mimi has suddenly stopped and turns around. "What's wrong?"

"I don't know. Have you ever seen so many autobikes in one park before? Look at them; there must be hundreds of them," says Mimi.

"Hm. You know, it's not even a real Autobike Park. I mean there's no clearing of any kind that has been made for them. They are just parked all together on the grass," says Doc.

"Maybe that's because this could be a newly built Shelter, which is probably just up ahead. We won't actually see the Shelter, though, until we are practically there, you know," says Mimi.

"Why not?" asks Doc, who has never been to a Shelter before. "Have you ever been to one?"

Mimi bites her lip, recalling what happened to her in the past.

"Yes," she says and pauses for a moment before looking Doc squarely in the eye. "But it is not something that we should talk about right now. Not until we leave here safely."

As an afterthought, looking at Doc with a more relaxed expression, Mimi adds, "I can hear the Golden Poppies in my pocket telling me to just shut up and keep going!"

This elicits a snicker from Doc. "Oh my! But you *ARE* learning, Sister." says Doc.

"Yes," sighs Mimi with a slight chuckle. "I suppose I am."

At that moment the two women hear the sound of autobikes behind them. They turn around to see a caravan of what looks like a hundred or more people.

"Good grief!" says Mimi. "I know I have never seen anything like THAT before heading toward a Shelter."

"Hello!" calls out the front rider as the caravan catches up with Mimi and Doc. "Why are you stopped? My Buddy just reported that there are neutralizers on the way right now."

The women look at him rather quizzically, so he stops and pulls over to tell them the rest of the latest news and instructions. "The Council has decided that whoever gets to a Shelter first, *anyone*, regardless of age or health condition, will get the first available neutralizers! We don't know how many there are or how long the supply will last. So don't stop, ladies! Get moving!"

The caravan begins to pass them by and the man quickly rejoins them racing to the front of the pack.

"Good grief," exclaims Mimi once again.

"Yes," Doc says, as they both look at each other and suddenly blurt out: "LET'S GO!" They ride faster, careening towards the Shelter.

Standing in line in front of a factory-made house Mimi and Doc run into a mob scene at the front door. As Mimi looks around, she notices another small structure. This one is no bigger than a small hut reminiscent of the restrooms on the Amber Beach boardwalk. Memories flood back to her when she sees the Hut, remembering the last time she was at a Shelter.

It was a long time ago during the last major viral outbreak when Mimi was 13 years old. She remembers how her parents ran for their lives to a similar place. The greeting place was an outdoor tent, and those who showed no signs of infection were given a neutralizer and kept in the tent to rest for a while.

However, those who were feverish or symptomatic were sent to the little Hut, which was actually a dug-out underground room, and where Mimi and her parents got separated. They had symptoms and Mimi did not. She remembers her mom and dad holding her tight and telling her how much they loved her. They instructed her to wait for them in the tent because the Overseers said they would be out within 24 hours. As

Mimi watched them go down the step ladder, and descend into the underground room, (or the "hole" as it is referred to by the people), she never felt so frightened and alone. Each day that passed that her parents did *not* emerge from the hole terrified her more, with the growing realization that she might never see them again.

Mimi stayed in the tent for six days. She never knew how many people were actually down in the Hut; although, she did see seven or eight people come out during that time. Then, on the morning of the seventh day, a bulldozer showed up. It scooped up the pile of dirt that was sitting in front of the Hut and threw it all back in, filling the hole from which it came, and burying the people who were left down there, including Mimi's parents, without a trace of evidence of what had happened to them. Not knowing where to turn, she was left alone in the world at the age of 13.

It was many years ago, but Mimi has carried the pain of that day in her heart always.

"Are you okay?" Doc asks, noticing that Mimi is looking off into the distance with tears in her eyes.

Brushing her tears aside as she comes back to the present moment, Mimi says, "Yes, I'm sorry. I was just remembering what happened the last time I was at one of these places. I promise to tell you all about it, Doc. Once we are safely away from here."

Doc lays her hand on her friend's shoulder and nods.

As Mimi wipes away the last bit of moisture from her face something else comes into view. Just behind the Hut and a little way off in the distance, Mimi sees something that suddenly lifts her spirits.

"WHOA! GOOD LORD! HOLY SCHMOLY! HOLY— *WHOA!*" Mimi exclaims wildly.

"WHAT, SISTER?!" Doc is startled by Mimi's sudden change in demeanor.

Hardly able to contain her excitement she points to a whole field of Indian Paintbrush wildflowers off in the distance.

"That was part of my dream last night. They were in my dream, Doc!" Mimi says with great excitement.

"Awesome!" Doc replies. "Those are called Indian Paintbrush."

The two women reach the front of the line and an overseer is staring down at them.

"Well," he says smiling, "I am glad to see how enthused you both are because you are, in fact, just in time to receive one of the last available doses of the neutralizer."

Mimi and Doc try to tone themselves down and show a modest level of enthusiasm more appropriate to the situation. They plaster smiles on their faces and express their gratitude, careful not to let it show that they are not really there for neutralization but rather information about what's going on in the Shelters.

"Oh my, that is wonderful," says Doc.

"Thank you, thank you, yes *indeed!* It is truly wonderful," says Mimi.

"So, you gals can just go over to that Hut and go down the steps to receive your Ebola neutralizers."

Doc is still smiling and blabbering words of gratitude, but a cloud has come over Mimi's face. However, feeling the energy of courage flowing into her from the Golden Poppies in her pocket and looking at the Indian Paintbrush in the distance, she proceeds with caution to the Hut.

As they walk toward the hole, Mimi tells Doc the full details of her dream: about the Indian Paintbrush, the ocean, and the beautiful sunset. When she mentions Ryan's appearance in the dream, she becomes worried that Ryan may possibly be sick with Ebola.

"I wonder if the Indian Paintbrush has some answers for you," Doc says. "Look, there are some right over there by the Hut."

Mimi runs over to them and bends down to pick a handful of the Indian Paintbrush flowers. She holds them against her chest the way she had seen Doc do with the Golden Poppies. As she closes her eyes and breathes gently, Mimi finds herself back in the dream dancing with Ryan and holding him close. Only this time instead of seeing Ryan bleeding from his eyes, he is telling her to trust her inner-voice and continue to follow the course, even in the face of fear, knowing that she is protected and that he is always there with her too.

"Thank you, my darling Indian Paintbrush . . . Ryan." Mimi kisses the flowers gently just as she did when saying goodbye to her sweetheart. She puts them in her pocket, looks at Doc, and the two of them descend the stairs to the underground shadows of the hole.

It takes a few moments for their eyes to adjust to the dim light. As they look around, the two women see that they are in a sort of covered trench with the walls, ceiling, and floor all earthen. There are bunk beds with colorful string-lights hanging on them, which are intended to give the people down there some semblance of hominess—and probably security.

Mimi and Doc notice a group of people who are seated at a table with a male Overseer standing nearby. Another Overseer, a woman is administering a hypodermic needle into people's arms, which Mimi assumes is the neutralizer. The male Overseer tells them to come over, sit down and wait their turn.

Mimi notices a shower curtain hanging from the ceiling being used as a partition to block off the other end of the Shelter. She looks at Doc and whispers, "I wonder what's behind that curtain."

"I don't know," Doc whispers back, "but look what's over there on the *side* of the curtain."

In the dim light, Mimi and Doc begin to move toward what looks like a person sitting on the ground curled into a tight ball and holding him or herself around the legs. They approach slowly and the ball tries to back away from the two friends.

"It's okay, it's okay. My name is Mimi, and this here is Doc. Are you okay?" she inquires in a voice barely audible.

A pair of enormous brown eyes filled with terror stare back at the two friends.

"I'm sorry," says Doc, "we didn't mean to frighten you."

The young woman continues to stare at them as her body starts to tremble. She points her shaky finger at the shower curtain.

Curious, Mimi grabs the corner of the curtain and just before peeking behind it, she is struck by an unpleasant odor wafting from the other side. Drawing the curtain back slightly, Mimi takes a look. Piled, one on top of the other, are human bodies, dead and saturated in blood.

Choking back the urge to vomit, Mimi drops the curtain turns to Doc and whispers, "We are getting the hell out of here. Now!"

Hearing this, the young woman balled up on the ground holds out her hands, pleading with her face, *please don't leave me here.*

Mimi takes the young woman by the hand and says to Doc, "I am going to distract the Overseer. When you see the guy's back, take this one and the two of you climb up those stairs. Don't worry about me. I will be right behind you."

Doc did not see what was behind the curtain, but what she saw in Mimi's face was enough and nods in response.

Mimi walks over to the Overseer and strikes up a conversation. "Excuse me, Sir, I just want to thank you so much for the opportunity to have this neutralizer. I didn't think I would be so lucky as to be among the first. I really appreciate it, yes indeed."

"Indeed, yes! And you are also a very smart woman to realize how fortunate you are. Yes, yes indeed," says the Overseer.

"Sir, I'm obliged to report something to you. A moment ago, when I was standing behind the table, I think I may have seen something, you know, uh, forbidden. I believe it might be some kind of monetary currency, Sir, which of course someone could get in trouble for if it is found down here. So, I thought I had better report it to you at once. I'm sure you will want to confiscate it before, heaven forbid, one of *us* finds it!"

The Shelter Overseer is suddenly concerned about what might happen to him if such a contraband item were to be found on his watch, and what a feather in his cap it could be for him if he turns it in to his Master.

"Sure thing! Thanks. Where did you say you think you saw it?" asks the Shelter Overseer.

"Right over there in that corner behind the table, Sir. It is very dark so it's hard to see anything. I think you might have to get down on the ground and search with your hands. It is not very large though, and I believe it appears to be paper currency; that is, we learned about what that looks like in school, Sir, just so we would never touch it if we were ever to come across any. I think you should have no trouble finding it," Mimi babbles on, giving her two companions ample time to get out of the hole.

Greed creeps in, and the Overseer begins to think about what would happen if he should decide to keep it for himself. He knows of Masters who are corrupt and who could probably be bribed in some way with precious metal coins or currency. The Shelter Overseer believes that perhaps he has come into a small fortune.

"Thanks for reporting this to me, woman. I will take care of it at once."

Approaching the spot where Mimi directed him, he squats down on the ground running his hands through the dirt. Mimi wastes no time. She is up the stairs in seconds where Doc and the young woman are anxiously waiting for her.

"Don't run," says Mimi. "We do not want to attract any attention to ourselves. We just have to keep moving at a normal and steady pace."

The three women leave the area without attracting any undue attention, looking as if they have simply been neutralized and sent along their way. They head to the Autobike Park never looking back and having no further desire to check out another Hut ever again.

"Where to now?" asks Doc, as the two of them ride off with their new companion seated in Doc's sidecar.

Mimi replies, "I was wondering if it would still be okay for us to look up your friend Judy and have a rest on her farm for a few days. Do you think she would mind?"

"I'm sure Judy would be honored to have us there," reassures Doc.

"Okay then!"

The young woman seated in Doc's sidecar is listening to the other two as they are making plans. Mimi and Doc glance at her for a moment to make sure she is okay.

In a soft voice their new companion says, "Thank you. My name is Angie."

"You are quite welcome, Angie," says Doc.

Mimi chimes in, "Glad to have you on board."

Angie puts her head down in her hands and begins to weep softly. Mimi and Doc realize they need to stop and tend to their new, young companion.

"Would you like to tell us what happened, Angie?" asks Mimi.

The two women both notice that Angie has something clutched in her hand as she begins to share her story.

"A few days ago, my mom and dad went to the Center Market to get me a birthday present. I just turned 18 years old, so they wanted to give me something special."

Angie opens her hands to reveal a small box of crayons.

"They knew how much I love to draw, but we only ever had a few pencils that I could draw with. So, they used a few of their own food points to get me this very special birthday gift: a box of colors."

Angie begins to sob and she can say no more.

But Mimi puts two and two together and says to Doc, "There were about 10 or so bodies, Doc, behind that shower curtain and they were saturated in blood."

Turning back to Angie, Mimi asks her gently, "Angie, were two of those people lying there your mom and dad?"

Curled up into a ball again, Angie is rocking back and forth weeping and nodding her head, yes.

* * *

Back at the Hut, the Shelter Overseer is sitting on the dirt floor seething in rage: *Did this woman take the currency for herself? Was that why she and her friend were both so happy to be down here? Was it all a diversion to get themselves out of here? Terrible woman! Terrible, greedy slave!*

The Shelter Overseer is consumed with hatred at what has been taken from him and terrified of what might happen next. He knows that he cannot even report the incident and get a reward for it; not the usual way at least, as he runs the risk of his own loyalty to the UC being questioned. They could say that he grabbed it for himself to make a deal with a corrupt Master and is now using a cover story to try to gain favor in a most disloyal way.

And so, the Shelter Overseer sits on the ground enraged by the thought that he has been outsmarted by a slave. But worst of all, by a *woman.*

Chapter 4 – Rebels

WHILE THE SHELTER OVERSEER is ruminating about how to get even with the treacherous female slave who tricked him, another woman comes down into the Hut to see him. The woman does not introduce herself, but the Shelter Overseer recognizes her face, having seen her several times before.

"I have a message for you, from . . . *above*" says the woman, with a faint smile. "It is the usual. You do what we ask of you and you will be, well, you know *rewarded.*" As she says this, the woman shakes her skirt and an object drops out next to her shoe; she steps on it quickly before the Overseer can see what it is.

"Overseer, you are to neutralize as many people as you can today as quickly as you can, and you may earn another one of these by this time tomorrow." She taps her foot upon the item she's covering. "The Shelter Overseers with very high numbers of Ebola neutralizers administered will be rewarded in this manner," she says, patting the object with her shoe. "This is just a taste of what you can receive every day if your numbers are high. Do you understand me, Overseer?"

"Yes Ma'am, indeed I do!"

Without further ado the woman leaves. The Shelter Overseer moves quickly to the spot where the woman was just standing and retrieves what has been left for him: a gold coin. Swiping it from the ground and clutching it to his chest, he is overjoyed at his good fortune. And he instantly realizes how he can get even with the treacherous slave woman.

* * *

The Major is waiting in the outer-reception area of his father's office suite. Master Howard has summoned his son for a private conference regarding the business of the day as well as a rumor at hand.

A soft, feminine voice on the Master's Communication Device instructs the Major, "Your father will see you now, John."

He rises from his seat in the reception area and slowly meanders toward the door where his father awaits him on the other side.

"Come on in, son!" Master Howard beckons in a gentle yet searching tone.

"Hello, father. You wanted to see me about something in particular this morning?"

"Oh no, no, John. Just wanted to see how my boy is getting along, and, of course, go over the usual day's business."

The Major reads his father's face to see if he can figure out the real purpose behind his being summoned. They did their usual business meeting the other day, and, as a rule, such encounters between father and son only occur once a week, or so. "Okay, what do you need from me?"

"Well, as I'm sure you've heard, our company released the first batch of newly modified neutralizers for this variant of Ebola. What you may *not* be aware of though, and what I am proudly telling you is that they were injected into the first slave's arms yesterday! Yes indeed, son! Yes, indeed!"

"Indeed," parrots the Major still searching his father's face.

"Well, aren't you impressed?" Master Howard watches his son's facial expression, not seeing the glow of enthusiasm he expected anywhere in the Major's countenance.

"Oh sure, father!" the Major replies brightly, not wanting to arouse any suspicion. "How ever did you manage to pull it off so fast?"

"Oh, the usual way," Master Howard says with a sly grin.

"Aha! It sounds like the plan worked then and all is well. Congratulations, father," the Major says with a wide-eyed grin. He is playing his part well.

Master Howard's evil-genius smirk fades for a moment. "Well, there seems to be a little glitch somewhere. In fact, I wanted to talk to you about that this morning."

Ah! Here is comes, the Major thinks to himself. He listens to his father and asks him in earnest, "What do you mean 'glitch'?"

"Well, you know what we do when we want to get something done quickly with the Overseers."

"Sure."

"Even though it is illegal for a slave to obtain and have in its possession any piece whatsoever of a precious metal or currency, and the Overseers are, of course, nothing more than slaves themselves who have been put in charge due to their more aggressive natures. Well, the Lords do not seem to mind when we use such a gift on occasion as a form of, you know, *persuasion* with the Overseers," Master Howard pauses for a moment.

"So?" inquires the Major.

"So, I put out a message to our moles to use this method with the Shelter Overseers, that the ones who get high numbers of slaves neutralized in a given region at the end of each day will be rewarded with a gold coin the following morning. And this reward will continue every day until all the slaves everywhere have been neutralized."

"Okay. And your point is?" asks the Major who is now fidgeting, showing signs of irritation.

Master Howard leans into his son and in a subdued tone reveals, "At approximately 11:40 this morning, I got word from one of my Shelter Overseer contacts at the Floraville Shelter. He said, that after the mole delivered the coin to him along with my message, another woman, a slave who was there for her Ebola neutralizer apparently overheard what was happening. He reported that she must have seen the Shelter Overseer put the coin in his pocket. In her treachery, she walked over to him and started flirting with him, even rubbing herself up against him. Sometime after she left, he noticed that the coin was gone and realized that the slave woman had picked his pocket!"

"Huh?" The Major is getting more irritated with his father and trying to cover his annoyance with short responses.

"If this is true, do you understand the serious implications of this? A one- ounce piece of gold bullion in the hands of a slave woman!" says Master Howard.

"What?" asks the Major, still managing his irritation by feigning ignorance.

"It isn't just that the slaves are not allowed to have gold, or any form of currency in their possession, son. It is also the idea that she was privy to the whole interaction and can start rumors flying about what happened. I mean we do not want to rouse any suspicions amongst the slaves as to why we are anxious to inoculate them so quickly; that we are using bribery to do so." Master Howard is beginning to get a bit irritated with, what appears to be, his son's apparent lack of concern. "Pay attention John. This is serious! This is a very delicate matter with these creatures. The Council has always stressed the need for great cunning when dealing with the slaves. It is why they have had the Lords spend so much time and effort on perfecting their mind-control methods."

"So, who is this woman, then?" asks the Major.

"That's what we must find out and without a moment's delay. Otherwise, things could get seriously ugly for us very quickly."

Father and son look at each other for a moment in silence, and then look away. Each one is lost in his own private world of angst, unbeknownst to the worries and concerns of the other. After a long pause, the Major speaks.

"What do you want me to do, father?"

Master Howard answers his son in a loving voice, the likes of which the Major has rarely heard since his childhood, "That's my boy." Looking into his son's eyes and smiling, Master Howard instructs the Major. "Go and find this slave woman, my son. Find her; find out who she is and what she knows, and then, you know, take care of business."

"That's what this is all about, isn't it, father? It's all about taking care of our business—the pharmaceutical business."

"Yes, John. And one day it will all be yours."

The Major regards his father sadly for a few moments before walking out of the room and closing the door behind him.

Stepping into his Autocar, the Major programs his destination into the AI autodriver. He also programs some peaceful music to help him relax as he contemplates what he has just learned and decides what he will have to do about it. In order to track down this woman and her alleged gold coin, there is someone else whom he must go to first: his Overlord and best friend, Kookie.

Riding along lost in nostalgia, the Major begins to reminisce of his younger days with Lord Kenneth, or Kookie as he has always been called. In those days, Masters and Lords did not communicate too much or too often with each other except when business called for it, or the Council gave them specific instructions to do so. Kookie was a few years older than the Major and had a distinctly innocent personality. He was especially known for his extreme, off-the-charts level of intelligence.

The Major was Kookie's polar opposite in that regard. Although by no means stupid, the Major was not even in the same stratosphere of Kookie's intellectual abilities; a point over which the Major was very sensitive, especially since he could never be quite smart enough to please his father. Master Howard let him know it on many occasions, joking sarcastically about Kookie's abilities compared to the lesser brain power of his own son, little John.

But one thing little John had in abundance over Kookie was attitude. Little John was never really little, or so it seemed. He was born tough, had a mean streak, and became a pit bull of protection over his family and friends. That is how he earned his nickname, the Major. When the little-boy-major snapped an order at anyone, they instinctively said, "Yes sir!" while looking down at the little tyke. But the Major had jealousy issues over Kookie due to Master Howard's public humiliation of his son. So, in their adolescence the Major began to bully Kookie.

During the summer months, the children of the Lords and Masters were strategically sent to sleep-away camp together. The Council recognized that even though the Lords were above the station of the Masters, they would have to learn how to work together as they got older in order to keep the slaves under control. It was during one summer retreat that the Major and Kookie's lives were transformed by each other.

Having gone through a particularly difficult time with his father during the prior winter months, the Major was feeling especially mean-spirited when he ran into Kookie the following summer. Kookie was in the camp band, and he played the tuba. Music was his way of reaching out to the other youngsters since he was so painfully shy that he wasn't able to say much to anyone most of the time. The Major began to tease Kookie mercilessly. The bullying was relentless, and Kookie was such a sensitive young man that he just didn't know how to fight back.

The bullying was also bothering the other campers who witnessed the Major's cruelty day after day. Kookie got very upset one day and he grabbed his tuba and took off running. When the others realized Kookie was gone, they all got worried and went looking for him. Something inside of the Major began hurting too, and he joined the campers in their search. When they found Kookie, he had gone down to a spot on the lake that was peaceful and soothing to him, and he was playing his tuba alone.

A young girl in the group approached him. "Hey there, Bud, are you alright?" she asked. But Kookie looked out over the lake and kept on playing. A few others tried to talk to him too, with the same results, until the Major could stand it no more.

"Hey, you big dodo brain! Can't you hear everyone talking to you?" bellowed the Major.

Kookie looked up and stared the Major square in the eye; he removed the tuba mouthpiece and blew the most thunderous noise into the thing. The sound reverberated like massive human flatulence sending ripples across the lake. Everyone started screaming in fits of laughter, including the Major who was roaring away with merriment. Kookie sat there smiling at everyone as he put the tuba mouthpiece down and began tapping the tips of his fingers together.

After that special moment at the lake, the other campers warmed up to Kookie, and he learned to get past his shyness and talk to them. That summer was the last time the Major ever bullied or teased Kookie, or anyone else for that matter. By the end of the summer, Kookie and the Major had become best friends.

Now, pulling up to Kookie's Kastle, the name Kookie has given to his 24-bedroom mansion, the Major looks forward to seeing his old friend again. In recent years they have both gotten caught up in their respective lives and do not get a chance to see as much of each other as they would like, except when connecting on their communication devices for official business.

The Major announces himself into the intercom at the entry way. "Hey Kookie! It's me! Major-Pain-in-the-Ass! Thought I'd mosey on over and bother you for a spell."

After a few moments a sultry electronic female voice responds. "Take off your shoes and step inside. The Lord will see you today." Kookie gets a kick out of his biblical references.

The Major knows the drill and where to find Kookie in his enormous abode. Walking softly, shoes in hand he comes to a long dark tunnel, which of course, has a light at the end of it. The mansion is Kookie's lair, his living quarters, his workstation, his hideaway, his monastery, his retreat, and the place he rarely ever leaves. Basically, the house is Kookie's prison.

Walking into Kookie's workstation the Major is greeted by the back of Kookie's head as Kookie is staring at three giant monitors in front of him. "Great to see you again, Major," Kookie says without taking his eyes off the monitors.

"Great to see the back of your head again, too, Kookie." The Major distinctly hears Kookie chuckle as his friend swivels around in his chair and the two men come face to face with each other.

"How goes things with you, Brother?" asks Kookie. "Have you come to tell me what's up in that great big world out there? I guess I don't get out very often."

"Hey, Bud. *I* know that *you* know just *exactly* what is going on in that great big world out there," the Major says while shaking his head and the two of them sigh.

"Yes. I suppose I do. So, what *does* bring you here then, so unexpected?"

The Major fills Kookie in on the meeting he had with his father earlier. "Can you help me, Kookie? I really need to find her, the woman who allegedly stole a gold coin."

"Well," Kookie thinks for a moment, "if she actually does have one, I can use an electronic metal detector program and give you her exact location."

"And what if she does not have a gold coin?"

"Then it gets a bit more complicated, but I can still give you her general whereabouts," says Kookie.

"I must find her, Kookie. You know what I am talking about," the Major says.

"Yes, my friend, I do. And I will do the best I can to help you."

Kookie turns back to his monitors and gets to work. The Major looks on with fascination as Kookie puts his hands on the massive terminal in front of him, pushing buttons, pulling switches and lighting up panels like one of those historical arcade games. Kookie's genius fully comes to life, and the Major smiles inwardly to himself. Remembering what he hated so much about Kookie as a kid is now the very thing that he so desperately needs from him. The first thing that Kookie does is access the Shelter Hut security camera. Since Master Howard mentioned 11:40 am as the alleged time of the robbery, Kookie goes back to about 11:00 am and does a security check on everyone who passed by the camera and went down into the hole during that time. There were only two women who left without getting neutralized, which is a red flag. Kookie's surveillance system ID's them as Mimi and Doc.

"Well," says Kookie, "I can tell you one thing for certain. The woman you are looking for does not have a gold coin. There were two women who showed up together and did not get neutralized. Their names are Mimi and Doc. My guts are telling me that the one you are looking for is Mimi."

The Major bows his head in silent relief letting go of a long exhale. "I still need to find her though, Kookie."

"Okay then, here it is."

He prints out a map with a circle on it. "Within that circle is a ten-mile radius of her probable location. She could be anywhere within that ring, especially if she moves around. There is just too much nature around there, and it gets in the way of the tracking system. I'm afraid you'll have to do the rest of it the hard way; that is, going down there and asking around."

"Yes, I figured as much. Thanks for your help."

"You can count on me, Major. Remember that and don't be a stranger. Oh, and here is something that will help you." Kookie hands a small, hand-held device to the Major. "This is not Council issued, and as such it is not monitored."

"What is this?" asks the Major.

"You know that all of our communication devices are monitored by the Council, and even though the people are not allowed to communicate with each other right now due to the emergency alert, we are through our own systems. However, it doesn't help us much if everything you and I communicate to each other on one of the Council issued devices is monitored, does it?

"Kookie. What in the world are you talking about? And where the devil did you get this thing?"

Kookie rolls his eyes as if to say, *good grief man, don't you know me by now?*

"You . . . you mean . . . you made this?" the Major asks.

Kookie lets out a snort with a sheepish grin and says, "Uh, yup!"

"And I suppose you are going to tell me that you also have another one for yourself, and that we now can communicate with each other anytime, anywhere and any place without anyone else being the wiser?"

"Yup!"

The Major lets out a laugh. "You sly old fox, you!"

They both have a good chuckle together. Then something occurs to the Major. "Do you happen to have another one of these gadgets that you can spare? I have an idea where another one of these might be very helpful."

"Sure thing," says Kookie as he retrieves another one of his personal communication devices. "Just remember that this device needs to be kept under our own concealment."

"Thank you, Bro', thank you for everything; especially that incredible brain in your head. But most of all thank you for caring and for being a part of this mission we have been planning for such a long time now. We have talked about this for so many years, Kookie, and now our time has come to help our fellow people all over One World."

"Yes. Thank you, too, Major. We will do whatever we can together to help the people."

"We certainly shall."

* * *

It is dinnertime, and Mimi, Doc and Angie have just arrived at the front door of Judy's cottage. As the door opens, they are greeted by warm lights and an exquisite aroma suggesting something wonderful is happening in Judy's kitchen. Sprawled out on the living room rug in front of a toasty fire burning in the hearth are Doc's friends from Floraville: Blake and Maureen, Jerry and Linda, and their little girl Suzie.

The three women are filled with gratitude for the friendly invitation into the homey cottage. The horrors they experienced earlier in the day are quickly fading into a distant memory as Judy greets them all with a warm hug.

"I'm so happy to see you, Doc! And thank you for sending all these wonderful folks here today," Judy says, referring to her guests on the rug. "We were just about to sit down to some soup, potatoes, fresh-baked bread, and all the coffee you can drink. Come on and join us."

"Bless you, Judy" says Doc as the other two lower their heads and nod in agreement. "Thank you for this most welcome meal."

Judy has known Doc for many years, and although her friend's words express appreciation, Judy detects that all is not well with Doc and her two companions.

Everyone gathers around a large wooden table in the center of the dining area. They pass food around while Mimi and Angie introduce themselves to everyone without going into the details of their day and how they met.

There will be time enough for all of that later, Mimi thinks to herself, wanting to simply relax and put the Shelter and Ebola aside for the moment. They are all enjoying the antics of little Suzie, who is a joyous ball of entertainment as only a two-year-old can be.

"I wuuuv da bwead!" squeals Suzie with delight.

"Me too!" others chime in, holding up their chunks of bread to Suzie, laughing around the table.

The hearty meal and good fellowship fill the moment with gaiety, until a knock sounds at the door.

The revelry quiets down for a moment, and Judy moves to the door to see who else is calling on her today. *Another blessing,* she thinks, smiling to herself as she opens the front door.

A strange yet handsome man is standing on her porch. Judy estimates that he is about forty-something and not one of *the people.* He is definitely too well dressed to be one of them. His curly black hair spills down over his deep, brown eyes, and the hungry expression of his slightly parted full lips adds to the intrigue of who he is and why he has come to Judy's remote location.

"Hello there," she says to the stranger. "Can I help you?"

He steps forward into the cottage so that all present can see and hear him.

"I have come about a woman," he says. "She was at a Shelter in Floraville today, and, let's just say that I know her name is Mimi.

"Apparently, ma'am, I have also come to learn that you are friends with one of her traveling companions; a woman who goes by the name of Doc."

The man looks around the table where everyone is seated.

"Ah. Having some guests for dinner, are you? Well, I will not keep you long, then. I am looking for this woman, Mimi, and would like to question her and your guests for just a moment. Perhaps you'll allow me to introduce myself," he says while producing his credentials. "I am Master John of Howard Pharmaceuticals, but people just call me the Major."

Chapter 5 – Safehouse

MIMI AND DOC STARE AT EACH OTHER from across the table, confused and apprehensive.

Oh, Lord, how did he find us? Mimi agonizes in thought. *Is this to do with the lie I told the Shelter Overseer about currency on the floor of the Hut?*

She remembers the Indian Paintbrush inside her pocket and shoves her hand in there grabbing hold of the flowers as the Major approaches the table. Mimi does not know that he recognizes her and Doc at once from Kookie's security camera scan. Courage and the message of *stay the course* instantly transfer to Mimi's heart when the Major begins to speak.

"That's quite a nice spread you've got there. Mm . . . Smells really good, too!" The Major realizes he has not eaten all day and the feast in front of him looks enticing. He stares at Suzie in particular who is chewing on a piece of bread.

Feeling uneasy by the stranger's stare, Linda pulls Suzie in closer to her, eyeing the Major warily.

"Is there something we can do for you, Sir?" Jerry pipes up, putting his protective arm around mother and child.

"This woman Mimi did something today that has gotten her into a bit of trouble." Lowering his voice, he says, "And I need to find her." the Major is hoping that Mimi will identify *herself,* without him having to point her out.

Mimi realizes that she is putting her friends in jeopardy. Hearing the "voice" in her pocket—*Stay the course, Lady, stay the course*—she decides she must face the consequences. She bravely speaks up. "I am Mimi, Sir."

"Oh no!" cries Doc. "MIMI!"

The Major looks at both women before moving over to Mimi. He lowers himself so his face is level with hers. Staring straight into her frightened brown eyes, the Major says, "Do not be afraid. I have come here to protect you."

Something about the urgency in his eyes and voice causes Mimi to feel that he is speaking to her in earnest. She also feels a trust growing within her and an inner-knowing that she is just beginning to understand, that her true powers are greater than she has ever known.

Everyone is intensely fixated on Mimi and the Major as Judy emerges from the kitchen bringing a serving tray with a large bowl of soup, a plate of potatoes, a flask of coffee, and a great big chunk of her homemade bread. Setting the tray down in front of the Major she invites him to join them.

"Please, good sir, won't you break bread together with us?"

"Thank you, ma'am. This sure does look like a feast!"

They finish their dinner in silence, anticipating the rest of the news that the Major has come to give them. Although Doc is not as fearful as she was, she is still not inclined to trust this man completely; not yet, at least.

Why would a Master want to help any of us? Doc thinks to herself.

* * *

Back at the Floraville Shelter Cottage, a young Overseer by the name of Violet, or Vi as folks call her, is just finishing up for the day. She has been supervising Ebola neutralizers all day long and feeling good about all the lives she has just saved, but Vi is ready to go home. She hears from her Master Overseer on My Buddy.

"The Council is well pleased with you, woman. You did a good job today; yes indeed, *good job!*"

Vi responds, "Thank you, my Master, thank you. I am very happy to be of service to you, to the Council, and to the people. Thank you for the opportunity to serve. Yes indeed!"

"Good, my dear. And for tomorrow, because you are so well trusted by the people, I know that you will understand when I tell you that your assignment has been changed."

Oh? Vi thinks to herself, a little bit perplexed.

"Yes, dear. We have received reports that some of the people who are being cared for in the Shelter Hut are a bit wary of our help, if you can imagine such a thing. And that two of them actually got away from us today. I mean to say—" (he carefully corrects himself), "they just walked out without being neutralized! Can you just imagine? Yes, indeed!"

"Oh, indeed, sir?" inquires Vi. Her intuition has kicked into full hyper-alert.

"Yes, indeed!" replies her Master. "So, I am sending you down to the Hut tomorrow to see to it that everyone cooperates, quickly, calmly, and with no further incidents."

"Absolutely, sir. Thank you for the honor of placing me in such a position to help the people. I am sure that I am unworthy of such a special assignment as this one." If there is one thing Vi has learned from being the street-smart savvy survivor that she is, is that the UC in general, and in particular her Master, love to have their egos stroked and to be spoken to with utmost deference. It is also a maneuver she has learned how to use strategically when she is about to create a diversion.

"Well yes, Dear. You *are* such a good girl, aren't you! Yes, indeed!"

Yes, INDEED! Vi thinks as she smiles inwardly.

"Have a good evening, dear, get a good night's sleep and be ready to report to the Shelter Hut first thing in the morning." And with that her Master disconnects from My Buddy.

Vi leaves the Shelter Cottage, hops on her autobike and heads for her dwelling. As she is riding, her mind is churning away at something that has been gnawing at her for some time. Her gut instincts are sharp, and Vi knows when something just *isn't quite right,* as she likes to say.

"No." Vi says out loud, "Something isn't right." Thinking about the whole conversation with her Master just now, even the fact that he would contact her directly instead of going through the usual channels of the Shelter Overseer, Vi snorts and says into the wind, "And that *guy* isn't right, either! No sir, he just isn't right!" Riding off into the distance her fading voice whispers over the field of Indian Paintbrush, "Something is most definitely not right."

* * *

Mimi, Doc, and all the guests seated around Judy's dinner table are waiting for the Major to finish his last piece of delicious homemade bread. Pouring himself another cup of coffee, the others instinctively join him and do the same. Struggling with his thoughts and trying to decide just exactly what he is going to share with everyone, the Major looks squarely at Mimi and begins.

"I cannot reveal too much at this time for two reasons: one, because it would be dangerous for all of us, myself included, to have too much information out there in the open, so to speak. Two," he says lowering his eyes in shame, "because I'm not sure what I can do about any of it right now. What I *do* know is that I do *not* want to see any of you good people get hurt, and . . . and I just don't know what, if anything, I can do to stop it. But I am sure going to try."

Angie, who has been sitting quietly this whole time listening, speaks up.

"Sir does this have anything to do with the way we all say certain things sometimes? Like the way we all say, *Yes Indeed,* and stuff?"

The Major's jaw drops. He is astounded by the young woman's awareness. "Yes, Ma'am. That is part of it for sure. And it is not right. No . . . it is just not right; I am so sorry."

The others are in a state of confusion listening to the word INDEED spoken in a way that is somehow revealing a hidden darkness. The effect on all of them is that of a spell being broken, as if they are beginning to come out of a trance.

"Why do we all feel this way, Major?" asks Mimi. "It's as if we get kind of glazed over whenever we hear certain words or if we listen to My Buddy for too long."

The Major is too ashamed to even answer Mimi's question, and lowers his head.

"I've been having these recurring dreams lately," Angie says, "Dreams about butterflies. And in my dreams, they come and talk to me; sometimes they just dance around my head. I feel so much happiness coming from them. But then, suddenly everything turns black. The butterflies disappear, and I start falling into this deep hole of nothingness all around. And that is when I wake up, feeling an emptiness in my soul and a terrible loneliness for the *me* which has been lost in the darkness, forever."

Looking at everyone around the table she continues, "That is how I feel if I listen to My Buddy for too long, and then the dreams can turn into really bad nightmares."

The others can all relate to Angie's feelings. And the Major, whose head is still hanging cannot look anyone in the face.

"I like to draw them," Angie continues.

"Draw what?" Several voices mutter softly.

"Mostly, I like to draw the butterflies. But sometimes, when I hear them talking to me, they tell me to draw other things, as well."

Mimi reaches out to Angie, touching her hands and murmuring softly, "What do the butterflies tell you to draw, Angie?"

"Lots of beautiful colors, of things in nature; you know, like flowers and stuff."

Mimi glances up suddenly, connecting with Doc as they look on with great curiosity at what they are hearing.

The rest of the small group is also listening intently and everyone seems to have the same idea. Judy runs into the kitchen and retrieves a pack of colored pencils while Maureen remembers that she has a pad of drawing paper in her pack.

"I have been using this to write down and teach Suzie the letters of the alphabet," Maureen says, proudly producing the tablet for Angie.

Judy chimes in, "I was given these pencils by an old friend a long time ago, who thought I should do some coloring as a way of expressing my feelings, or some such foolishness!" Judy twitters, "I mean, I can't even draw a stick figure, for crying out loud."

The group chuckles, and Angie begins to draw butterflies. They are in a field of vibrant wildflowers, bright orange, yellow, magenta, violet and deep blue. She thinks of her mom and dad as she recalls the trauma of losing them earlier that day. They had all gone down to the Hut together to get neutralized. But it was too late for her mom and dad. Tears of deep sadness well up inside of Angie, and she beings to pour her broken heart onto the drawing pad with all the colors of the rainbow. She fills in the sky with the same brilliant colors of the flowers, as if they are all a part of the same world. She adds the faces of her mom and dad in the clouds.

Mimi is watching Angie sketch with the colored pencils and says to her tenderly, "Yes Angie, your mom and dad are home now."

Putting her pencils down for a moment and burying her face in her hands, Angie begins to cry mournfully. Mimi puts her arms around her, offering comfort to her new young friend. Each person in the room looks down or away thinking of their own recent losses and trauma; all that is except for the Major. He is staring straight at Angie and Mimi with a fire burning in his soul.

I must tell them something, the Major admonishes himself. Thinking of his pact with Kookie he thinks *this is for you too, Brother.*

"I'm sorry to have to leave you good people so soon, but my father is waiting for me to return. Thank you so much, Judy, for your hospitality, your warmth and the most delicious bread I have ever eaten."

"Oh, you are quite welcome, sir! The pleasure has been all mine. Let me go and get you another loaf to take home; you know, one for the road so to speak," she says with a smile.

"Thank you kindly, gracious lady." Turning to Mimi, the Major says, "May I see you outside for a moment, please?"

"Sure," Mimi replies, walking him to the door.

Once they are alone outside, the Major's tone turns serious.

"I can't tell you too much, Mimi, but I will give you enough information to help you stay safe and out of harm's way. Please do not ask me how I know what I am about to tell you. Just trust me and follow my advice, okay?"

"Okay," she says.

"And be careful with whom you share this information. There is a time and a place for sharing the truth with people, and if it is too much too soon it could all backfire. Do you understand me?"

"I think so," Mimi says sadly.

"First, you must know that the Buddy System and your Buddy devices are partly used for tracking."

"Tracking what?"

"Tracking you; the people."

Mimi sighs and says, "I figured as much."

"Second, there is a way of turning off the tracking device, but if too many people were to do that it would arouse serious suspicion amongst the UC and especially the Council. Last but not least, I was sent here to find you," choking on the tears in his throat he adds, "and to kill you."

"WHAT?" Mimi shrieks in terror and jumps back from the Major.

"Shh . . . It's okay, it's okay. I'm not going to hurt you." Pulling out a small sack that he has concealed under his outer cloak, the Major takes out two small bottles and hands them both to Mimi. "Take a look at these and tell me what you see."

Holding the bottles in her trembling hands, Mimi reads the labels: one is printed in brown ink with a bunch of medical jargon that she cannot understand, except for the bottom that reads EBOLA NEUTRALIZER—HOWARD PHARMACEUTICALS. The other bottle says the exact same thing, except the ink is orange.

"Okay," says Mimi in a hesitant voice, "So what gives?"

"I was sent here to give you the contents in the bottle with the orange label."

"So?"

"Mimi, that bottle is NOT filled with the Ebola neutralizer; only the brown one is."

"Well, so what in the blazes IS it filled with, Major?"

Hardly able to utter the words that will bear witness to the sins of his father, the Major finally says the unspeakable to one whom he grew up being told was his enemy; a slave.

"I'm so sorry, it is live Ebola. Please forgive me. Please forgive my father. Please forgive us all," The Major pleads.

Mimi gasps. She is barely able to speak, staring at the Major in disbelief. In disgust, she says, "You mean like some kind of *weapon*? To *kill people*?"

Shamefully, the Major nods in the affirmative, staring at the ground. "There are two things I need to do for you, before I go. You have become a target to the UC because of the incident with the Shelter Overseer in the Hut and a gold coin; I need to make it appear that I have done what they sent me here to do. One thing they will want is your

Buddy device. I must disconnect it and return it to the Lords for reprogramming.

"I will also set you up with another device that you can use to communicate with me, in a way that no one will ever detect. It is private, secure and *not* connected to the UC system. I have programmed it for you so that you will be able to receive your usual points for food and supplies, but most of all to the world at large you will appear to be deceased.

"The final thing, dear lady, is that I DO want you to be safe and protected. I hope you will trust me to inoculate you with the real Ebola neutralizer, the bottle with the brown ink that you are holding.

Somehow, Mimi believes from the bottom of her heart that this man can be trusted, but before she rolls up her sleeve, she just has to ask him, "Why Major, why are you doing this? Why are you willing to go against your family and the UC, putting your own safety at risk?"

"Dearest woman, throughout human history there have been corrupt and evil regimes, with evil rulers rising to power. And for a long time now, we of One World have been ruled by such as them. But not all who are in positions of authority are blind to the corruption and many are saddened and even angered by what we see. There are many of us who wish to do something to stop the evil; to do whatever we can when we have the opportunity to do so. I hope in time that you will come to see and understand this." And smiling at Mimi, the Major says, "We really are not *all* bad, you know."

Mimi nods, smiles back at the Major, and rolls up her sleeve. When it is done, she looks at him sadly and thanks him. The Major speaks to her gently and says, "You take care of yourself now, Mimi. And I will contact you soon on this." He hands her one of Kookie's devices.

* * *

Judy is clearing the table and the others are all helping to wash up when Mimi comes back inside. Doc looks at her with an imploring expression.

"I'm alright, Doc. Let's talk about it later, okay?"

"Sure," Doc sighs. "It has been a long day for all of us."

The others retire to their cozy corners of the cottage; the rug in front of the fireplace, the back porch overlooking the farmland, the two over-stuffed sofas in Judy's living room, and Mimi's chosen spot—the lounge chair on the front porch.

Settling down and searching through her pouch for her journal Mimi prepares to write when she pulls something else out of her pouch. It is a small chain of seashells that she brought with her from Amber Beach. Memories of the beach and of Ryan come back to her as she caresses the chain and thinks about her beloved. Instinctively, Mimi goes back inside the cottage to find where Jerry, Linda, and Suzie are all winding down for the night.

She holds out the chain to Suzie and asks her mom and dad if it is alright for Suzie to have it. Suzie squeals with delight as she takes the necklace into her hands and jingles it. Laughing, Linda wraps the necklace around Suzie's wrist several times so that she can wear it as a bracelet.

"Thank you so much, Mimi! This is very sweet of you," says Linda.

"Not at all, my friend, not at all," Mimi says, her heart feeling a bit lighter. "Thank you for accepting it from me."

Mimi returns to the front porch, feeling much calmer yet uncertain about what to do or to say to her friends regarding the whole incident with the Major. Her arm is a bit sore from the inoculation as she begins to write:

> *How am I to understand what is going on? This is all just too much for me. Whom do I trust, Lord? What do I tell my friends? What is really going on out there and what can I do about it? I am just a simple woman, one*

who misses her family very much. I think about Ryan, Lord, and wonder how he is doing. I miss him so much. Is he alright? Will I ever see him again? Somehow, in my heart I feel that he is okay, but whether or not we ever see each other again is another story. And what about this horrid news from the Major, that there is a live Ebola weapon of some kind! Good grief! I cannot even begin to wrap my brain around that one. And how much of all this do I tell the others? And Doc? And yet, there are the flowers, the Indian Paintbrush, the Golden Poppies and what next? I'm just feeling so alone, but I know that I will do whatever you ask of me. Your faithful servant, Mimi.

Judy and her four guests, Jerry, Linda, Blake and Maureen, are making arrangements for them to stay at her place and help out with the farming and anything else that needs to be done on the property. She tells them about the vacant dwellings that are available and will be provided for them if they decide to stay as helpers. They are willing to do just that and are grateful to Judy for all of her help. As everyone settles down for the night, their Buddy devices all come on simultaneously; all except for Mimi's, that is, which has now been disconnected and is in the Major's possession.

"Hello, hello, Dear Ones! What a truly wonderful day this has been, indeed! Yes, siree! I have great news and instructions for all of my Dear Ones this evening. We have just been informed that Howard Pharmaceuticals has manufactured almost ALL of the doses needed to neutralize the ENTIRE GLOBAL POPULATION against Ebola! Woo Hoo! Whoop-Dee-Do! Yes, indeedee-doo!! So, of course you all know what THAT means, don't you? Tomorrow, bright and early, the Shelter Overseers all over One World will be ready and waiting at your local Shelters to neutralize you, Dear Ones. So do not hesitate, do not delay. Go get your Ebola neutralizer today! Ha ha!! And when you do there will be another wonderful gift waiting for you. Each one of you will

receive extra bonus points on your food card just for being so good and cooperative. Yes indeed! Go on down to your local Center and find the Shelter nearest you. See you all tomorrow, then. Good night, my dears. Sleep tight!"

"Well, I guess that takes care of that!" says Blake as they all start turning their bed rolls down on the rug. He gives Maureen a big hug. "I guess life will be back to normal after that, eh Sweetie?" he says giving her a kiss.

"Oh, you bet! I'm so ready for that. And so happy that we have this wonderful place where we can serve and live now."

"Yes indeed!" the whole house chimes in, laughing together as they can now see the end of Ebola just around the corner. The only one who is not laughing is Mimi.

As the lights go out, everyone is in bed looking forward to the next day. Drifting off one by one, Judy and her guests fall into a peaceful sleep. Angie is thinking of her mom and dad in their beautiful new home in Heaven, and Doc is thinking about making plans for her trip with Mimi and finding out what the Major told her. As Mimi drifts off to sleep, she sees herself in a flower garden . . .

It is warm and sunny, and the vivid colors of the wildflowers lift her spirits. Off in the distance someone is coming toward her. It is Ryan, and he is holding a bunch of Roses in his hands. She rushes to him and they grab hold of each other in a tight embrace. Hugging and kissing, Ryan and Mimi express how much they love and miss each other, and Ryan gives her the Roses. She is overcome with joy and thanks her sweet lover over and over. . . and all of a sudden, the light turns to dark and she begins falling into a hole of nothingness.

Mimi begins to cry out when she hears Ryan off in the distance calling to her, "Don't cry, my darling, everything is gonna be okay. Ryan loves you. Ryan is just fine! Don't cry, my darling." And then Ryan is gone . . . and everything goes pitch black.

* * *

The Major is sitting in his Autocar, a little way down the lane from where he just left Judy's cottage. He watches the cozy little farmhouse for a long time as the lights eventually go out one by one for the night. Finding his courage, he messages his father on the Master's Communication Device. Master Howard appears on the screen:

"Well, hello, Son! I was beginning to worry about you. Everything okay?"

"Everything is just fine, father. Yes, indeed; everything is just fine."

"So, did you find the slave woman?" Master Howard asks.

"Yes, sir, I did."

"Good! Excellent! Were there uh, how shall we say, any problems?"

"No, sir. There were no problems."

"Well, did you, you know, take care of things?"

"Yes sir, I took care of things," the Major says.

"I see. So, you gave her the shot?"

"Yes, Father," the Major hesitates for a moment, "I uh, I gave her the shot."

"And did you *dispose of things*, you know, the *usual* way?"

The Major pauses before answering. *"INDEED!"* he says, forcing himself to sound enthusiastic.

"That's my boy! Now come on home, son."

"I'm on my way, father."

Chapter 6 – Venom

"GOOD MORNING, DEAR ONES! Hoping you are all doing well. Just a reminder that you are to report to your local Shelter and get your Ebola neutralizer today. There is plenty to go around for everyone, so after you have eaten a good healthy breakfast be on your way."

There is a pause for a moment before the Buddy Overseer continues.

"I have just received word that some of you are coming in and testing positive without any symptoms. Indeed! But not to worry, Beloved. There is another neutralizer that is just a teensy, weensy bit stronger, and it will work just fine for those of you who need it, provided that you are neutralized immediately; so, do not delay in coming in. The stronger neutralizer may make you feel a bit woozy and drowsy when you first get it so be prepared to rest in the Hut for a little while before going home.

"This concludes your news and instructions for the morning. Be seeing you soon, Dear Ones, at the Shelter. Yes indeed; yes indeedee-do."

* * *

Vi has just arrived at the Floraville Shelter. She has been listening to My Buddy along with everyone else this morning and is somewhat apprehensive about the day that awaits her. The early morning shift is getting ready to start, and Vi is there to provide back-up support in the Hut. It is expected that they will need more hands on deck down there today since there are more folks coming in who are testing positive. The people who are showing up with more advanced Ebola symptoms also seem to be on the rise this morning, which means that additional room might be needed down in the hole in the area behind the shower curtain.

In fact, Vi heard from another Overseer that a crew of diggers came in before the Shelter opened this morning to dig a deep trench in the area behind the curtain and bury all that remained there. The UC discovered that burying the dead in a massive trench is a more efficient way of dealing with the remains.

As hard as it is for her to know about these things, Vi understands that some folks come in just too sick to be helped; although, the people have been told that the new Ebola neutralizer has a promise of helping the more advanced cases. In light of the stronger neutralizer, it is especially hopeful to treat those who are extra sick down in the hole, regardless of their condition.

Vi walks into the Shelter Cottage to sign in for her morning shift.

There must be hundreds of people here, she thinks to herself. *I am so glad to be of service to them.*

Everyone in line is anxiously waiting to get tested and then neutralized, hoping they will not test positive and require the stronger neutralizer. As she heads for the Hut a small group of concerned folks trot up behind her.

"Ma'am?" one man calls out nervously, "Ma'am?"

"Yes!" answers Vi.

"Is that the Hut over there, ma'am? We were told that we needed to go to the Hut."

"Yes, it is," says Vi in a calm tone. She can hear the apprehension in the man's voice and tries to allay his fears. "I am headed that way myself," says Vi smiling at him. "Would you all care to walk along with me?"

"Yes ma'am, we sure would appreciate that."

The others nod in agreement and are already feeling reassured.

"We were all just told that we are positive for Ebola. We can't understand that, ma'am. That is, we are all feeling fine. And what about you? Can't you catch it from us if we are infected?"

"No, sir, I have already been neutralized. But it is kind of you to think of me. Anyway, you have nothing to worry about; any of you, really. The neutralizer you are getting is just a little bit stronger so you will need to stay there and rest while the light-headedness and feeling of weakness passes. Then you can go home."

"Oh, okay! Thank you, Angel Lady," the man says as the little group smiles at Vi.

"That's quite all right," Vi says, grinning back at everyone. "My name is Vi. What are all of *your* names?"

"I'm Jerry and this here is my Woman, Linda."

"And the little one is our daughter Suzie," adds Linda.

"And I'm Blake and this is my Woman, Maureen."

"We don't have a little one just yet," chirps Maureen gaily, "but we expect to start trying right away, now that we just found ourselves a place to call home."

"Well, my goodness!" exclaims Vi, "So let's get those Ebola neutralizers into your arms first thing and get you on your way!"

Blake and Maureen look at each other romantically and start laughing at the thought of the fun they will have once they get home.

The group reaches the Hut and they all descend the stairs into the dark hole. As they are the first of the day to arrive, Vi is able to take them immediately. One thing she is aware of and grateful for, is the smell that was down there previously is now gone.

"Okay folks let me get this box open and take out the bottles. While I am getting everything ready for you all, why don't you just sit down make yourselves comfortable and roll up your sleeves."

"Sure thing, Vi," they all chime in.

Although it is dark and somewhat oppressive down in the Hut, there is a feeling of hope and gratitude amongst the five people eagerly awaiting their Ebola neutralization, and the new life that is waiting for them as soon as they leave the Shelter and go back to Judy's farm.

Suzie is playing with her seashell bracelet, and the cheerful jingle sound it makes is brightening up the somber place, bringing in a feeling of hope. Vi in particular notices the jingly sound of the seashells since they are so out of the ordinary and lovely. Somehow the joy they create seems to sanctify the dark and dreary place.

When it comes to little Suzie's turn, she starts clinging onto her mama and whimpering, so Vi immediately puts the hypodermic needle out of sight.

Holding her hands out to Suzie, Vi says, "It's okay sweetheart. My what a lovely bracelet you have! It makes such a pretty noise, doesn't it!" And for a moment Suzie forgets to be afraid as Vi continues, "Why don't you keep jingling those shells and look at your mama, honey, and before you know it this will all be over."

Between Vi and Linda, the deed is done before Suzie can give it much of another thought, and Linda takes her to one of the bunk beds with the colorful lights to rest up before they leave.

As she continues administering the neutralizers, Vi notices something different about these little bottles. They do not have the same brown labels as the many, many bottles she has been handling day after day.

I guess the stronger neutralizer has this orange label now instead of the brown one, Vi thinks to herself.

* * *

It has been several days since Mimi's departure from Amber Beach, and Ryan is by himself picking up trash along the shoreline. The sun is shining and the salty sea air is refreshing to his spirit. Pausing for a moment Ryan stands still to watch the waves crash and come up to his feet. He is a little sad thinking about Mimi and the wonderful walks they had together on the beach. It seemed that she did not even mind while he picked up the trash and scattered some of the more tightly packed seaweed. She would walk alongside of him collecting seashells for the jewelry items she made for her Beach Master Overseer of boardwalk craftspeople. Mimi even made a necklace for Ryan one time, which she proudly put around his neck. He did not have the heart to tell her that he was not really into wearing necklaces, so he simply kept it in his pocket after that and put it on whenever he saw her coming. But now, looking out over the Pacific Ocean with memories flooding back to him of Mimi, Ryan is wearing the seashell necklace. He cannot bear to take it off.

"Ry-aaaan!" a voice yells out from the boardwalk.

He turns around to see his Beach Master Overseer frantically waving his arms motioning for Ryan to come on over. Ryan heads toward the boardwalk, but his Overseer is still waving frantically. Sensing the urgency in the guy's body language, Ryan steps up his pace and is at the boardwalk in a flash.

"Hey, what's up?" Ryan asks.

"Hasn't anyone told you, my man?"

"Uh, no. Told me what?"

"The Ebola neutralizers are ready for us. We are to report to the Shelter immediately and get neutralized; today, right now. There is a Shelter that has just opened up this morning right here on Amber Beach. It is down by the marina and folks are already lining up. Come on and let's beat the crowd and get over there."

"Uh, I haven't finished my morning clean up yet, sir," Ryan says as he is remembering Mimi's admonition to *not* go to a Shelter: 'S*tay away* *from people and if things start to look or sound serious get out of Amber Beach altogether.'*

"Don't be ridiculous, Ryan! This is serious! Get your things together now! I will wait for you and we can go together."

The Beach Master Overseer is interrupted by another man who is walking quickly down the boardwalk heading towards the marina.

"Hey!" the man calls out. "What are you standing there for? Things are getting out of hand at the Shelter, with swarms of people coming in. You are needed there immediately! Move it!"

The Overseer looks at Ryan and says, "Okay then, I gotta run. You grab your stuff and meet me over there immediately. I can get you taken care of first since you are a beach maintenance helper."

"Sure thing," says Ryan as he quickly runs into the restroom, allegedly to gather his belongings from his locker. Peeping out of the door a few moments later Ryan barely makes out the two men's conversation as they are charging away down the boardwalk towards the Shelter; something about building a Hut on the end of the pier. *Whatever a Hut is* he thinks to himself.

When he is sure that he will not be seen Ryan steps cautiously outside, finds a spot behind the outhouse and furiously starts digging. He excavates his travel gear, which he prepared and buried in the sand after Mimi uttered her last words to him. Included in the paraphernalia is his folded-up autobike wrapped in plastic. Ryan unwraps his bike, unfolds it, swings his legs over the seat, and takes off heading north up the California coast. He remembers where Mimi said she was going: Salena, Oregon.

* * *

Vi has spent much of her day in the Hut, neutralizing countless people who are sent down there after testing positive for Ebola. They are young and old, male and female, frail and strong, and all different ethnicities. All of them are sent to the Hut, and as far as Vi can tell, all of them appear to be asymptomatic. They start to show some kind of reaction to the shot almost immediately and are sent to the triple decker bunk beds to lie down and rest.

The next day when Vi reports back to work and goes down the dark hole in the ground once more, she is happy to see that the folks who were sent to recover in the bunk beds yesterday are no longer there. The Overseer informs her they all left later in the afternoon, feeling much better. Knowing folks are neutralized and feeling better warms her heart; Vi feels that she is being helpful to humanity.

She wants to do her part in ridding the world once more of the ravages of a disease known to cause a painful, slow and unstoppable death. She has heard that once the Ebola bleeding starts it is relentless, and a person will bleed to death within 6-16 days or so.

Vi is partnered with another Shelter Overseer down in the hole this morning, who is a bit abrasive with people and not very well liked by any of his peers. She notices him coming down the steps and he says that he is there to relieve her so she can take a break. Collecting her things, she begins to climb the steps when a breeze hits the hole, causing an updraft. Suddenly Vi becomes aware of something familiar. Some days she smells a faint unpleasant odor, but merely dismisses it as nothing and carries on with her service. But on her way out today, she smells the stench again.

There's that trace bad odor again, she thinks to herself. Only this time, the odor is stronger than usual, perhaps because she is standing right in the breeze. The gnawing sensation that she had in her gut the other day that told her *this isn't right,* returns and she can no longer ignore it. Vi climbs down from the ladder and begins to look around, trying to appear casual in front of the unfriendly Overseer. He is too busy neutralizing people to notice Vi anyway.

She follows the smell and notices the trail is drawing her in one direction: to the shower curtain. Standing in front of the curtain, the odor there is unmistakable. Slowly and with a bit of apprehension, Vi glances behind the curtain. As far as she can see, there is nothing there. But the smell is stronger now; strong enough to make her feel nauseated.

Thinking perhaps she has been down in the hole for too long and is imagining things, Vi begins to turn away and head for the steps again, when something catches her eye. As she moves aside, the light hits something small and white on the ground. Vi approaches the object and stops dead in her tracks.

Sticking out of the ground is a bracelet of seashells wrapped around the small wrist of a child. The fingers of the little girl's tiny hand are balled into a tight bloody fist as if she died fighting extreme pain. In pure gruesome horror, Vi's nausea turns explosive and the contents of her stomach spew out of her mouth and onto the ground.

Vi's soul is torn asunder as she drops to her knees and gently removes the seashells from the sweet little girl's wrist. Softly caressing and kissing the precious bracelet in her hands, Vi's tears are bathing the seashells with a sorrow beyond anything she has ever felt, and the sweet jingle sound that the bracelet made the day before has become the shattered pieces of Vi's broken heart. She does not yet understand what has happened here but she does know that she was lied to this morning. She must not show any emotions just yet. Vi must get out of the Hut and away from the Shelter as fast as possible. She climbs the steps and leaves the dark hole, never, ever to return.

Once outside, Vi walks as casually as she can to her autobike and rides away at a normal pace until the Shelter behind her is out of sight. Then she stops, gets down on the ground and begins to scream gut wrenching cries from the bottom of her soul; screaming at the darkness of hell that took this innocent sweet life. Her screams turn into frantic wailing with her arms outstretched and holding the seashell necklace up to the sky:

"Oh why? Why? *WHY?*" Vi cries out in agony, bowing her head low to the ground and then up again at the sky, rocking back and forth totally inconsolable. "Oh, dear Lord, *WHAT HAPPENED?* I don't understand! They said everyone got better and went home. Dear Lord! WHAT HAPPENED? Why did they lie to us?! *What happened?!*"

Vi is unable to go straight home after her horrible experience. She needs the comfort of people that a Coffeehouse provides, to sooth her shattered nerves and overwhelming grief. She stops at the Floraville Center to have a cup of coffee, relax and try to make sense of what happened today. Her mind is reeling; all Vi can think about is the sound of the little girls laughter while jingling her seashells, and the sight of her bloodied little fist sticking up out of her grave. Vi is not especially hungry, so the thought of dinner does not appeal to her. But, seeing a few other people sipping on coffee and quietly chatting with each other is reassuring. Vi is thinking about what she is going to do with herself now. She knows she cannot ever go back to the Shelter and administer neutralizers again.

The food points card will take care of most of her needs. Vi is a wilderness survivor, so she has survived before and knows that she can do it again if need be. However, something is burning inside of Vi, and she knows that she cannot simply go off on her own and turn her back on people. She must take action and promises herself that she will have some kind of a plan by the next morning. She knows that she must figure it all out very quickly as there will be no dwelling for her to go to, now that she has stopped serving as an Overseer at the Shelter.

Breathing a little better and beginning to feel her appetite return, Vi decides to get a bite to eat. She looks around and notices a man sitting at the table in front of her; something around his neck catches her attention.

"Wait, what? Can it be?" she whispers aloud to herself.

She takes the seashell necklace out of her pocket and tenderly holding it in her hands looks very intently at it, then at a seashell necklace around the neck of the man seated in front of her. Looking back and forth between both necklaces she sees that they are exactly the same. Vi is awestruck and shakes her head. After staring for a while in disbelief, Vi realizes she simply *must* go over and talk to this man.

"Uh, excuse me, sir, might I inquire as to where you got that necklace?"

"My friend made it," he replies.

"I see. So, you mean it was made for you personally?"

"Yes, ma'am."

"Okay, so what would you say then if I were to show you this?" Vi says, showing him the seashell necklace she has in her hand.

"WHOA!!"

"Yes," she chuckles. "Whoa is right! Uh, my name is Vi. Mind telling me your name?"

Remembering all that Mimi told him about staying away from people and such, Ryan thinks that it may be a good idea to identify himself to this woman. "My name is Ryan," he says to her, hoping that he just did the right thing.

"Hello, Ryan. Would you be so good as to tell me where you got that necklace and I will also tell you how I got mine."

"My very special friend gave it to me. Can I see yours?" Ryan asks Vi.

"Have you been neutralized yet against Ebola?" asks Vi.

"No."

Vi sadly explains to him, "Then you had better not touch this one. At least, not until I have had a chance to thoroughly sanitize it. It belonged to someone who died very recently of Ebola."

Ryan jumps up from his seat, his eyes filling with tears. *"What? Mimi?!"* he cries.

"I can't remember her name just now," says Vi with great sorrow, afraid of being the bearer of bad news to this man. "But I do remember her age. She was only two years old, and her mom and dad were with her. I am afraid that they all seem to have died together."

Ryan collapses back into the chair. "Oh, oh, thank you!" He mutters looking up to the heavens. But he is confused, wondering how Mimi's necklace ended up on a two-year-old child.

"So, what is your friend's name then, Ryan?"

"Mimi," he says softly, tears of relief rolling down his cheeks.

Vi and Ryan share their stories with each other and their uncertainties about which way to turn, and what to do next. Vi also realizes that she must get some super-sanitizer for the little girls necklace before leaving the center market.

* * *

At Howard Pharmaceuticals, Master Howard is enjoying an exquisite dinner with his wife and their son. He is sitting at the head of the table, laughing and joking with them and telling favorite family stories of days gone by, when the pharmaceutical business was just a fledgling organization.

He turns to his wife wistfully, "Do you remember those days, honey, when I was just getting started?"

Mistress Henrietta looks at her husband with an adoring smile, "Oh my yes, dear. Yes indeed!"

Turning to the Major, Master Howard says to his son, "It was the Council, my son, who really got things going for our little company, which has now grown into a global success all over One World. My

Overlord fixed things with the Council and well, here we are today! Yes indeed!"

"Yes, sir, yes indeed," the Major absent-mindedly replies looking out the window off into the distance, his mind elsewhere. "Speaking of which, father, *my* Overlord has requested a meeting with me. Something about receiving further instructions. So, it looks like I will have to be on my way fairly soon."

"Oh of course, of course. It is so good to see you finally taking your duties as a Master seriously," he says a bit tongue-in-cheek, then turning to his wife adding "Isn't that so my dear Henrietta?"

"Yes, Howard, yes indeed."

Master Howard realizes that there is something he must discuss in private with his son before the Major takes off again. "My sweetness, there are a few things the Major and I need to talk over; things that I am afraid are just a bit over your head; you know, *man talk.*"

Mistress Henrietta touches her fingers to her lips in lady-like fashion and giggles, as her husband continues, "So I'm afraid I must ask you to take your leave of us. Perhaps you can retire to your boudoir and make yourself all, you know," he winks at her, "prettied up! I shall be there shortly, my cherry blossom."

The dutiful mistress of the house excuses herself from the dinner table, leaving her husband and son to their *man talk.*

"Well John, I think I need to fill you in a bit more on what is going on, especially now that you have taken care of things with that slave woman who caused us a bit of trouble. You have shown your fealty to the UC and the Council."

"Yes indeed."

The Major perks up and wants to hear what "bit more" his father has to tell him.

"As you know, the whole concept behind bioweapons was developed a very long time ago when all the world was at war. That was before the Council came to power and rescued us from our savage ways. Now we all live together in harmony as everyone knows his place; the Upper Crust and the slaves. Of course, the slaves are not fully human as we of the Lords and the Masters are. They are like little children at best, and uncivilized animals at worst; there are *way* too many of them. The Council began to realize that they had to develop ways and means of controlling them and their population growth."

Master Howard pauses for a moment to make sure his son is truly understanding what is being explained to him. The Major is transfixed with glazed-over eyes staring at his father. *GOOD!* Master Howard thinks to himself and continues.

"Well, we feel that we have been reasonably successful with the mind control but not so with the population control. It seems that with all the time these children have on their hands, all they want to do is loaf around and well, make other children! In fact, there was an expression they once had a long, long time ago, before our time: *MAKE LOVE, NOT WAR.*" Master Howard laughs for a moment. "It's too bad they didn't make more war than love, if you catch my drift, son, or we wouldn't be overrun with the vermin today!"

"Indeed," says the Major, looking hard at his father.

"It was during that era that a few truly brilliant Master-minds came up with an idea for using bioweapons as a means of population control, should things ever get out of hand with over-population. But no one ever thought that if such extreme measures became necessary, we could pull it off successfully--*UNTIL NOW!*" Master Howard suddenly shouts with a vengeance, causing the Major to nearly fall out of his chair. "And *that* is how we are now doing it! With Operation Snake Bite!"

After a moment's pause, Master Howard sits back in his chair, relaxes, and smiles at his son. "Well, my boy, I guess you had better go on and keep that appointment you have with your Overlord."

He looks up towards the stairs with a romantic sparkle in his eye and removes a Red Rose from the vase on the table. "And *I* have an appointment to keep with my honey bunny!"

* * *

The Major cruises down the road, en route to his appointment with Kookie, ruminating over all that Master Howard has just told him. He is trying to digest the indigestible and comprehend the incomprehensible; or in this case the *re*prehensible.

With his head bowed down low, he keeps dwelling on one thought over and over in his mind: *Please Lord, forgive me. Please forgive me for the sins of my father.*

Sitting there in silent sadness, his autodriver in control, the Major sits back and closes his eyes. Not knowing what the future will bring to him, to One World, or to anyone, the Major feels a vibration going off in his pouch.

Pulling out the secured, private hand-held device which Kookie gave him he sees a hologram appear on the screen. It is a golden pyramid, turning slowly with the numbers 333 displayed underneath. He recognizes it at once as the ID code of his Overlord when he gave him the hand-held device. Activating the voice control the Major speaks into the pyramid:

"Hi there, Kookie."

"Hi, Major. You okay?"

"Yeah, I guess so, Bro'."

"I got worried when I didn't hear from you," says Kookie.

"Sorry, man. Things were tougher than I thought. I'm on my way to see you now."

"Okay then. See you soon."

A few moments after the Major and Kookie disconnect from each other another vibration comes in. Anxiously grabbing his device, the Major sees the numbers 393 appear. Recognizing who *that* ID code belongs to as he himself programmed it, the Major is overcome with a deep sense of relief blurting into the pyramid:

"MIMI!! WHERE YOU BEEN, WOMAN?!"

PART 2:
ANCIENT WISDOM

Chapter 7 – Sequoia

MIMI, DOC, AND ANGIE ARE TRAVELING up the coast, passing through the Redwoods of California. The grandeur of the magnificent old trees is uplifting to their spirits and comforting to the three women. Riding through the greenery with the sunlight sparkling through the conifers, they can feel the healing effects of nature in all its glory. They come to a quaint little town and decide to stop at the Center for a relaxing break at the Center Coffeehouse. Mimi takes out her journal and begins to write.

Doc, Angie, and I have been traveling for the past couple of days and we've just come to the most beautiful part of the world ever! It is called Arbor Vista, California, where the trees are so huge and magnificent! We are mellowing out here at the Arbor Vista Center Coffeehouse after a gorgeous ride through the Redwoods. Angie is working on a drawing, Doc has found someone to chit chat with, and I figured this would be a good time to do a little journaling.

*I'm sorry to say that I haven't found the gumption within myself to tell either one of them what happened with the Major back at Judy's house. What I did tell them is that he wanted me to have the Ebola neutralizer, so he administered it to me right there on the porch. Then he gave me a device of his so we can stay in touch. I also told Doc and Angie that he had to deactivate My Buddy, but I did not tell them why. I guess I'm just not really sure that I believe all of what the Major has told me. I mean, the UC having created something in a neutralizer bottle to **kill** people?! That just doesn't make any sense! It makes NO sense at all! No indeed!*

Doc sees Mimi putting away her journal and waves to her. "Come on over here. There's someone I would like to introduce you to."

Mimi gathers her things and approaches the table where Doc is seated with an elderly gentleman. He has long, white hair tied back in a braid. He is wearing a wide-brimmed, flat topped hat, decorated with turquoise, in the style of the Native American culture.

"Mimi, I would like to introduce you to Phil. Phil, this is Mimi," says Doc.

Phil lights up with a bright, infectious smile, causing her to feel instantly at ease with him. "Well, hello there, Phil," Mimi says, extending both of her hands to him.

"Phil here has been telling me all kinds of fascinating stories about the Sequoia," Doc says.

"Is that right?" says Mimi rather intrigued.

"Yes, ma'am. Your medicine-lady friend here tells me that you have visions and dreams about flowers. The flowers and the trees are our Brothers and Sisters who care very much about us and our wellbeing. They speak to us all the time, but we usually do not listen very well. However, in times of great trouble they will come to us with even more persistence than usual. I think they must be trying hard to get our attention these days, you know. My Brother the Sequoia has been coming to me in my dreams nearly every night. He is insistent that I listen to him and take heed."

Mimi is most fascinated. "Wait a second Phil, hold on," she interrupts him for a moment. "There is another one among us who has intense visions and dreams as well. I think we should bring her in on this conversation." Turning to Angie who is still drawing, Mimi calls out to her, "Angie, would you come over here please? There is someone whom I would like you to meet."

"Right there," Angie says putting away her crayons and walking over.

"Hello young lady, my name is Phil."

"Hi, I'm Angie."

"Mind if I see your artwork?" asks Phil, gesturing to the drawing Angie has in her hands.

Angie smiles timidly and holds up her drawing for all to see. Mimi and Doc praise her handiwork, especially making references to the unusually bright colors. But when Phil looks at the drawing, the blood drains out of his face and his eyes glaze over.

Doc notices his reaction. "Phil, is anything wrong?"

He can hardly get the words out as they seem to be stuck in his throat, "Uh. Uh." After a few moments he collects himself and looks up at Angie. "Young lady, can you tell me about your drawing?"

"Sure," she says, feeling pleased that she has grabbed his attention with her artwork.

"When we were riding over here today, I kept looking at all the *gorgeous* trees. They seemed to be the usual tree colors of browns on the outside, but on the inside, I could see they had much brighter colors. It seemed as if they were talking to me, like they were speaking *tree talk* or something with colors." Angie pauses for a moment to consider how she is going to explain what happened next.

Meanwhile, Mimi and Doc are nodding in a mindful sort of way, but the color has not yet returned to Phil's face. Angie continues, "Then it seemed as though I could feel what they were feeling, and, well . . ." she hesitates and looks at the other three for a moment, "the trees seemed to be crying. Then they all got drenched in a bright-colored orange liquid, as if it was pouring out of them, like they were bleeding or something. So that's what I drew: beautiful, giant Redwood trees bleeding orange and crying,"

"Wow! Oh my!" exclaims Mimi.

"Good grief! Gracious me!" says Doc.

Phil is quiet and still as a stone. With his hands over his mouth, still staring at Angie's drawing he finally says to her, "Angie, what you were told by Sequoia is, um, exactly what I dreamed last night. I saw the trees bleeding orange, too, and they were not only crying, but also burning."

With all this talk about the color orange and the dreams and visions from the others, Mimi knows that she can no longer delay in telling everyone the full story of what happened with the Major, including the orange-labeled bottles filled with live Ebola virus. And although Phil is new to them, Mimi feels that she can trust him. In fact, she feels as though the Redwoods are *instructing* her to tell him, along with Doc and Angie.

Hmm, instructions from a TREE! Ha! What next? Mimi wonders to herself.

* * *

Later that day Mimi receives a message from the Major on her communication device. She connects with him and speaks into the pyramid on the device, "We're in Arbor Vista at a small campground. It's *magnificent* here, Major! And did you know that the trees can talk to us?" she twitters, knowing full well that he will have no idea what she is talking about.

"Uh, yeah. Sure . . . I knew that!" he stammers, making a mental note to himself to ask Kookie to research that one. "So how are you all holding up?"

"We're okay, all things considered. How about yourself?"

"Alright I suppose. As you say, all things considered. I'm on my way to see my Overlord. He is a good man, Mimi. He made the device you and I are communicating on. He wants to help people, too, and his name is Kookie."

Mimi laughs to herself. *Lord Kookie?*

The Major continues, "There are a few things I need to take care of for you and your friends, and then I will catch up with you as soon as I can. But I am going to need my Overlord's help to fix a few things so you, Doc and Angie will all be safe. Please sit tight and be careful as you travel toward Oregon. The UC is moving quickly with the Ebola neutralization of the people, but it's not the Ebola neutralizer that they are getting aggressive with."

Mimi is confused. "What are you talking about?"

It is a moment of truth for the Major; he can no longer conceal the terrible burden he has been carrying around inside of him. "Yes, some of your people *are* getting the real neutralizer so the rest do not get suspicious, but too many are targeted--" he chokes on his own words, "for, uh, a *special treatment* as it is called."

"And what exactly is this *special treatment?*"

"It is the contents of the orange-labeled bottle. You know, the one that I was supposed to give to you? It was mass produced by my father many years ago in anticipation of the moment when the Council would order the UC to use it. And now--" the Major has difficulty speaking the words which are unspeakable, "and now, it has been so ordered. People think they are receiving the real Ebola neutralizing agent, the one with the brown label, and some of them are, as a deceptive decoy. But the truth is, most of them are receiving the orange-labeled bioweapon."

Mimi whispers to herself, *A . . . Bio-what? Good Lord!* "Just how many of the people are targeted for this *special treatment*, Major?" Mimi asks horrified at what she is trying to understand.

In a barely audible, grievous voice, the Major answers, "Ultimately, Mimi. . . the entire populace . . . Everyone."

* * *

Settling down in their tent for the night, Angie turns to Mimi and asks, "So how did your conversation go with the Major? Is he going to help us?"

"I believe," says Mimi "that he is a good man, and that he will do everything in his power, everything he *can* do, to help us."

Angie smiles as she lies back in her sleeping bag, feeling comforted by that thought.

"The Major says that he will catch up with us as soon as he can and that we need to be careful and stay safe," says Mimi.

Doc nods, "Yes, yes. Phil also told me that the whole town of Arbor Vista has been given their news and instructions to go to the Shelter immediately and get neutralized."

Mimi is worried considering the news the Major just shared with her. She knows that he does not want her to go around telling everyone about the bioweapons. She must trust him and Lord Kookie "to fix things for them" as the Major put it.

As the women begin to drift off to sleep, Mimi becomes aware of a presence emerging into her dream state.

It is the sensation of a soothing heartbeat rocking her gently in the center of its being. Mimi feels enveloped in bliss, falling deeper into the other dimension of her nocturnal reverie. The emerging presence begins to take form. It is a Sequoia with the spirit of a woman stepping out if its bark and coming toward Mimi. She is amazed at the beauty of the woman's spirit, radiating to all the life forms around her giving off sparks of life and love. Mimi feels the energy of Sequoia Woman entering her own heart.

Suddenly Mimi awakens from the dream and immediately memories of significant events in her life flash in front of her.

She begins to have visions about her life's good times and the unfortunate times, along with all of the consequences that came down as a result of each event: the love and fear, life and death, joy and sorrow. Each memory comes flooding back to her, especially the painful ones, as if she is experiencing them all over again. Mimi begins to weep remembering the pain not so much from those who have hurt her, but, even more sorrowful, the pain she has inflicted on others that is only now being revealed to her.

One such memory was when she was first getting to know Ryan, a gentle soul who would never hurt anyone. Mimi saw him talking to another woman on Amber Beach one day and holding a Red Rose. She was immediately hit with pangs of jealousy, and as she approached, instead of keeping their date at the picnic table, Mimi just looked at him and kept on walking. And now, through the spirit of Sequoia Woman, Mimi is being given a vision of what really happened.

The other woman was Ryan's sister whom he hadn't seen in many years. He was ecstatic to see her as they laughed and chatted away reminiscing about their growing-up years together. Ryan was so happy, and he was eager to introduce his sister to Mimi. He was going to give Mimi the Rose when he confessed his love for her. But when she looked at him and walked away, he was heartbroken.

Mimi is now feeling his heartbreak in her own body. In her sorrow and guilt, she wails, "Oh Ryan! I am so sorry! I didn't know. I am so sorry. Please forgive me, my darling!"

Turning to Sequoia Woman in her vision, Mimi cries, "Why are you showing me these things my Sister? Why? I can do nothing about it now, except to feel deep sadness and terrible remorse."

In Mimi's mind's eye, her Sequoia Sister takes her gently by the shoulders and says, *"But there is something you can do sweet Lady of the Light. That is why I have come to you."*

Mimi looks at her through tear-filled eyes. "What is it, Sister? What can I do? Please tell me; I will do anything to make things right with the one I love.

Smiling ever so tenderly Sequoia Woman says, *First, you will remember that all humans are made imperfect. The Creator has made you that way so you will have a reason to find your way back to Him. Through your imperfections you will hurt each other, even when you do not mean to. You will also remember that the Creator loves you and forgives you, as He wants you to love and forgive each other. But most of all the Creator wants you to forgive yourself.*

Looking deep into Mimi's eyes Sequoia Woman continues, *And now I will give you my medicine so that you may forgive yourself, and forgive others who have hurt you, so that you may become a power of forgiveness for others who seek good medicine from you.*

Suddenly Mimi feels the pain and sorrow leave her heart. In its place a sensation of peace and understanding pours into her soul from the spirit of Sequoia.

In her state of renewal and harmony her tears transform into a desire to profess her love to Ryan. Calling out to him, Mimi speaks softly, "Oh Ryan, my angel. I love you, my darling! I love you so! Hear me, sweet Ryan, wherever you are. Hear my words reaching out to touch your heart, that you may know that I am your Woman, and I love you, forever and ever."

Coming out of her meditative state Mimi opens her eyes, peeps outside the tent and sees a beautiful old Sequoia nearby. Softly she whispers to the tree, "Thank you, my Sister. Thank you for the healing and the message."

Smiling peacefully, she drifts off back to sleep.

* * *

Just a little way south Ryan is lying in his sleeping bag, looking up at the stars and thinking of Mimi. He hears a small voice inside of his head whispering to him, *I love you my darling, I love you, so! I am your Woman, and I love you, forever and ever!*

Suddenly his heart is filled with a rush of ecstasy and he says out loud to the stars, "I love you too, Mimi. I am your Man, and I love you, forever and ever."

* * *

The three women awaken with the morning sun and thoughts of starting their day, wherever the road will take them. Angie is the first one to climb out of her sleeping bag and prepare something for all of them to eat. She notices something red on Mimi's sleeping bag.

"What's that?" asks Angie.

With one eye half open Mimi looks around and says, "What's *what?*" Then she sees it; a beautiful single Red Rose. "Oh my!" she exclaims and takes the rose tenderly into her hands.

Doc is fully awake now and sees the Rose. Mimi regards both of her friends with a knowing smile. "This is medicine, ladies," says Mimi. "It is healing medicine, just like the other flowers and the trees of the forest."

"What does it heal?" Angie and Doc ask simultaneously.

Mimi holds the Rose against her chest, breathes in deeply and closes her eyes. "It heals a broken heart," she says.

"But where did you find it?" asks Doc rather inquisitively.

"I didn't find it. It found me."

Packed up and ready to leave, Mimi walks over to the Sequoia nearby and says, "Thank you, my Sister. Thank you for giving your love and sharing your wisdom. Might I perhaps take a few pieces of your bark for my pouch so that I may pass on your message to others?"

A sudden breeze passes through the air sending loose twigs and a gentle rain of needles to the ground. "Oh, my goodness! Thank you! Thank you, Sister Sequoia! I will treasure this and remember you always." As Mimi turns around to leave, her sweater catches on the bark of the tree (or perhaps, the tree catches her) and a piece of bark comes off burying itself in her clothing. She laughs and says once more, "Thank you for the bark, my Sister!"

Mimi hears a small voice inside her head calling back to her, *You are very welcome, Lady of Light.*

The three women go to the Arbor Vista Center to freshen up, stock up on food, and spend a little time at the Coffeehouse before beginning the day's journey. Just as they are about to enter the Center, they run into Phil outside. He is distraught as he approaches them cautiously looking around.

"What's wrong, Phil?" Doc asks him with concern.

"It is . . . my family," Phil stammers, trying to remain calm with all the fear that is welling up inside of him. "I came here this morning to get some provisions and when I came back, they were gone. A neighbor said that a van came with Overseers, collecting people to take to the Shelter. She heard them reassure my Woman that they would only be gone for an hour or two. My Sister, I did not tell my Woman what you told me yesterday about the Major's warning. I needed some time to think about it, you know. Now I am asking the Creator to forgive me for not trusting and believing all of your words yesterday!"

Phil is terribly anxious, overcome with guilt and fear for his family. "So I came right back over here to find out from the Center Overseer where the local Shelter is. What can I do? What can I do?"

"I know what you can do," says Mimi feeling the pouch in her pocket. "Thanks to you, Doc, and Angie, and all that is happening, I am learning about a whole new world."

She takes out the pouch and opens it, pulling out the Red Rose and pieces of Sister Sequoia. "Last night I had a dream followed by a vision about Sister Sequoia and a Red Rose."

After sharing her dream with all of them, Mimi says to Phil, "I believe that the flowers and the trees are here to help us be strong and brave, holding true to our course."

Handing a few leaves, twigs, and Rose petals to Phil she continues, "Please take these, bless them and put them in your medicine pouch, and if you think your family needs them, there should be enough here to share with everyone. Then, Phil," she looks at him seriously, "create some kind of diversion and *get your family out of there!*"

Phil takes Mimi's hands and all three women put their arms around him. "Be brave. Be strong," they each say to him.

Phil stands up straight and tall. "I will not let my family, my friends, and the Creator down!"

"I'm sure we will all see each other again, my good friend," Doc says to him as the others nod in agreement.

"Yes, yes, we will, good Sisters; until then . . ." Phil takes off heading toward the Arbor Vista Shelter.

Doc looks around nervously and says to the other two, "Maybe we should just take care of business and get out of here quickly. I will feel a whole lot better when we are away from groups of people, even small groups."

With her eyes glazed over as if in a trance, Angie murmurs, "I do not think it is a good idea to go into this Center at all today. There is another one about two hours north of here and my guts are telling me that we will be okay at that one for a quick stop."

Mimi is holding the medicine pouch against her chest. With a far-away look in her eyes she says, "Yes, you are right. We will be safe there for a little while, but we have to get out of here immediately!"

"I'm right behind you, girls! Let's go!" Doc chimes in.

The three of them turn away from the Arbor Vista Center and head north.

* * *

Phil sees the Shelter coming into view. There is a van parked out front and a few people milling around. Off to the side there is a cottage where folks are lined up waiting to go inside. As he approaches, Phil notices that a few of the people emerging from the cottage are going back into the van, but most of them are going someplace else.

Pulling up in front of the Shelter, Phil is full of dread. He is just in time to see his Woman and their two teenage children leaving the cottage and being escorted somewhere around the back and out of sight.

Rushing to catch up with them he just makes it to the Hut as he sees them disappearing down the steps. His Woman looks up and sees him. She is wide-eyed and full of fear calling out to her Man, "Phil! They said we tested positive for Ebola! You too?" He tries to shush her as he reaches his family at the bottom of the hole.

"No," he whispers, "Just get in line quietly."

While Phil's family all wait to get their super-strength Ebola neutralizers, he quietly reaches into his medicine pouch and pulls out a few Sequoia needles and Rose petals. Slipping a few pieces in each one of their hands, they all look at him quizzically.

"Just be quiet," Phil says softly with a loving, but anxious gaze. They all lift up their sleeves and prepare to receive their neutralizers. Remembering what Mimi and Brother Sequoia told him, he looks at the labels on the bottles in front of his loved ones—they are orange.

Closing his eyes, Phil says a silent prayer: *Great Spirit, Creator of the universe and all life upon this earth, please protect my family.*

Phil hears the Shelter Overseer explaining to his family that they need to go over to the bunk beds and lie down for a while as the super-strength neutralizer causes a bit of a reaction. The Shelter Overseer tells them that they will feel fatigued and a bit head-achy for a little while. But not to worry, the symptoms will soon pass and they will all feel better within a few hours.

As if in a dream, Phil hears a seemingly far-off voice telling him that he is next; roll up his sleeve. With just enough mental capacity left, Phil barely has time to look at the bottle that just filled the hypodermic syringe with the needle that is now plunged into his arm.

The label on the bottle is brown.

* * *

Mimi, Doc, and Angie are nearing the Center of a little coastal village. They are tired, ravenously hungry, and badly in need of some freshening up.

"I'm really glad we waited until we got here to do a rest stop," Angie says, "This place feels SOO much better than what we just left behind at the Arbor Vista Center!"

The other two nod vigorously in agreement.

"Any news and instructions from My Buddy this morning?" Mimi inquires.

"I guess I should turn My Buddy on for a moment," Doc replies, "Just before we go in and have some lunch. Wouldn't want to spoil my appetite, listening while eating," she snickers as the Buddy Overseer comes on.

"Well, well, well! Hello and good morning, My Children! What a wonderful morning this is. Yes indeed! The Council is so pleased at how our efforts are going at getting everyone neutralized. Yes! And we, your trusted friends and Overseers have been doing our part as well to see to it that you are all escorted quickly and safely to the Shelters, in the vans that we have provided for you. As most of you have already noticed we are even providing you, dear ones, with door-to-door pick-up and delivery service. Yes indeed. We are coming right to your door with our comfortable vans and taking you down to the Shelter where you will be taken care of immediately, and then brought back home all safe and sound. Ah, yes! It is all moving along very well, very well indeed! This whole thing will be all over before you know it, Precious Ones. So be sure to get down to your Shelter right away or be waiting

when we get there to pick you up. And now for the day's programming; something to make you laugh and smile. Yes indeed, yes indeed!"

"Yuck!" Mimi, Doc and Angie murmur in unison.

"You know," says Mimi, "there is something about the Buddy Overseer that has me rather puzzled all of a sudden. I mean the three of us are obviously irritated by this guy, and rightfully so. But what seems weird is that he never really bothered me all that much before."

"Me neither," says Doc, looking thoughtful and considering this idea as being a bit strange.

"Same here," says Angie.

"So, what's *that* all about, then?" Mimi continues. "I mean, nothing has changed, not with the Buddy Overseer anyway."

Doc looks at both of them and says, "Could it be that somehow *we* have changed?"

"Why, yes! Yes, we *have* changed. All *three* of us. Mimi says. Feeling the presence of Divine Love glowing within their souls, the three women are all beginning to understand their new, budding state of mental and emotional awakening.

* * *

Phil Joins his family on the bunk beds. His son turns to him and says, "They said we just need to rest a while, Dad, until the effects of the super-strength neutralizer pass. Then we can leave whenever we are ready."

"Yes David, I know," Phil says.

He is beginning to relax, feeling a bit more comfortable with everything. Once again, he is not quite so sure about there being any truth to Mimi's story of the bottles with the orange labels.

"My son, I have never told you how proud I am of you. Like the time when you were only nine years old and a new family came to live nearby. They were separated from their relatives and seemed very lonely. There was a little boy about your age who looked sad all the time and did not want to play with the other children. I remember how most of the others just ignored him when he did not seem interested in playing with them. But you went over to him and left him a drawing you had made of a colorful sunrise. You did not try to make him play with you, but just left a gift for him, a gift from your heart. Do you remember him son?"

David smiles, nodding at his father.

"When I saw what you had done, I lifted my arms to the Creator and said *thank you for giving me a son with a heart as big as the whole universe.* But I never said anything to you."

Phil continues with tenderness in his eyes, "You have always shown so much kindness to others, my son, and yet I have never told you how much I love you, and how proud I am and blessed to be your father."

"Dad, it is *I* who am blessed to be your son!"

The sun is going down and some of the people have already left the Hut. Like Phil they seem to have not been affected at all by the neutralizer. The Shelter Overseer is also packing up and heading up the steps reminding everyone that they can just leave when they are ready.

Phil is breathing a bit easier, feeling that he and his family will all be going home together soon.

Sometime later, shortly after the Overseer leaves, the horror begins.

A spray of blood shoots across the small underground room, splattering a few others in its violent release. Phil looks up to see another bloody spray coming from the other direction. Forceful eruptions of vomit spew from one person after another . . . and another . . . and another.

Terrified, Phil looks down at his Woman and two children who are asleep on the bunk beds. Wailing and crying begins to resound through the hole, and there is more vomit and blood everywhere. Phil tries to stretch his arms out to embrace his loved ones as if he can protect them from the cries of fear and the blood that is drenching the small underground space. He practically lays down on top of his family but does so mindful not to disturb their rest and grateful that they are asleep!

The vomiting and the blood and the moaning and the agonizing horror of a violent, massive Ebola bleed-out continues for what seems like an eternity to Phil, as he lays there covering his family with his own body.

Gradually, the horror subsides and an eerie stillness is left down in the Shelter Hole. There are no more moans and the vomiting has ceased. All is quiet and still without a breath to be heard.

Phil looks down at his family and he realizes that none of them are breathing either. They have all gone to be with their Creator, having left peacefully in their sleep.

Bowing his head low and crying over his loved ones, Phil turns his face upwards and weeping, says to the Creator, "Great Spirit, I do not understand all of this. But I am grateful that you did not let my family suffer. I now know what it is that I must do for them, for You my Creator, and for all of mankind everywhere on this earth."

Kissing his Woman and children good-bye, Phil leaves the Shelter Hut.

* * *

Kookie is seated at his consol. He is lost in a world of numbers, shapes, colors, and a multiverse of kaleidoscopic patterns. Due to his inordinate level of superhuman intelligence, the Lords have charged him with the responsibility of designing, programming, and maintaining systems for which the primary function is to track the whereabouts of the people, and to control their minds. The Council has designated all Lords to track and control people in whatever way they can, including the creation of new and improved methods of mind control.

However, the Lords also have the responsibility to track and spy on the Masters. As everyone is encouraged to spy on everyone else and there is no real loyalty that is recognized among the UC. The only fealty of the Lords which they *must* show is to the Highest of the Council; PA, ES and SPA. And they are always spying on the Lords through the Council moles and other Lords.

The intercom switches on from Kookie's entryway as the Major announces his arrival. "Hey Kookie, it's me!"

Pressing a button on the control panel Kookie unlocks the front door and plays the AI greeting, "Take off your shoes and follow the light at the end of the tunnel. The Lord will see you today . . ."

"Yeah, yeah, yeah," the Major smirks, "But is the Lord *happy* to see me today?"

Kookie softly mutters, "Yes, indeed!"

Chapter 8 – Metatron

"HELLO THERE!" THE MAJOR STATES WITH CHEER, staring at the back of Kookie's head.

Disengaging himself from the whistles and bells of his console Kookie turns around to greet his friend. "Hi there, Major. Glad that you could get back here so quickly. How did things go with your father?"

The Major's smile fades as a dark cloud appears over his heart. "It's hard Kookie, very hard. I don't know how much longer I can keep this charade going." Looking at Kookie with great sorrow he continues, "My father is telling me for the first time since I was a kid, that I am a good son. The sad part is that for the first time I *am* a good son because I am not supporting his . . . genocide," the Major struggles to say the word, turning his head to avoid eye contact with Kookie.

"You know, since I was a kid, I wanted to be like him—to be *liked* by him—to make him proud. I now know that I will never be able to do that. He is a bad man, Kookie, but he is still my father."

Feeling much empathy for his friend, Kookie leans forward to offer him comforting words. "You know, even though Master Howard is doing something bad I do not believe that he is a bad man." The Major looks down and shrugs his shoulders. "In fact, I believe that somehow, someday your father will see the truth and turn back to the Light. And when that day comes, Major, he will see you for all that you truly are and be *very* proud of you."

After a moment of recollection Kookie adds, "Just as I did the day I blew those badass raspberries at you across the lake!" The two men start howling with laughter at the memory and remember how it led to a new understanding between them and formed a lifelong friendship.

"So, tell me what is happening with the woman, Mimi, and her two friends?"

The Major replies, "You know, I am amazed at how strong they are. It almost seems as if they have gotten stronger since I first met them, which is really strange because I haven't known them for all that long."

"Good. That's very good," Kookie says with a wink and a knowing nod.

"What? Have you been up to something?"

"Who me?" Tapping the tips of his fingers together, Kookie is giddy with delight.

"Yeah, *you!*"

Kookie fesses up, "Yes, it is time I told you the whole thing." Taking out the small black device that lights up with a pyramid, he begins to share the real purpose behind his invention:

"As you know, my friend, we are all being monitored all the time, either by someone who is higher-ranked than us or by each other. But what you do not know and what I am about to tell you, is that I have created something to manage all that; in this room right here in my workstation. No one knows this, Major, and it is going to be our secret."

The Major nods and is humbled by the trust that Kookie is placing in him.

Kookie continues, "The Council and a few other Lords think that they have the ability to monitor me 24/7 like they do with everyone else. But that is not the case. With some ancient wisdom and quantum theories of Metatron's Cube combined with modern technology, I have created a shield in here.

"When I flip this switch on the console or remotely from this little black device, anyone monitoring what is going on in here will see a hologram instead of the real thing. It creates quite a seamless shift between reality and fantasy, if you follow my drift. In fact, I have a program running right now that shows me sitting here diligently monitoring some people in a Center Coffeehouse."

"Well, if that doesn't beat all!" the Major mutters sarcastically.

"Yep. I can make anyone who's watching believe anything I want them to about what is going on in here. Of course, the story I create does have to be believable. I mean, I can't exactly project an image of me petting a T-Rex dinosaur at my console and expect anyone to buy it now, can I?!"

The Major grins and shakes his head at Kookie, who is having a knee-slapping guffaw over that idea. "Anyway, that is only the beginning," Kookie goes on to explain. "That is just the diversion. The real purpose of my work here is embodied in this small black device." The Major instinctively takes out his own device as his friend goes on:

"Like Metatron's Cube, one of the purposes of this device is to connect to a higher form of communication and transformation, among other things of course. I'm working on it every day to improve its capabilities in many areas, as well as learning what all of its energetic properties are."

"Like what, for instance?" asks the Major.

"Like giving off energetic and healing properties to those who use it; including courage, strength, knowledge, wisdom, cleansing, protection from negativity, and even restructuring DNA."

"Whoa, Bro!"

"Ha ha!" Kookie sits back for a moment in his chair, joyously tapping the tips of his fingers together. "Yes, it is rather amazing, isn't it?"

"Uh, wait a second. Do you mean to tell me that this electronic thing that I am holding in my hand can do all of what you just said?"

"In theory, yes. I'm sure it can do even more things that I am unaware of and learning about. Actually, I can program it to emit different frequencies which ought to presumably manifest, well, just about anything, I guess."

The Major sits back in his chair with his mouth hanging open, alternating between staring at the little black device and gawking at his friend.

Kookie interjects with an idea. "You know, I have been considering what to call this thing and I do believe that a good idea has just come to me. You know how the people are all forced—I mean, *asked* to carry My Buddy around with them at all times? Well, what if a few of them, like Mimi and her friends, were given one of these little guys to carry around, not only for communication but also for protection against the negative energy that they are receiving from My Buddy; not to mention the potential consciousness raising effects. I can program a safety factor into this device which would alert someone when danger is near, sort of like warning about a nearby red zone, if you want to look at it that way. Then they can easily avoid the suspect area and any conflict that might ensue by simply staying away from it. That would certainly help to keep them safe from harm, wouldn't it?"

The Major, who is still dumbfounded over the black box and it's capabilities simply nods in agreement.

"So, the name I have come up with for the device is Metatron. What do you think?"

"Huh? What?"

"Now, snap out of it Major. No time for mental fatigue and idle brain farts! We have much work to do."

* * *

Continuing their journey up the northern coast of California, Mimi, Doc and Angie are still enjoying the scenery, but the grim message from the Overseer on My Buddy this morning has dampened their mood. The exponential rise in the death toll from Ebola is being blamed on the people. According to the morning news and instructions, the people are not coming into the Shelters fast enough to receive their Ebola neutralization. Mimi thinks about everything the Major has told her, and in spite of what he has said and what she is now hearing, she still finds it hard to believe that anything as evil as bioweapons are somehow behind all of this.

The group thinks about stopping soon and settling down for the night. Using their intuition and medicine pouches as guides to a safe location, Angie shares her own thoughts. She has been having visions of a crystal-clear lake in the middle of a sea of wildflowers; a place which is calling her to spend the night there.

Mimi says, "There is a campground right up ahead. Perhaps we should just stop there for the night?"

Angie insists, "Oh, I just *know* that the lake and the field of wildflowers are not far away. Not much farther at all!"

"I guess we can go just a little bit farther," says Doc, even though she'd prefer to stop sooner rather than later since it has been an exhausting day and their stomachs are all empty by now. Then, out of nowhere, a clearing appears before them. The late afternoon sun casts a brilliant light across a field of blue wildflowers. Just beyond the field is a shimmering crystal lake.

"Woo Hoo!" cries Angie, "There she is!"

Grateful to have found their resting stop for the night, the three exhausted women begin to slowly unload their gear and set up camp. They are just about ready to turn in for the night. Doc notices that the wildflowers around them are Baby Blue Eyes. Searching her memory for the energetic properties of Baby Blue Eyes, Doc seems to remember something about trusting one's own vulnerability, being open to experiencing the lessons to be learned from pain and suffering. She ponders the vague memory and writes it down in her notebook where she's been tracking the messages of the other flora they have encountered along the way.

Mimi is preparing dinner for the three of them consisting of fruit, raw veggies, bread, and some packaged items that they picked up at the last center. She notices Doc observing the wildflowers and writing.

"What are they, Doc? They are so pretty, aren't they?"

"They sure are," agrees Angie. "In fact, it was these here Baby Blues Eyes that I believe were calling to me that we should spend the night with them."

"Is that so?" exclaims Mimi. "So then, what do *these* lovely little things have to say to us?"

"Well," says Doc, "there was a song once that had a line in it which I think pretty much sums it all up. It goes something like this: *No, it won't harm you to feel your own pain.* Basically, I think the song was about fearlessly facing our own truths; whatever they might be and wherever they take us."

"Wow!" says Angie. "That is truly awesome!"

"Yes," sighs Doc. "Those were the days when people still had a mind of their own, let alone the courage to speak out and even write songs about life and how they felt. I don't know how but it seems like somehow and somewhere since the time of our ancestors we have lost both of those things."

"Or maybe it was taken away from us," says Mimi. With a sudden inexplicable awareness filling her heart, she takes out the little black device the Major has given her. "I wonder what else this thing can do?" she wonders aloud.

* * *

After leaving the Floraville Shelter, Vi has had a lot of soul searching to do. She made excuses to her Master Overseer about her family needing her so she would not be able to return to her work at the Shelter Hut.

The Master Overseer accepted her excuse in a manner that suggested he was almost relieved to see her go.

Now she must consider what to do next. She is thinking about the encounter she had with Ryan, the synchronistic fact that his necklace was made by the same woman, Mimi, who also made the little girl's necklace and is now headed north to find her family. Vi doesn't believe in coincidences and is feeling the pull to head in the same direction as Mimi.

Riding along on her autobike with her sidecar full of camping gear and supplies, Vi is enjoying being out in nature again. She rides down back roads soaking in the energy of the plants, trees and flowers. They soothe her emotional pain as she passes them by. They seem to be telling her that they understand her feelings of helplessness and grief from the horrors she witnessed at the Shelter Hut, but the experience is part of what is guiding Vi to her true work, seemingly along the path that is currently being laid out before her.

By late afternoon Vi decides to stop for the day. She finds a secluded area, pulls off the road, and begins to prepare her meal. However, Vi realizes that the nourishment she needs is not so much from the food she is about to eat but from the positive energy vibrating around her. As the sun begins to descend into the west, misty shadows and sunset colors dance together among the tree trunks of the towering Redwoods.

Vi's private natural sanctuary calls to her: *Bear witness, Angel Lady. With love, you are healed and with love, you will heal others.*

Vi feels a rush of energy filling her entire being, pulling out the darkness and leaving a deeper feeling of serenity within her soul. Falling to her knees, taking the little girl's seashell necklace out of her pocket, and bowing her head low, Vi tenderly places the necklace over her head and around her neck. Looking at the golden colors of the setting sun, Vi makes a solemn vow:

"In the name of all who have died of this dreaded disease, and especially the precious child who died holding this necklace", she cries out loud, "I will discover the truth of what happened to them. And I will not let them die in vain."

* * *

With his family taken away in a scene filled with horrific suffering, Phil knew exactly what he had to do next. He could not stay at Arbor Vista anymore, but he was feeling compelled to get at the truth of what was going on all around him. He felt a driving force within him to help others in whatever way the Creator would have him do, which is how he found himself at the Emmonsville Shelter. Upon arrival at the Shelter, Phil told the Master Overseer that he lost his whole family to Ebola but was spared himself. He said it was his son's dying wish for his dad to help others through this terrible disease. Phil revealed he was there to help and humbly be of service in whatever way he could. He even bowed his head when he said the word "humbly."

The Shelter's Master Overseer bought into Phil's story and was impressed by Phil's willingness to serve. He told Phil that they were desperately short-handed and put him to work immediately.

This is how he came to be of service at the Emmonsville Shelter.

A few days later, Phil is at the Shelter Cottage opening boxes of bottles that have just arrived from Howard Pharmaceuticals. There is one of three labels on each box: one is marked "Ebola Neutralizers"; another one is marked "Super Neutralizers for Ebola Positive"; and the third one is marked "Ebola Marker Test Kits." It is Phil's job to see that the boxes are distributed to the right stations, and the contents of the boxes are all laid out and prepared to be used by the designated Shelter Overseers.

As he looks around to observe the setting, he is aware of various peculiarities that just don't add up. One oddity in particular is the number of people who test positive and those who test negative. Although Phil has only been there for a few days, each day the number of people testing positive has gone up exponentially. The day before, everybody who came in was testing positive, and they were sent to the Shelter Hut, presumably to receive the Super Ebola Neutralizer. However, he notes that not one of those people have emerged alive.

Great Spirit, Phil prays quietly to himself, *what can I do? Please, please, tell me what to do.*

A voice responds inside of his heart saying, *"Witness, my brother; bear witness, and in time you will do more."*

* * *

Kookie and the Major have just finished a sumptuous dinner of roast leg of lamb, roasted vegetables, and scalloped potatoes. They are sipping on ambrosia tea accompanied by petit four tea cakes and almond fudge. The Major's thoughts have been preoccupied with everything Master Howard and Kookie have told him; from the Council's dreadful agenda to Kookie's creation of Metatron, and the possible uses for the device.

"I'm really intrigued by the possibilities of what this thing can do," the Major says to Kookie. "For something like healing, how does it work?"

"Well," says Kookie, leaning back in his chair with a full belly and tapping the tips of his fingers together pensively, "It's all about programming the little guy to emit the correct frequency."

"Come again?"

"Ah HA! Yes!" Kookie exclaims, pointing his index finger in the air. He gets excited when given the opportunity to explain something technical, especially when it is one of his own inventions. "Everything emits a frequency of some kind or another and that frequency can all be quantified into a number called hertz. The challenge is to discover what the correct frequency is for each thing so that you are in effect, imitating or sounding like that thing."

"Is it all about sound waves?"

"It can also be light waves, or radiation, or other such things."

"I see." The Major is holding Metatron in his hands as he continues with his line of thought. "So basically, if you tell Metatron here to sound or pulsate like a butterfly by programming the frequency of the sound waves or whatever that a butterfly emits, then a girl butterfly might go *OO Baby* and come running, thinking she has a hot date with a guy butterfly, when in fact it is Metatron. Yes?"

Kookie is having a good chuckle at that one, "I guess you could put it that way."

"Hey, Bro that's the best *my* brain can handle! So how do you know what the frequency is, let's say, for a butterfly for instance?"

"There are different ways of discovering frequency and it's not all that complicated. In fact, one of my programs works really well for that," says Kookie.

"Wow! So, in theory then, you could create something medicinal if you knew its frequency?"

"Well yes, but you also have to be sure that you've got the right medicinal for the right ailment."

"Hmm, makes sense," the Major says reflectively. "So how are we going to figure that one out, then?"

"We?"

"Absolutely! Count me in. After all, I *am* the pharmaceutical guy, am I not?"

"You've got a point there," says Kookie smiling. "Ok, partner!"

The two men shake hands.

* * *

Mimi and Doc have gone to sleep, but Angie is sitting in the middle of a patch of Baby Blue Eyes looking up at the stars and thinking of her mom and dad. She is remembering the way her dad always explained things to her as if she were an intelligent adult and how good it made her feel to be treated with so much dignity and respect. She's also reminiscing about all the times she would wake up during the night frightened from a nightmare and run to her parents' bedroom. Snuggling down next to her mom made her feel safe and loved, and she easily fell back to sleep. Then the vision of her very last memory of her parents invades her consciousness, sending her soul crashing to the depths of darkness and grief. The brutal memory of watching her parents vomit blood to death along with other people suffering the same way is unbearable for Angie.

For the first time since that terrible tragedy, Angie is hit with the full force of horror of what she witnessed. She looks up to the stars and cries out over the agony of losing her mom and dad, tearing handfuls of Baby Blue Eyes out of the ground with both fists, throwing them everywhere.

In the little tent nearby, Mimi and Doc awaken to the agonizing sounds of Angie's cries. They go outside and approach her gently, reaching out to offer all the love and support that they can. As Angie is crying and clutching two handfuls of Baby Blue Eyes, she suddenly reaches out to Doc and Mimi, accepting their comforting arms. The three women remain there holding each other letting Angie release the pain of her unspeakable tragedy.

At last Angie calms down, spent of all energy. She is still holding the Baby Blue Eyes tightly bundled into her fists as she begins to realize something; the emotional pain is subsiding and she knows that she is going to be okay. A wisp of a smile crosses her face and she thanks Doc and Mimi for being there. She looks down at the flowers in her hand and thanks them too.

Later that night, Mimi has a dream:

She is sitting next to a lake surrounded by wildflowers. They are radiant in all of their colors and fragrances and they all seem to be calling to her. "Take me! Take me!" they call out to her, one after the other. "I want to be your medicine! Take me!" Suddenly a giant golden pyramid begins to rise out of the lake, rotating slowly in the sunlight casting radiant beams of light. Circling the pyramid as if skating on top of the water she sees and hears Ryan dancing and singing and reaching his arms out for her to come and join him on the lake. The sound of his laughter and the warmth of Ryan's smile makes her heart break open with intense longing to be with him. Mimi steps out onto the lake and Ryan catches her hands. He twirls her round and round as the golden pyramid shimmers in the sunlight, growing bigger and bigger until it encompasses the two lovers in a golden halo.

Mimi awakens from her dream in a state of ecstasy and gradually rolls out of her sleeping bag and looks outside the tent. It is early in the morning and the sky is beginning to discard the shadows of the night. It is just light enough that she can see the lake in the distance and the large field of Baby Blue Eyes stretching out before her. Mimi feels the passion of her lover, and in her mind's eye she sees the golden pyramid.

All at once, everything becomes as clear to her as the lake, and she reaches for the little black device that the Major gave her.

The Major wakes from a deep sleep at the sound of Metatron vibrating with great insistence. Assuming it's Kookie summoning him, he doesn't bother to read the incoming code of 393 flashing on the screen across the rotating golden pyramid.

The Major answers the call like a sleepy grizzly bear, "Jeez, Bro! I'm sleepin'! Wassup?"

"Well, when I last checked, I was a *Sis*, not a *Bro!*" Mimi exclaims with indignation. But then she realizes what time it is and quickly adds, "Oh my! I *am* sorry, Major! I didn't even think about how early it is! I just have something monumental to talk to you about."

"Sure thing, Mimi." The Major is wide awake now and sitting up straight. "What's going on?"

"It's about this little black communication device you gave me." Mimi now has the Major's full attention.

"Yeah?"

"Major, I know this is going to sound crazy, but I do believe that this device can do a whole lot more than just give us a private and secure means of communication."

"*Yeeaaaah?*" The Major is fully alert and becoming animated. Waving his arm in the air he continues, "*SOOO?*"

"I don't know; I just had this dream. I believe that this device has some kind of life force and it is connected to some kind of higher form of energy."

Dumbfounded, the Major scratches his head as Mimi continues, "And in addition to that, we have been receiving messages from flowers including their healing properties. Major, I think this here device is making us all, well, I guess the word is *intuitive*, or something. Is this possible or am I going bonkers?"

Shaking his head in amazement the Major says, "Well, Mimi, if you are going bonkers then join the club." He proceeds to fill her in on the dinner conversation he and Kookie had the night before.

"My goodness, Major! We have been receiving all kinds of messages from the natural world around us. Do you think it is really possible to program their frequencies into this device?"

"According to Kookie, that's exactly what it can do," the Major replies. "Oh, and by the way," he continues, "Kookie gave the device a name. It is Metatron."

"Wow, that's awesome!" says Mimi. The Major promises to meet up with the three women very soon.

As they are preparing to get back on the road, Mimi fills Doc and Angie in on the conversation she just had with the Major. They are excited about the possibilities of Metatron, especially as they are all learning new things about the properties of the natural world around them.

"I'm also beginning to understand the heightened intuitive abilities we are all becoming endowed with. It is truly remarkable!" Doc says, and the other two agree.

"Actually," says Angie, "I have been feeling that perhaps we should not return to the open roads that we have been traveling on. Something is telling me to take back roads instead."

"Yes," agrees Mimi, "I have been feeling the same way."

"Me too," says Doc.

The women take off, traveling a bit more inland on their journey north. At this point, they are only a few more days away from the California-Oregon border.

* * *

The village Center is coming into view, and Vi decides to stop for food purchases and a quick freshen up. Thinking about the morning news and instructions from My Buddy, she is preparing for a very special kind of "confrontation" at the Center. It seems that the Overseers are on the lookout for anyone unfamiliar; that is, those whom they do not recognize from the area. They are concerned that everyone should receive their Ebola neutralization "in a timely manner." To Vi, the urgency is a code way of saying they are watching out for folks who know they are being lied to, that something scary is going on, and they are choosing to run.

But then she wonders, *run where?*

Apart from the fact that she is following her gut instincts to go north and will probably end up somewhere in Oregon, she really doesn't have much more of a plan. But one thing Vi does know for sure is that anytime she is in a public place, she will have to rely on a method of self-cloaking that she learned as a child.

It is an effective way to not be noticed, like now.

Pulling up to the Center and getting off her autobike, Vi closes her eyes for a moment. She puts her hands across her chest and relaxes as her breathing begins to slow down. Visualizing a blanket of loving light covering her entire body Vi whispers softly, *I am safe in your love; I am protected in your love; I am seen only through YOUR eyes by those who are righteous, and so it is, and so it shall be; it is already done.*

With that Vi enters the village Center.

Shortly afterwards an Overseer's van pulls up.

* * *

"There is a Center just up ahead," Mimi says to Doc and Angie. "Let's stop there for a moment.

As they approach the Center all three women suddenly get a sick feeling in their stomachs. They stop just in time to see an Overseer's van pulling in front of the Center.

"I heard something about this on My Buddy this morning," Doc says. "This doesn't feel good." Mimi, Doc and Angie stay out of sight a safe distance away as they witness the unfolding of the scene before them.

Two Security Overseers get out of the van while three more emerge from the Center, surrounding a dozen or so people. The Center Overseers hand the people off to the two Security Overseers who proceed to load the folks into the van. Meanwhile, the three Center

Overseers have gone back to escort more people out of the Center and to the van. Mimi, Doc and Angie are watching anxiously as some people are getting pushed and shoved while being told to "Move along."

"Oh No!" says Angie as she is gripped with fear, "What is happening?"

Just then, as the Security Overseers are locking up the van and preparing to take everyone to the local Shelter, a young woman emerges casually from the Center, carrying a bag full of food to her autobike.

"*HUH?*" Mimi, Doc and Angie all blurt out at each other, watching in disbelief while the woman moves about unnoticed.

"Good Grief!" says Doc, "It's like they don't even see her!"

Mimi's eyes go wide, as if they will pop right out of her skull. "*HOLY, SCHMOLY!*" Mimi blurts out to the other two. "Well, *I* certainly see her and what she is wearing around her neck!" Mimi nearly faints when she recognizes the seashell necklace the mysterious woman is wearing.

Chapter 9 – Unseen

"WE'VE GOT TO CATCH UP WITH HER! We can't let her get too far ahead of us!" Mimi is anxiously exclaiming to the others.

"Yes, but we obviously aren't invisible the way she seems to be, and the van is still sitting there," Doc says.

"You're right, but we can't let her get away either. What can we do?" Mimi wonders. She notices Angie standing with her hands on her chest and her eyes closed. Her lips are moving in what looks like either prayer or feeling the surrounding energy field, but Angie is doing neither.

Doc whispers to Mimi, "Look," pointing in Vi's direction. "The woman is looking around like she's hearing something but can't make out where the sound is coming from."

They both look at Angie and then at the woman and then at each other. It suddenly hits them at the same time; Angie is *talking* to the woman with her mind. And the woman can *hear* her.

Finally, the van drives away. Mimi, Doc and Angie waste no time barreling down to the Center where Vi is getting on her autobike ready to leave. She starts heading toward the lane that leads back to the road when suddenly, urgent voices call out behind her. "Hey there! Hey! Whoa! Wait!" Vi turns around and sees three women frantically waving her down.

"Hi!" Vi calls out to them as they finally catch up with her.

Jumping off her autobike Mimi says, "Hello there! My name is Mimi. I know this is going to sound strange, but would you mind telling me where you got that necklace?"

A sullen look overcomes Vi's face. "It belonged to a little girl. She died from Ebola not too long ago."

"Was the little girl's name Suzie, by any chance?" asks Mimi, her heart sinking.

Vi's jaw drops. "I think so! That sounds familiar!" she exclaims, as the memory comes flooding back to her of meeting little Suzie's family at the Hut. Watching Mimi trying to digest the sad news of little Suzie's death, Vi says to her, "You wouldn't by any chance be Ryan's friend, would you?"

Mimi's grief turns to instant shock, "Yes! I am, have you seen him?" "Where, when? Is he okay?"

"Yes, it was just a few days ago in the Arbor Vista Center."

"Was he all right?" asks Mimi, feeling anxious and hopeful.

"He was just fine," Vi says smiling, happy to give some good news to these women.

"Oh, thank you, sweet Father in Heaven!" Mimi cries. Burying her hands in her face she continues crying and repeating, "Thank you, Lord, thank you!"

"He was wearing the same seashell necklace around his neck that belonged to Suzie, which is why I wound up going over and introducing myself to him." Vi explains.

With a gentle smile, memories come flooding back to Mimi as she relates the story, "I could tell he didn't like to wear that thing, so he kept it in his pocket. Whenever he saw me coming, he tried to *discreetly* slip it out of his pocket and onto his neck. Of course, I never let on that I saw what he was doing," she chuckles.

Holding out her arms, she calls out to Ryan, "Bless you, my darling. I love you, too!" And to her Heavenly Father she calls out, "Thank you, thank you for sending me this beautiful message and for keeping Ryan safe. Thank you!"

Mimi turns to Vi. "We have much to talk about, my friend. Would you like to join us? We are headed to Oregon."

Vi sees Doc and Angie nod in agreement to the invitation. "I would love to, thank you. I've got plenty of provisions here for all of us for the next couple of days if necessary."

"Oh yeah." says Angie, "How on earth did you get past all those Overseers without them noticing you?"

"We really do have quite a lot to talk about." Vi chuckles. "May I tell you all about it later, when we stop and make camp for the evening?"

"Sure thing," they all agree, and head north on the back roads.

* * *

Kookie is sitting in front of his consol. He has been listening to the people's news each day in order to project an appropriate hologram of his own activities at his workstation. Currently, he has a live image from an onsite camera inside an actual Shelter Hut feeding into the Holographic Imager. This way Kookie's High Overlord Contact (HOC) of the Council will think Kookie is diligently working on Council orders.

The Lord's Communication Device activates, waiting for Kookie to accept the incoming message.

"Good morning, Lord Kenneth. How are you today?" asks the HOC.

"I'm fine, sir. And how are you?"

"Very well, My Lord, very well, indeed!"

"Indeed, yes indeed, sir," Kookie responds to his HOC, intentionally repeating the word "indeed" while holding onto Metatron, which has been activated with the updated 369 Program he developed.

"Good. I have your instructions for the day, My Lord. There is growing suspicion there may be a rogue element operating within the Upper Crust."

"Oh my!" says Kookie gripping Metatron.

"Yes, indeed!" says the HOC.

Kookie parrots back the words, "Yes, indeed! Yes, indeed!"

"Good. Your instructions are to find out if there is any truth to these suspicions. We want you to carefully monitor your associates of the UC, and with the usual chain of command use any and all means of, shall we say, *discovery* of their true fealty."

"Yes, sir."

There is a pause, then the HOC continues, "My Lord, I am asking you to spy on your own brothers and sisters of the UC, as well as two others: The High Lord and High Lady of the Council. Do you understand me, Lord Kenneth?"

Clenching Metatron tightly in his hands, Kookie thinks to himself, *SHOOT!* but his words come out, "Yes, indeed. Yes indeed, I do."

"Good. I'll check back with you later." The High Overlord Contact signs off and Kookie is left sitting there stunned.

So is the Major when he steps out of the shadows.

"Sorry, Bro. I was on my way in here, and when I overheard the last part of the conversation, I thought it would not be a good idea to make my presence known."

Looking down at his hands still clutching Metatron Kookie says, "Well, at least I can be grateful for this."

"What do you mean?" asks the Major.

"I guess that's something else I need to share with you, now that we are officially the UC Rogues Gallery." Kookie continues, "Major, you know that the Lords are charged with various duties and responsibilities, just as the Masters are. And our *main* function, apart from surveillance of the populace, is the ongoing improvement and implementation of various means and methods of mind control and manipulation of the human will.

"Yes," the Major nods, "which is a whole lot more serious than the 'dumbing-and-numbing' of the people with My Buddy and various other tactics we use to supposedly take care of them."

Kookie replies, "Yes, well, that is how it is supposed to look on the outside, all for the greater good of the so-called 'childlike people' who can't really think for themselves. In reality, it is because of what *we* are doing to them that is causing them to be incapable of using their rational minds anymore. Funny thing is, they still have their intuitive skills intact. Sometimes I think their intuition is even a bit better than it used to be as a kind of overcompensation. It seems that we just haven't been able to gain control of that part of the human spirit.

"It is too much for me to go into it all at once, but I'll tell you that the mind control and manipulation is totally pervasive, infiltrating every part of their lives. And some of it even extends to us; after all, the Council must keep their Lords and Masters under their domination too, *especially* the Lords, as we are their guardians. And especially the three who were chosen as youngsters, who presented the most promise, to be taken away from their true families and reared in a very special way." Kookie pauses for a moment and takes a deep breath.

"Go on," says the Major gently to his friend.

"I was chosen as one of those three, Major. We are referred to as the Council's Three High Lords, or the High Lords for short. Although we are not technically a part of the Council, we are the bridge between them and the Lords. Each one of us was chosen for the unique gift that we possess; one for extreme intelligence, one for extreme intuitive skills, and one for the highest combination of intelligence *and* intuition."

"And which one are you, Kookie?"

Smiling sadly Kookie says, "Another time I will share all of that with you. But for the moment, let me just finish by explaining that the trigger word for all of us which I'm sure you are already aware of by now is: INDEED."

The Major nods, "Yes. Go on, Kookie."

"I have developed a program that is able to counteract the effects of that word, among other things. It is a function of the 369 Program."

The Major glances at Metatron still clutched in Kookie's hands. "Have you figured out how to install the 369 Program onto Metatron?"

Kookie nods in the affirmative. The Major adds, "And does that give you some kind of protection against the trigger word?"

"It is not merely *some kind of protection*. It is *ALL* kinds of protection."

"Okay," says the Major, "How does it work?"

"Metatron is a communication device and it is also an amplifier."

"Aha!" interrupts the Major. "So, if people are tuned into My Buddy and hearing the word INDEED at whatever the current frequency My Buddy is set to, then people are basically being dumbed-and-numbed, hypnotized, propagandized and basically *stupid*-ized into receiving their daily news and 'instructions.'"

"Yep," confirms Kookie.

"Good Lord!" says the Major.

"I try to be."

"Not you, *fool!*" The Major rolls his eyes; Kookie smiles and taps the tips of his fingers together, and the Major continues; "Okay, so it seems to me that your next move is to find out what frequency the Council is using in conjunction with the word INDEED on its daily broadcasts."

"440 hertz," Kookie says, grinning with delight.

The Major shakes his head. "I guess I shouldn't be surprised you already know that."

"Actually, my next move," says Kookie, "is to figure out how to destroy the Council's entire mind control system of the human race—before I am discovered, and they destroy me."

"You mean us, don't you, partner?" the Major asks with a friendly smile.

"Yes," Kookie sighs and smiles back. "Oh, and please let Mimi know as soon as possible that we should *not* use Metatron right now for communication. It seems that we are just too vulnerable to the UC's tracking system when using Metatron for communication purposes. However, Mimi *can* use 369's Safety Program, which appears to be under their radar."

"I will let her know, Kookie. Thanks."

* * *

Please promise me that you will do your best to keep your distance from people. And if you are ever told to go to a Shelter . . . DO NOT GO!

Ryan hears Mimi's words over and over in his head. He cannot forget her stern warning, or how she delivered it to him with so much urgency in her voice and caring in her eyes. His unexpected encounter with Vi a few days ago conveyed the same warning. The strangest part about meeting Vi was that the seashell necklace she had on was the same as his. Neither one of them could explain it, except that Vi's necklace most definitely was another one of Mimi's creations.

Vi's other warning to him was to travel the back roads. Ryan is by nature a beach person and has been traveling up the coast on the larger roads following the shoreline. He enjoys the ocean view by day and the sweet fragrance of the salty ocean air at night. However, the morning announcements said that since so many people are on the road trying to reach their loved ones, the Council is providing transportation assistance in comfy vans to help folks get to a nearby Shelter for their Ebola neutralizations. Ryan feels red flag warnings in his gut about the whole thing and decides that tomorrow he will start riding inland on the back roads, heading north.

Finishing his evening meal, Ryan looks out over the cliff where he has perched himself for the night. The sparkling ocean is stretching beneath him for as far as he can see. The sea appears to be an endless eternity of majestic blue, blending with the sunset colors on the horizon. Ryan watches as the sun sinks into the west, and he wonders when or if he will ever see such a magnificent scene again. *Take it all in,* he thinks to himself. *This may be the last time.*

Grasping the last rays of the setting sun, Ryan calls out in his heart to his beloved, *I miss you, Mimi. I wish you were here with me.*

* * *

Mimi, Doc, Angie, and Vi have just finished an excellent evening meal which Doc prepared from the food Vi picked up at the village Center— before *she* was almost picked up earlier that day. When Vi is distracted at the tent and Mimi has a few moments alone with Doc and Angie, she fills them in on her thoughts regarding what Vi told them about little Suzie.

"One of the things the Major warned me about was to use discretion in sharing what we know about everything that has been going on. I just can't imagine the horror Vi would feel if she knew the "medicine" she administered into all of those people was what killed them, *especially* little Suzie. I think we had better not say anything to her about it until the time is right, and we meet up with the Major again."

The others agree just as Vi returns. Mimi finally asks Vi what has been haunting her all day. "Okay, Vi. Could you please tell us how you walked past all those Overseers?"

"Sure!" says Vi. "It's a technique I learned when I was a young girl and first learned about the powers of the natural world. I wanted to learn a new way to protect myself, so a friend of mine taught me self-cloaking. I believe it has other names as well, since it has been practiced through the ages going all the way back to ancient civilizations."

"Wow. So how does it work?" asks Angie.

"Well, it helps to first understand a bit more about what it is. Have you ever walked down a street and seen someone coming from the other direction who kind of made you feel creepy?"

"Oh sure," Angie replies.

"When that happens, we tend to look down, look away, or maybe walk a bit more quickly and try our best to appear unnoticed."

"O-*kay*," says Angie, trying to follow.

"Well, this is sort of like that only taking it one step further," Vi explains. "In essence, you are going out-of-body with your spirit and telling others energetically that you are not there, even though physically you still are. The spirit is more powerful than the physical body, a fact most people do not realize. Also, the mind can easily be tricked into seeing, or *not* seeing almost anything. . . kinda like magic tricks."

Mimi, Doc and Angie are enraptured by what they are hearing, as Vi continues, "So the rest of it is all about practicing, and eventually mastering, the technique of becoming more and more unseen. Of course, being unseen provides protection."

"Can you teach us your technique of self-cloaking?" asks Doc, thoroughly amazed.

"Sure thing." says Vi. "Are you all ready for your first lesson?" They all nod in the affirmative with great eagerness. "Well, okay then; let's begin!"

Vi invites her friends to lie down on top of their sleeping bags and get comfortable. She guides them through a simple but effective meditation to help them relax. When she feels they are ready, she tells them to imagine that they are enveloped by a white cloak of energy. The cloak feels like being wrapped in a warm embrace; loved and protected. Then she instructs the three women to repeat after her, one phrase at a time, in their state of total relaxation:

I am safe in your love. I am protected in your love. I am seen only through your eyes by those who are righteous. And so it is and so it shall be— it is already done.

She invites Mimi, Doc and Angie to stay in their relaxed state for just a little while longer, soaking in the protection and inner peace in their state of relaxation. As they return to their fully conscious state Mimi is the first one to speak.

"Oh, my goodness! That is truly amazing. I mean if nothing else it is most certainly soothing and relaxing." The others agree and all are feeling very calm from the experience. "You know," adds Mimi. "If this is so effective as we have all witnessed with Vi here today, I wonder what it would be like adding Metatron to it?"

"What's that?" asks Vi. Mimi, Doc and Angie proceed to fill her in on the whole story of their meeting with the Major and the creation of Kookie's Metatron device. She is fascinated to hear about the Major and the courageous work that he and Kookie are involved in for the people.

"I didn't know that Lords and Masters could be so caring about the rest of us," says Vi. "I am certainly happy to learn that there are such souls as theirs living amongst all the bad ones and yet remaining pure and decent within themselves."

Mimi adds, "It does give me hope, *much* hope for us all."

* * *

Mimi is feeling encouraged as she prepares for bed and grabs her journal.

> *I truly meant what I said to the ladies this evening about feeling much hope right now. Even after Vi told us about the murders of Jerry, Linda, Blake, Maureen and Suzie, I still feel that the best of us will shine through before this is all over. I believe that there is a depth of love in the human soul which we have not yet experienced or discovered, and that we are awakening to that kind of love. Thank you, Lord. Thank you for the news that Ryan is still okay. I know that if I should ever see him again in this life, I will let him know each and every day just how precious he is, and how much he means to me. Your faithful servant, Mimi*

As Mimi and the others are preparing for their night's rest, Metatron begins to vibrate and the number 363 appears on the screen.

"Hey there, Major! What's the good word?" greets Mimi.

"Hi Mimi. I can't talk long, but there is much that I have to tell you. However, the UC seems to have caught on to the presence of the Metatron device; although, they are unable to lock down our coordinates as of yet. Kookie says that we are most vulnerable when we are using it for communication, so this needs to be our last transmission, at least until we see each other and Kookie can figure out what to do. Meanwhile, you can still use it for the safety program, and Kookie and I will use it to track you."

"Okay," Mimi says with a sigh.

The Major continues, "I can see from your coordinates that you ladies are only about a two-day ride from the California/Oregon border. You *must* be careful Mimi; all of you. There is a small town called Emmonsville, just a few miles up the road, with a Center that is remote and quiet and has not had any trouble. You should all be fine to freshen up, replenish your supplies and have a little rest while you are there. I was even thinking that an outdoor spot just outside the Emmonsville Center might be a good place for us to gather. What do you think?"

Mimi replies, "As you know, Doc has connections with safehouse food farms. She knows a trustworthy couple that is just on the other side of the Oregon border. It is called Bear River Farm, and that is where we are headed and will likely stop for a rest. Things are changing so quickly right now, especially at the Centers, that what may seem safe today, may not be safe tomorrow. So maybe we can plan on meeting in Emmonsville and then see where things are at by the time we get there."

The Major considers Mimi's idea for a moment. "Okay, I have a few things that I must attend to first, but I will meet you at Emmonsville Center tomorrow, provided, as you say, that things are still all clear there. If not, then I'll check your coordinates on Metatron so I'll be able to find you. Mimi, it is imperative that we meet. Is that understood?"

"Yes, Major. You can count on us. Thank you again, for all you are doing to keep us safe."

"That's okay," he mutters softly. "Don't mention it."

The Major returns home at the urgent request of Master Howard. Kookie has installed the 369 Program into the Major's Metatron, and they are both anxious to see how the device affects the meeting with his father.

With Howard Pharmaceuticals mass producing live Ebola as a bioweapon, the Major and Kookie are on an urgent mission to stop the genocide, whatever way they can. And Kookie believes he may be onto something with the 369 Program and Metatron.

* * *

"Well ladies, in the next two days we should be at the California/Oregon border," says Mimi as they all gather their gear, preparing for another day's ride.

Checking Metatron for the Major's directions to Emmonsville, Mimi notices Kookie's safety guide.

"Oh my, take a look at this, ladies."

"What is it?" asks Vi.

"It seems that Kookie figured out how to rate all the Centers according to their safety factor. Check it out."

There is map on the screen showing a color-coded system categorizing red for danger, green for all clear, and various shades of pink and light green notating levels of danger in-between.

Angie laughs. "You know, I think I'm gonna like this guy, if I ever get to meet him, that is."

"Yeah, but how would he know what's safe and what isn't anyway?" asks Vi.

Mimi responds, "From what the Major told me, the Lords are in charge of propaganda, brainwashing, and total dumbing-and-numbing of the people as he calls it. And another part of what they do to control us is surveillance, which includes track and monitor everything we do."

"Everything?" asks Vi.

"Everything that may pose a potential risk at any given moment. It is their job to stay on top of it all and keep the peace with 'us children,' in a manner of speaking," Mimi says, disdainfully. "So, I guess it is no surprise that he could program this device to help lead us to places where we can stay out of sight and unnoticed."

The four women pick a route according to the Major's map and set out in that direction. They decide it would be a good idea to take his advice and stop at the Emmonsville Center, get refreshed and reload on provisions. However, when Mimi checks Metatron she notices that the green light on the Center is suddenly flashing red.

"Good grief!" she exclaims and lets the others know.

"I know this sounds weird, but I have a gut feeling we are supposed to go there anyway," says Mimi, "you know like maybe hang back at a safe distance and see what's going on?"

Mimi holds Metatron to her chest and is suddenly seized with a massive panic attack. "Whoa!" she gasps. "Oh no. Oh no! NO, NO, NO!"

"WHAT!" they all shout at her in unison.

"Wa . . . Wa . . .Witness!" Gasping for air, Mimi continues to stutter out, "Witness . . . Wa . . . witness. W-w-we . . . must . . . witness."

Doc, Angie and Vi try to calm Mimi down while also feeling Mimi's same sense of urgency. They agree to proceed to the Center with great caution, staying far back and out of sight. The four women do not have very far to go when Angie is the first to see the Center.

"There it is," she says nervously, pointing to the Emmonsville Center.

Approaching slowly and with caution, they notice a patch of trees with the Center in close range. The spot appears to be well hidden, so they decide to use it as their secluded lookout point.

They do not have to wait long.

Coming down the road from the opposite direction are three vans. They pull up in front of the Center and three Security Overseers jump out of each van and storm the front entrance with guns. Within seconds, the women hear shots fired and people screaming. Moments later the Security Overseers emerge one by one, dragging some people out with their hands tied around their backs and forcing others to move at gunpoint. One woman is holding a baby. As an Overseer tries to wrench the baby from her arms she begins to scream, clutching her baby close to her chest. The Security Overseer points his gun at her head and pulls the trigger.

Catching the thrashing baby as it falls from her arms, he hands the little one to one of the people being escorted to the van. "Here, take this thing on board with you," he demands gruffly.

All pandemonium breaks loose as the people begin resisting and fighting back. More shots ring out, leaving people dead or fatally injured on the ground. Mimi and the others catch themselves from crying out in horror at what they are witnessing. The doors of the vans are locked from the outside and the Security Overseers take off with what remains of their captives.

All falls quiet for a moment as the air hangs heavy over the massacre. In their state of shock, the women see a man emerge from the entrance of the Center, badly shaken and barely standing on his two feet.

Suddenly, Mimi lets out a blood-curdling scream and races toward the man crying out to him, *"RYAAAN!"*

Chapter 10 – 369

RYAN'S BRAIN IS IN A FOG. The last thing he remembers is being ordered by a Security Overseer to go outside and get in the van. He was standing there, frozen in confusion until the Overseer came toward him with a club yelling, "MOVE IT, MAN!" Then everything went black.

Now, as if in a dream, he can hear Mimi calling his name. *"RYAN! OH LORD! RYAN!"*

Squinting through his clouded vision he sees her running toward him with three other women following behind. As Mimi reaches him and holds her arms out, Ryan realizes this is not a dream. He opens his arms with weary relief to receive his beloved as she falls into his embrace. They stand together holding each other tight, crying, unable to speak and unable to move. Doc, Angie and Vi stop at a respectful distance as the two lovers reunite, surrounded by broken bodies, blood and death.

Angie, Doc and Vi begin to check each person lying on the ground, hoping that someone may still be breathing, but all is still. As far as they can tell no one is left alive. They go inside the Center to check for survivors there.

Mimi is crying, "Are you okay, my darling?" She notices a huge swelling on the back of Ryan's head and blood in his hair.

"I, uh, don't know," he says.

Mimi takes him gently by the hand and says, "Let's get you inside and clean that up."

In the Center, Mimi and Ryan catch up with Doc, Angie and Vi in the deserted food market.

"Doc, Angie, this is Ryan." Turning to Vi she says, "I believe you two have already met."

They all smile meekly and sadly at each other, welcoming Ryan with a hug. Observing the bump and the blood on his head, each woman wastes no time in gathering antiseptics, bandages and assorted first aid items to tend to Ryan's injury. They also gather a pile of food and prepare to head back to their autobikes. On a sudden instinct, Mimi checks Metatron for Emmonsville's safety-status. When last she looked it was flashing red, but now it does not register at all, as if the Center does not even exist anymore. Sharing this with the others, they all get a creepy feeling that they had better get the heck out of there *immediately*.

Meanwhile, another red light has been flashing on Kookie's screen. It is connected to Metatron that is tracking Mimi. Kookie stares at the screen with great anxiety and concern, wondering why the women went to that center. *Did they not see the flashing red light?* he wonders, also concerned that Metatron may have malfunctioned. But then he sees their signal begin moving north away from the terminated center. *Oh, thank heavens!* Kookie exhales with a sigh of relief. But he remains greatly perplexed as to why the women went there in the first place.

* * *

Off in the distance Phil sees the two vans coming. He knows that they are carrying human beings who have just been taken, most likely against their will, to a place where most of them will not survive. He watches as the back doors are unlocked from the outside and a group of frightened people emerge. They are brusquely escorted to the Emmonsville Shelter Cottage. "Get moving," he hears a Security Overseer yelling at them. Phil makes his way over to the reception area. He knows that his presence will help calm the people down and allow them to have some kind of hope.

They are lined up for processing and testing when all of a sudden Phil hears a baby crying. Going down the line, he comes to a man who is holding the crying little one. "May I help you?" Phil asks kindly.

"Yes, please," the man says. "This is not my child." As he fearfully glances around, the man tells Phil what happened to the baby's mother when they were all taken captive.

Overcome with compassion for the little one, Phil sees from her clothing that she is a little girl. He takes her into his arms and holds her snug against his chest saying a silent prayer to the Creator: *Do not let them hurt this little one, Great Spirit. And* **I** *will not let them hurt her either.*

When no one is looking, Phil takes the baby and tucks her inside his button-down shirt so she's partially hidden and carries her to the autobike park. Placing her carefully in the sidecar, he rides away from the Emmonsville Shelter for the very last time.

* * *

The Major arrives at the Howard Pharmaceutical plant and heads straight to his father's office. Master Howard is waiting for him.

"Hello, father! What's going on?"

Master Howard looks at his son with a grave expression. "Sit down."

The Major instinctively grabs Metatron in his pocket and fearing the worst, holds onto it for dear life.

"We seem to have a problem, John."

Unable to say a word the Major is locked in his father's stare.

"Something appears to be, how shall I say, not working?"

"What do you mean, father?"

Leaning forward and staring hard into the Major's eyes, Master Howard says, "It's the live Ebola. There are reports coming in of people surviving Operation Snake Bite!"

The Major sits like a marble statue, still and mute. Until he suddenly manages to let one word escape out of his mouth. "*INDEED!*"

"Indeed, my sorry butt!" says Master Howard, standing straight and flinging his arms in the air. It's going to *be* my sorry butt if I can't figure out what's gone wrong in production!"

"So, do you want me to snoop around in the plant and find out what's going on?"

Drawing in a long breath and exhaling it slowly, Master Howard says, "Yes, my boy . . . yes."

"Okay then. I got this covered."

"Thank you, son. Thank you."

As the Major leaves his father's office, heading for the factory floor, his father calls out to him, "John, you are a good son."

"Thank you, father," he says sadly, "I try to be."

When he is out of sight the Major quietly takes Metatron out of his pocket and makes sure everything looks good for what he is about to do with it. A few days ago, Kookie began remotely transmitting the DNA restructuring function of the 369 Program to the boxes of orange-labeled Ebola bioweapons at Howard Pharmaceuticals. Kookie knew the effects of a remote transmission would be limited at best, but it seems the remote test run was effective if people are surviving the live Ebola injections, much to the horror of Master Howard.

However, in order to ensure more survivors, the Major will have to restructure the rest of the live Ebola DNA using the 369 DNA restructuring program installed in Metatron, in person at the factory. He must get to the remainder of the bioweapons himself without being detected.

* * *

Mimi and her friends have ridden a good distance away from the nightmare in Emmonsville, and they come to a meadow off the road with a tranquil field of wildflowers. It is the perfect spot for a badly needed rest, and for tending to Ryan's head injuries. Before they had left, Mimi made Ryan as comfortable as she could in the sidecar of her autobike where she is grateful to now see him sleeping peacefully. She does not want to disturb his slumber, so she and the others have a meal together while Ryan sleeps.

Mimi shares with Doc, Angie and Vi the last conversation she had with the Major about meeting up with him at the Emmonsville Center.

"Obviously that's not going to happen now. We also talked about meeting up at our next rest stop if for some reason Emmonsville didn't work out. I told him that we were probably going to the safehouse in Bear River Farm. He said he would track us with Metatron and get our coordinates once we stopped there. We aren't too far from there now and will probably be there tomorrow around midday.

"Also, apparently our communications on Metatron are rousing some suspicion within the UC, so we are not to use the device for communication purposes at this time. However, the safety program is still okay for us to use. Maybe we should listen to My Buddy to see if the news is covering what happened at the Emmonsville Center."

The others all agree and Doc turns on My Buddy:

"Hello Dear Ones, and how are you all doing this bright and lovely day? It feels like spring has truly sprung, as the saying goes, ha ha! Yes, Indeed! Yes, indeed it has, spring has sprung! What a wonderful time to get those lovely fruits and veggies now, especially as more of them will be coming into season soon! Yes, indeed they will! Isn't it simply fabulous that the Council has given us all those wonderful local Centers where we can do our shopping and get all of those yummy and healthy foods fresh from our local farms? Yes, indeed, it is! So that is all the news and instructions for all of you boys and girls today, which I will be repeating throughout the day. Stay healthy, stay happy, and for those of you who haven't already done so, be sure to go to your local Shelter

and get the Ebola Neutralizer. Yes . . . GET YOUR EBOLA NEUTRALIZER TODAY! INDEED!

And now, children, I will leave you with today's program, LAUGHING YOURSELF SILLY, with today's episode called 'HENRIETTA HOO HA'S HYSTERICAL HIPPOPOTAMUS.' Ha ha, Henrietta! Yes, Indeed!"

* * *

The four women sit in amazement looking at each other.

"What the *hoo ha* was that?" Angie asks.

The others shake their heads with a sarcastic chuckle. Vi notes with some uneasiness, "So I guess they're not saying anything about what happened this morning. Just an all-is-well-and-good message and don't forget to buy your fruits and veggies today from your local Center Market."

"Yeah," says Mimi, "and what about the folks who have been taken captive, beaten, or murdered at their local Center? No mention about them, I suppose." They grow quiet, pondering the tragedy that is unfolding before them.

"Ow." Ryan's voice breaks the silence. Mimi runs over to her autobike sidecar to check on him.

"Hi there, sweetie, how are you feeling?"

"Ow."

"Ow?" Mimi inquires with affection.

"Ow," Ryan repeats while gingerly touching the back of his head.

"We cleaned you up and bandaged you as best we could. Now that you are awake, I can also give you some painkillers if you like. I grabbed a couple of bottles of the stuff before we left the Center Market. By the look of that welt on the back of your head I figured you'd be needing some."

Mimi retrieves the medicine bottle from her gear pack and offers it to Ryan with a bottle of water. "Would you also like a bit of food? We seriously raided the place, since it was left deserted and all."

Lying back and closing his eyes Ryan moans, "Just a little, not really hungry yet, thanks."

Mimi begins to walk back to Doc, Angie and Vi, but Ryan slowly opens his eyes and meekly calls out to her.

"Mimi?"

"Yes?"

"Mimi, thank you."

She nods and smiles at him.

"Mimi, I . . . uh, I love you."

"Oh my" Mimi cries, rushing back to his side and gently touching his hands. "I love you too, my darling."

Ryan closes his eyes again and drifts off into another peaceful sleep.

"So, what is Metatron saying now about our road ahead, Mimi?" Doc asks. Turning to Angie she continues, "And what about your gut feelings? It seems we've got the best of both here as a guide for us; modern technology combined with body wisdom."

Mimi checks Metatron as Angie closes her eyes and checks in on her guts. "I'm feeling," says Angie, "that we are okay for the moment, but there may be trouble at the California/Oregon border."

"I'm getting the exact same read from Metatron," Mimi agrees.

"So," Doc asks anxiously, "how are we going to get across to the safehouse and our meeting point in Oregon, then?"

Vi thinks for a moment and then a thought occurs to her. "You know ladies, I think there is something that just might work here."

They all look at her with quizzical expressions.

"Here's what I'm thinking: I know that you guys are basically newbies at the whole self-cloaking thing and that it does take some time to master it. However, let's take a look at just how many things we've got going on here. That is, we've got the tracking capabilities of Metatron as well as the 369 Program on this thing."

"What exactly *is* 369 anyway?" Doc asks looking around at all of them, but especially at Mimi. "Did the Major ever give you any details about it?"

"Not exactly, but one thing he did say is that it is a program that holds powerful energy around the matrix of all creation and can affect life itself. He said he would tell us more about it when we actually meetup."

"Wow, okay," continues Vi. "But in order to *get* to our gathering point, it seems we are going to have to figure a few things out for ourselves."

Mimi and the others all agree. Looking at the wildflowers off in the distance, Vi notices several butterflies fluttering around amongst them and says, "Maybe what we need to do is give it some thought for a little while, each one of us tuning into our own gifts and the voice within ourselves." Turning toward the butterflies she continues, "For me I find answers quite often in the sweet little sounds of nature's smallest beings. Excuse me while I go off for a moment to commune with those arthropods over yonder."

"The *what?*" laughs Mimi.

"Oh, excuse me, the Monarch Butterflies," Vi smiles as she heads off in their direction.

* * *

The Major is looking for the Shop Overseer on the factory floor of Howard Pharmaceuticals. Meanwhile, he is also walking around to make his presence known to the few people who serve there in case they need him for anything. Since most of the functions are performed by AI, there aren't too many human beings serving in the factory, and those who are don't really need much from the Major. He is well liked by the few servants who are on the floor, which is one reason why Master Howard always prefers to send his son whenever there is a problem of any kind. One thing the Major does that no one else does is greet the people with a friendly smile and an air of respect, creating an unusual mutual bond between the Major and the factory servants.

"How's everything going, my man?" the Major asks one of the people.

The policy of Howard Pharmaceuticals is to forbid servants to be called by their names or anything too familiar as they are considered to be not worthy of such respect. Instead, they are referred to as servants or servers, but the Major simply refuses to do that.

"Just fine and dandy, sir, yes, indeed!"

"Ah, Major, I hear that you are looking for me," comes a voice from behind him.

"Yes, Shop Overseer. How is everything going here today?"

"Very well, sir. Very well indeed. What brings you here if I may ask, sir?"

"Oh, not much," the Major lies. The Overseer can sense that something is afoot. "Just checking up on your progress with the Ebola neutralizers. You know, I think we are about to turn a corner with the outbreak."

"Really, sir?" the Shop Overseer says.

"Yes, yes—" the Major clears his throat trying not to sputter, "yes . . . *indeed*."

"Oh my, yes indeed! That is just remarkable, sir!"

"Actually, Shop Overseer," *Aha! Here it comes,* the Overseer thinks to himself as the Major continues, "I was wondering if you could show me the supply of neutralizers that are ready to be shipped, specifically the ones that are super- strength."

"You mean the ones that are for treating people who are already infected with Ebola sir? The ones with the orange labels?"

"Yes, those are exactly the ones I need to inspect."

"Is something *wrong* with them sir?"

"Oh no, no, not at all" the Major says calmly.

The Overseer has no doubt that the Major is totally lying.

"We have just heard reports from some of the Shelters that a number of bottles are arriving broken or in some way defective." Inexplicably, the Shop Overseer believes the Major *is* telling some of the truth this time. "So, my father has asked me to look things over with the orange-labeled bottles, especially the ones that are all packed and ready to be shipped to the Shelters."

"Oh, absolutely sir." The Shop Overseer begins to relax his guard, satisfied the Major is simply here to check things out. He takes the Major to the shipping room. "Right this way, sir."

There is a sea of boxes, hundreds, stacked one on top of the other. The Major knows that he is going to have to make this "inspection" look good. He grabs the Inventory Quality Control Device, which is sitting on a table nearby. The quality control device is a small, gray piece of hand-held equipment that electronically detects any defects in the products that are already packed and ready to go. The user enters the code specifically generated for a particular medicinal product and holds the device against the box. If there is anything wrong anywhere inside that particular box, the Inventory Quality Control Device will automatically start pulsating with a beep-signal and flashing red light. *Another one of Kookie's inventions*, the Major thinks to himself and smiles when he picks up the thing. He is thoroughly amused by his friend. *Kookie sure does love his little flashing-red-light gadgets.*

The Shop Overseer leaves the Major, attending to other business elsewhere in the factory. Cautiously looking around, the Major puts the gray device aside. Checking to make sure no one else is in the shipping room with him, he retrieves Metatron from his pocket and turns it on.

Standing in front of countless boxes of deadly, weaponized live Ebola, the Major is sickened to know it is his own father who has created this weapon of genocide that is intended to murder 94 percent of the world's population.

He hears his father's voice saying, *We don't really need all those people, boy. We've got AI to do everything for us now, everything son! Everything! All those slaves out there? They are just useless eaters. And if there really is such a thing as reincarnation, do you know what I would like to come back as? I would just love to come back as a deadly virus and wipe out all that human trash!*

Turning on the 369 Program, the Major mutters under his breath: "Well father you almost did it. You and your kind *are* the useless eaters, the deadly virus and the biggest pile of human trash ever. And now it's time for your son to take out the garbage!"

The Major takes Metatron, with the DNA restructuring function of the 369 Program activated and ready to go. He places it on top of the first box. There is a ball of light on the screen flashing red (naturally) and within the count of five, just as Kookie promised, the light changes to a steady and smooth, pulsating green. The DNA is now restructured, turning the Ebola bioweapons, in that box, into Ebola Neutralizers; to save lives rather than destroy them.

The Major works as quickly as he can touching each and every box with Metatron. If he suspects anyone coming to check on him, he discreetly takes out the gray Inventory Quality Control Device and pretends to be using that instead. The Shop Overseer comes to check on the Major's progress.

"How's it going there, sir? You sure have been given one major task, Major! Ha ha!"

You have no idea, you sorry schmuck! the Major thinks to himself. "Oh it's just a labor of love!" The Major replies out loud.

Never a truer statement has he ever spoken. Before he leaves, he remembers one more thing Kookie showed him how to do. He takes the Inventory Quality Control Device and reprograms it with a cloaking screen similar to the hologram program that Kookie uses at his workstation to fool the Council into thinking that he is doing what they want him to do. Every box with the genetically altered real neutralizers will still flash red. Only the 369 Program will be able to discern the true contents.

A few hours later the Major returns to the executive suite looking for Master Howard. Finding him getting ready to leave for dinner, the Major calls out, "Hello there, father. I wanted to check in with you before you leave."

"Of course, son. Of course. How did everything go on the factory floor?"

"Just fine. It's the strangest thing. I checked every one of the boxes marked orange and they all flashed red; each and every one of them. You can go down there and check for yourself. Not a thing wrong with any of them. Not a thing."

Master Howard is perplexed. "Then what the devil is going on?"

"I just don't know, sir. Sounds like we may have to launch an investigation or something. You know, all that new AI stuff. Could be some tiny little flaw in any one of those thousands of pieces of equipment."

That should keep the old man distracted for quite some time, thinks the Major.

Master Howard shakes his head in frustration and throws his hands in the air. "Oh bother. Let's go have some dinner then, shall we?"

* * *

Ryan is still sleeping, which Mimi knows is probably good for the healing of his head injury.

The others are off, regrouping and replenishing their energies. Mimi takes a break to do some journaling.

Thank you, Lord!

(She begins to cry and writes through her tears)

Thank you! Thank you! Thank you! Thank you for bringing my man back to me! Thank you for the sweet love that we share. Thank you for the message of hope that you are planting in my heart; and Lord, grant me the courage to share your message with others. I believe this is what you are calling our little group to do. I believe you want us to be strong, to discover the Truth, YOUR truth, and be a living light of Love and Truth to others. I believe you want us to rise up from bondage; to awaken to our true nature; our true power and our true purpose here on earth. I believe that you want us to take back that which has been taken from us; our true selves and our free will. And Lord, I shall do my best to be your servant and do whatever you ask of me. I truly am your humble, faithful servant. Mimi.

Ryan begins to wake, feeling hungry and sore. Mimi fixes him a meal, which he scarfs down like a bear coming out of hibernation. Mimi smiles, relieved that he seems to be on the road to recovery.

Angie is off in the field of wildflowers soaking up the afternoon sun. She is deep in meditation over concepts of the power of numbers, matrices, creation, and how beautiful and perfect the universe truly is. She is remembering stories that her mom used to tell her about ancient days and civilizations when people knew about such things, and a sadness overtakes her spirit for a moment. But then Angie remembers Kookie and his inexplicably brilliant brain (and kind soul) to have figured out how to use such wisdom in combination with modern day technology.

I hope I get to meet this guy! Angie muses, smiling to herself.

Doc has gone exploring in the direction of Vi and the butterflies, (who seem to be having an enchanting time with each other) when she notices a little stream nearby. Approaching the gently flowing water Doc realizes that it has been quite some time since she or any of them have bathed. The thought of getting cleansed in that refreshing water is tantalizing. Doc rushes back to get her toiletries and tell the others.

The group takes off for the stream each finding their own little spot along the meandering waterway. They enjoy the refreshing combination of water, sun, and the fragrances of nature all around them. The weary little group is finding much comfort while basking and washing away all the debris that is clinging to their bodies, minds and spirits. The Monarch Butterflies nearby see them and join in their cleansing delight, flying in joyous circles around the human creatures and sending them loving energy to relieve the darkness that has intruded into their lives.

Each of the human creatures—Mimi, Doc, Angie, Vi and Ryan— are uplifted into a renewed feeling of strength, courage and hope for the future. They know that they will be strong, move forward together and do whatever it takes to share the message of hope and love.

"Thank you, my friends," Vi says to the Monarchs.

You are quite welcome human creature, she can hear them saying to her heart as they smile down upon her.

As much as they all want to stay right where they are for a while, the friends are aware that they have an appointment to keep with the Major. They regrettably pack up their things and prepare to leave. Mimi takes out Metatron and checks the road ahead for safe travel and a place to camp for the night. There are a few places up ahead which feel safe enough and show no red lights at the moment. The group feels it is okay to wing it this time, and just stop and pull over for the night whenever they get tired.

The countryside is indescribably beautiful near the California/Oregon border, with tall trees, grassy fields, wildflowers, lakes and streams. They lose track of time as the sun slowly begins to descend and Mimi notices that it is getting dark. She turns to the others. "I guess we should look for a place to stop."

The traveling companions come to a clearing with just enough sunlight left to set up camp and begin unpacking their gear. Since the ladies don't want Ryan helping with the physical labor just yet, he decides to stretch his legs after sitting in the sidecar all day and go for a little walk.

While the women are about ready to prepare their meal, it occurs to Mimi that she has not checked Metatron for their exact location. She turns on the screen and immediately observes a flashing red light in their exact location! The pyramid on the screen is spinning and pulsating with the message:

Location: California/Oregon border. Status: Code red/flashing.

Off in the distance they suddenly hear the sound of gunshots, and from where Ryan is standing, he can see everything unfolding below.

Chapter 11 – Arthropods

"WHERE'S RYAN!" MIMI BELLOWS.

"It's okay, calm down," says Doc, trying to sooth Mimi while she herself is shaking. "He's right over there by those bushes."

More shots ring out and all four women make a dash towards Ryan who is paralyzed at the sight he is witnessing off in the distance. The group looks down across the field at the California/Oregon border crossing not more than a quarter mile away from where they are standing. They can hear a faint sound of commotion mixed with gunfire. Overseer Border Crossing Guards are yelling at a group of about 20 people who are being searched. Several people lie motionless on the ground, and the Overseer Guards are moving the bodies to an area behind the patrol station. People are crying and huddled together as their meager belongings are ransacked and left scattered on the ground.

Another Overseer Guard shouts to the others, "It's not here!"

Turning to the frightened people they bark orders, "Get your things together and move on out!"

Mimi, Doc, Angie, Vi and Ryan watch people in their fear and humiliation oblige the Overseer Guards and try to gather what few possessions they have. Many are crying, grieving the murder of their loved ones right before their eyes.

Ryan turns around to the others. "Come, let's go to our campsite," he says quietly.

* * *

On the large screens in his workstation, Kookie watches everything unfold. The murderous scenes and abuse of people are happening all over Panamerica, and he is wracked with guilt knowing what the

Overseers have been ordered to search for. The plan he has cooked up with the Major is going to be a race against time, and the best way they can *buy* more time is to continuously come up with diversions and decoys. But he had not anticipated that the Council would order searches on everyday people.

What could they possibly imagine . . . wait. His memory is suddenly jarred. Thinking back to his basic training days as a High Lord with his High Overlord Contact, he was taught that *there might be some members of the Upper Crust who will feel sympathy for these lower than low, useless eaters. If that happens it could turn into a dangerous, even threatening situation for the Council as well as the rest of the UC.*" Kookie was taught the extreme importance of *monitoring each other and being on the lookout for such weaknesses among themselves, and if such a situation is ever suspected there are guidelines to follow.*

Kookie remembers one of those guidelines loud and clear, hammering away in his head: *Use bullying techniques, torture, or even death with those worthless little bastards in a way that will cause EXTREME GUILT in the traitor who is helping them. He will know that it is **his** fault that the slaves are being made to suffer and this will stop things immediately. The suffering of the slaves may even cause the spineless traitor among them to trip up and expose himself!*

I'll bet that's it, Kookie ponders sadly. *Yes, I'll bet that's what is happening.*

Kookie understands now that he is caught in a mental trap of mind control against himself, with members of the UC potentially being pitted against each other by the Council. One way or another they will fight just as dirty as they can to see if they can smoke out the guilty party, using whatever psychological abuse they can on their own people. This gives Kookie an idea.Grabbing four Metatron devices Kookie prepares himself as an unexpected guest for the rendezvous at the safehouse. Pausing for a moment he holds his hands out in front of him and looks up. "Oh, Lord," he says, "Oh, uh . . . not me, *you the Divine Lord!* Ha ha!" Clearing his throat, he continues, "Dear Lord, please be with your people: Mimi, Doc, Angie, Vi and Ryan, and see them safely across the border."

* * *

Back at the campsite, the five companions must now consider their next move. Should they risk spending the night where they are and leave in the morning? They sit there quietly considering their options as Vi dishes up the evening meal. They seem to have lost much of their appetite for the moment, but they also know it is important to keep up their strength. So, the five of them slowly pick their way through the plate of food set before them.

"I don't think we should go anywhere just yet," offers Ryan. "But maybe if we get some rest, we can leave during the middle of the night, or the small hours of the morning."

Doc considers the idea. "Yes, that would seem reasonable, except during the night it is very quiet and whatever sounds we make while passing the Overseer Border Crossing Guards might be more easily detected. And they are probably on some sort of heightened alert right now, based on what we all just saw. At least during the day, we can get lost in another group of people as soon as we see others show up."

Mimi interjects, "So you think that leaving during the day might be a better idea, Doc?"

"I don't know." Doc says.

Mimi continues, "The idea of hanging around here that long, so close to trouble makes me feel very antsy."

"I have to agree with that one," says Angie. Then they all turn to Vi who has not said anything yet. She is lost in thought, watching a group of Monarch Butterflies playing nearby and wondering if these are the same ones they saw earlier during the day. She has been speaking to one of them with her heart, searching for answers to this difficult decision.

Vi is sure that this is the same butterfly who spoke to her at the stream, so she has decided to name her Angel. Finally, Vi turns to the others and has an idea.

"Okay, I know there are risks either way. Here's what I'm thinking. I realize that we are not familiar yet with all of what Metatron is capable of doing, but I do know that Angie here has some amazing energy and intuitive skills. And *I* know how to walk past those bozos out there without being seen."

Vi has everyone's full attention. "So, I say we leave here sometime during the night, walking our autobikes quietly but steadily right through the Border Crossing and past the Overseer Guards. I will get the four of you all psyched-up with the self-cloaking technique just before we cross. In fact, we can practice it a few times this evening, which will also give Ryan a chance to learn how to do it. Meanwhile, our mentally intuitive genius Angie here can figure out how to use Metatron in some sort of way . . . you know, doing that *woo-woo-that-she-do* so well!"

They all let out a momentary chuckle.

"And then we hope that the added effects of whatever Angie can tune into with Metatron will enhance our collective self-cloaking abilities."

Everyone looks at each other in a moment of reflection.

"Well? What do you all think, then?" asks Vi.

Mimi, Doc, and Angie blurt out, *"AMEN!"* or *"YOU BETCHA,"* and Ryan goes, "Woof!"

A little soul fluttering around nearby lifts her heart to the heavens and whispers, *Amen, human creatures, amen.*

Mimi has fallen into a restless sleep. She is tossing and turning when suddenly little Elli appears to her in a dream.

They are in a Center Food Market together, and Mimi is pushing a shopping cart around with Elli sitting in it, laughing and jabbering at all the colorful packages on the shelves containing all kinds of goodies. Looking down at her precious granddaughter she notices a butterfly hair clip in Elli's hair.

"Ooo, Gramma, I want this!" Followed by, "Ooo, Gramma, I want that!"

Gently touching her cute little face Mimi says to Ellie with a lovey-dovey-gramma-smile, "Well now baby girl, you just want everything, don't you?"

Elli squeals with delight, stretching out her little arms saying, "I want EEEVEREYTHING!"

Mimi coos at Elli, "Well then, my little princess must HAVE eeeverything then, mustn't she?!"

"Hee, Hee, Hee!" Elli is giggling.

As Mimi continues down the aisle people begin to suddenly materialize out of nowhere until it is too crowded for her to move. Mimi looks down at Elli only to see the shopping cart is empty. Looking around she sees a beautiful woman dressed in high black leather boots, a tight-fitting short black leather skirt with a matching top, and a snake dangling around her neck. She is walking out the front door holding Elli in her arms. Mimi tries to run and calls out after Elli, but there are too many people now between them, and by the time Mimi gets to the door the woman and Elli are gone.

Mimi starts to yell frantically, "ELLI! ELLI! WHERE ARE YOU!" running out of the Center and into an empty autobike parking lot. Terrified, Mimi starts crying, "Where is she? What have you done with her? What have you done with my baby?"

Suddenly a bright array of orange, yellow, brown, and red colors appear, shimmering in the center of a brilliant golden pyramid.

Mimi's spirits are calmed as the colors begin to take shape, forming a Monarch butterfly. It speaks to her soul, "Do not be afraid, little Elli is here with us."

Mimi feels a rush of loving energy pouring into her heart center from the Monarch. "Thank you, thank you," she says to the butterfly, "But I want to see my little one again; I want to be with her. I just miss her so much!"

"Be strong Lady of Light, take heart; we are right here with you too."

The lights fade, everything turns to gray and Mimi is aware of a pulsating sound coming from nearby.

Coming out of her dream and slowly waking up, Metatron is pulsating with a wake-up call. It is 3 am, the time that Mimi and her companions all agreed upon for the last leg of their journey to the border.

"Wake up ladies," she says to her tent-mates. She opens Ryan's tent which is right next to theirs, "Wake up sweetie. It's that time."

They all start moving about slowly, getting their gear packed and the tents put away; all except for their sleeping bags which Vi has instructed them to leave open for the time being. When everything else is ready to go Mimi, Doc, Angie, Vi and Ryan are agitated with nervous energy. Adrenaline is flowing through them, increasing their heart rates and pumping blood furiously through their veins.

"Okay folks," Vi begins, "let's get relaxed and ready here. We will have to slow our energy down quite a bit in order to not attract so much attention to ourselves.

"Angie, are you ready with Metatron?"

"Yep," she replies and turns it on.

Angie has figured out how to program Metatron to pulsate at 7.83 hertz, the frequency of the human brain and one of the "heartbeat" frequencies of the earth's pulse. Angie knows this beat will be soothing to listen to and a good combination for Vi to do a meditation over everyone.

Vi begins her meditation while Angie is projecting the 7.83 hertz frequency, slowing down the breathing and heartrate of their companions. Everyone relaxes in a short time, with their heartrates slowed considerably. Then Vi begins the self-cloaking meditation.

An hour later, Vi feels that Mimi and the others are ready. She instructs them to put their sleeping bags away and proceed quietly and steadily toward the border.

"We, and all of our gear are now unseen and totally silent," she says, as they move forward.

The moonlight and the stars cast as eerie shadow on the grassy field, accompanied by an unnatural stillness. Not a whisper, not a breeze, not a flicker of movement can be seen or heard. There are three Overseer Border Crossing Guards in the border patrol station; two are fast asleep and one, the Commander of the guards, is on guard duty. He is forcing himself to stay awake just a little while longer, knowing that it will be the other guys' turn to wake up and take over soon. Yawning and rubbing his eyes, the Commander glances out of the window.

All is quiet, he thinks to himself. *All is very quiet.* He suddenly becomes more alert. *All is too quiet?*

One of the other guards begins to stir and stands up to look out of the window. "What's up, Commander?"

"Dunno," he answers, "Just a weird feeling. I'm going outside to take a look."

The little group is moving steadily at an even pace; walking their autobikes just as quietly as they can and looking straight ahead. They are about 10 yards from the border patrol station when the door suddenly opens and out steps the Commander.

Vi can feel the fear growing inside all of them and in a barely audible voice she whispers, "Keep moving. We are unseen."

At that moment the Commander is sure he just heard something. The other two guards are now fully awake and they join the Commander outside to see what is going on.

"I *know* I heard something!" he says to them.

Suddenly a dark shadow fills the entire night sky blotting out the starlight, and a rush of black, fierce wind races toward them from the south. The three men look up in a state of terror when suddenly a swarm of thousands of Monarch Butterflies come screaming down upon them. And in a state of frantic, blind panic all three men begin to shriek. "*AAAAAAAAHHH!*"

The butterflies dive bomb all around them, flying low and circling around their heads. The guards jump up and down throwing their bodies around and swatting at the air in panic-stricken horror, but the butterflies will not go away.

"Quick!" yells the Commander, "get back inside the station!"

But the arthropods are relentless, and the men are unable to move from their spot for the next five minutes. Finally, the Monarchs fly high up into the night sky and the Commander and his men make a dash for the border patrol station, slamming the door behind them. They are panting, out of breath, and looking at each other in total disbelief.

When they are finally able to talk, the three Overseer Border Crossing Guards of the California/Oregon border vow to never *ever* tell a living soul about this strange occurrence, and their fear of being "chased" by butterflies!

And somewhere in the pre-dawn hours of the early morning, about seven miles north of the Oregon border, a grateful group of five friends collapse from exhaustion, followed by a hysterical fit of laughter over the "dancing guards" they left behind. Sleep overcomes them easily to renew their energy for the day ahead.

"Thank you, Angel," whispers Vi.

And in her heart she hears, *you are very welcome human creature. Sleep well now.*

* * *

Dawn is breaking and Phil is just waking up in his tent. Lying next to him safely cuddled up in her own little sleeping bag is the baby girl he rescued. Before leaving Emmonsville altogether he wants to go to the Center to pick up provisions for them. He figures he'll be safe enough there as a known Shelter server and that he can keep the little one safely tucked away in his autobike sidecar while he runs in briefly; especially if she is asleep. However, when he arrives at the Center, the place is deserted. Not a soul is to be seen anywhere. The entryway is open though, so he quickly runs inside, gets everything he needs for himself and the wee one in tow, and leaves as fast as he can. The place gives him an uneasy feeling, and something is speaking to his heart telling him to get out of Emmonsville altogether, without delay.

Back at the campsite, Phil is watching the little one fast asleep, wondering where they will go and what he is going to do now. He did not have much chance to think about anything other than her immediate safety when he took off with her in a great hurry.

Great Spirit, what do you want me to do now? Where shall I go with this little Wakanjeja[1] you have put in my care? We are both in YOUR care Great Spirit. Please give me a sign and tell me what I am supposed to do next.

He sits down on the ground next to the sleeping wee one. Bowing his head, Phil closes his eyes and begins to chant and sing. A gentle breeze is blowing through the grassy field of wildflowers and gradually the little one begins to stir.

"What shall I call you, little one?" Phil looks at her and asks. "We shall have to wait for a sign for that one too I suppose because you cannot tell me what your name is, now can you," he says smiling at her. "Meanwhile, I will just call you Little One."

Phil thinks this will suit her just fine when she begins to stir and slowly opens her eyes. Seeing Phil, Little One gives him a smile that fills his heart with happiness. "I guess you must be hungry" he says to her and takes out a bottle of infant formula. Not knowing exactly how old she is but thinking that she is about nine or ten months old, he took a

---

[1] *Wakanjeja: Native American (Lakota) term "sacred child."*

variety of infant and toddler foods from the Center Market, figuring he would find *something* suitable for her.

Little One grabs the bottle and starts to guzzle away, to Phil's delight. "I took some other things for you from the Center Market, Little One. It has been a long time since I have done this, but I guess I will have to change your diaper."

As Phil gets to work on the task at hand, his old "daddy skills" come back to him, and just as he is about finished getting Little One all cleaned up, he looks up and sees movement coming toward him from the field of wildflowers.

Fluttering over to Phil and Little One in the morning breeze is a playful family of Monarch Butterflies. They are sparkling in the sunlight, sending loving energy to their human friends.

Little One sees them and starts to laugh out loud, squealing and wiggling her whole body with delight. The Monarchs respond in kind, one of them settling on Little One's hair as if it is kissing her. The child coos and giggles as butterflies continue to dance around her, stretching her arms out to touch them. At that moment they gently flutter away with Little One's arms still reaching for them; Phil realizes that her arms are pointing due north.

"That's it!" He bursts out with the sudden revelation of the sign. "Little One! The Creator is giving us a sign! We are to go north!"

* * *

When Mimi and company wake up it is mid-morning. They feel refreshed, filled with gratitude and totally amazed at how they were able to evade the Overseer Guards at the border. Any time there is a mere mention of the "dancing guards" they all roar with hilarity.

"Well, I guess it's time to get moving," says Mimi as she takes out Metatron.

Doc asks her, "So what does Metatron have to say about the road ahead this morning?"

Turning it on Mimi sets the coordinates for their safehouse destination located in Bear River, Oregon. Checking the safety conditions, the lights are a smooth green. "All systems go! We can be there for lunch."

"Woo Hoo!" everyone chimes in.

"I just can't *wait* to have one of those scrumptious dinners from the farm folks!" says Vi.

"Amen to that," agrees Doc. Everyone nods, thinking about how delicious a nice hot bowl of soup and homemade bread will be.

They arrive in Bear River in the early afternoon and pull up to a quaint cottage on the Bear River Farm. Knocking on the door, they are greeted by a pleasant, down-to-earth woman whose name is Lisa. She is delighted to see her friend Doc arriving with other new friends. "Well, hello Doc! It's great to see you! Come on in!"

"Thank you, Lisa. It's great to see you, too," Doc says as she proceeds to introduce everyone all around. "And where is Kenny?"

"Oh, he's working hard these days in the fields. Not that much help now, you know," Lisa's voice saddens a bit. "Too many people have died from Ebola. Sometimes it feels like we are the only healthy ones left here to do all the planting and harvesting that needs to be done."

"I *am* sorry," says Doc.

"Yes, well, I'm just very happy to see you. To see *all* of you! Can I fix a meal for you folks?"

"You bet! Absolutely! Yes, please! Thank you, thank you!" they all chime in at the same time.

"Well then," says Lisa, "please feel free to freshen up and have a seat around the table. I will have everything ready for you in no time."

Doc thanks Lisa for her generosity and kindness, and also explains that they are expecting one more person to join them. She does not want to jump in right away with all the news that they bring; although, she is most anxious to hear from Lisa about what has been going on within the farming community; and any other news that is not filtered through the Council and My Buddy.

"Please let me help you with the meal preparation," says Doc. "In fact, we have quite a bit of provisions that I would like to offer you."

"Oh, thank you!" exclaims Lisa. "There are so many things we are short of these days. Whatever you can spare is greatly appreciated."

Lisa turns away for a moment so as not to let Doc see in her face the hardship and struggle that they have been through. Lisa is grateful to have guests visiting, and she is especially looking forward to hearing what is going on outside. Just like everyone else, Lisa and Kenny are also disturbed by the "news and instructions" that they hear every day on My Buddy. They are starving for some people's news, to know what is really going on.

Doc is getting the table ready for the midday meal where Angie has commandeered a corner of the table to do a drawing; Ryan is stretched out resting on the sofa as he is still recovering from his head injury; and Vi is out in the garden. Mimi smiles at the peaceful moment, thinking about her daughter Lydia, Sam and her precious little Elli who are not very far away now.

* * *

The Major has been watching Metatron's tracking program all morning for signs of Mimi and friend's arrival at the safehouse. Since Emmonsville seems to have disappeared off the face of the earth, he will have to follow her tracks, so to speak, and lock in on their location once they stop moving. Kookie, of course, is continuing to track them with his Metatron device too, relieved that they made it safely across the border.

* * *

Phil has come to a small village just south of the California/Oregon border and locates the Center. He brings in Little One wearing her in a front carrier papoose, which he created from a small blanket.

Smiling up at the heavens he says, *"Well honey, this may not be as good as the ones you used to make for our little ones, but at least it seems to be getting the job done."*

Little One is snuggled in comfortably against Phil's chest taking a nap as he goes through the Food Market grabbing provisions for the road. He goes to the Coffeehouse and decides to check out what is going on with the few people who are there, including the Center Overseer who is looking rather bored. As he moves over to a table, they all notice him carrying a snoozing bundle strapped to his chest. The people are nodding and beaming at Phil and his bundle and a man seated nearest to Phil speaks up.

"Hey there partner, that's a cute little travelin' companion you got there! Where you guys from?"

"We are from Arbor Vista," Phil answers, "Just on our way to Oregon to see how our relatives there are doing."

"I hear that, pal. Since Ebola, communication with our loved ones has been, shall we say, *limited*. It seems like we are all in the same boat. Lots of folks travelin' around right now."

Taking a sideways glance at the Center Overseer nearby, the man continues, "And we gotta be real careful who we talk to these days, if you catch my drift."

Phil nods, "Sure do, Brother."

"Yep. There some strange things a-goin' on around here these days. Heard that the Overseers Border Crossing Guards been givin' folks a hard time over there. Even rumors about shootin' and killin'. So, you and the wee one be real careful goin' across. Don't give 'em no trouble.

Folks say that theys a-lookin' fer somethin'; ransack folks belongin's, an' all. Though they probably won't give *you* much of a hard time with that cute wee bairn[2] in tow, now, will they?" he says, smiling sweetly at Little One.

"I sure hope not."

The men continue to converse about the goings on in the area, and then the man tells him about the Bear River Farm; how people who have worked there are suddenly gone, either off to look for loved ones or off to the Shelters. They tend not to come back and as a result the farm is short-handed.

Phil thinks about this for a moment and then says to the guy, "Say, Brother, I used to do lots of farming before Ebola and wouldn't mind helping out for a few days or so, if they need it. What do you think?"

"I think they would be more'n overjoyed, grateful to have ya man!"

"Yep. We've all got to help each other out these days, don't we?" Phil says while looking down at Little One.

"Ya got that right, partner."

* * *

Angie is just about finishing up with her drawing when Lisa comes out of the kitchen and announces that the meal is ready.

"Fantastic!" exclaims Angie as she goes to find Vi in the garden.

Doc starts bringing the food out to the table with Lisa, and Mimi goes over to Ryan, her sleeping sweetie on the sofa. Gently nudging him Mimi says, "I'm sorry to wake you up, honey, but there's hot soup, sandwiches and a huge fruit bowl on the table and--"

"And I'm up!" says Ryan before she can finish her sentence. "Up and hungry, my love!" He says with a shy, little-boy smile on his face. Mimi giggles at him and the two love birds join the others.

---

[2]*Wee Bairn: Scottish term meaning "little baby" or "small child."*

As they all sit down to eat, Kenny comes in to join them. "Ah, there you are, dear," Lisa says to her Man. Introducing him she says, "Everyone, this is my Man, Kenny. Kenny, this is everyone!"

They all proceed to introduce themselves one at a time and dig into the food. Kenny explains that he has been out in the back working on his pet project, inviting them to come and take a look after they finish eating.

"It's really fascinating," says Vi. "Kenny has a pigeon loft out in the back."

"Yes," he says. "Used to be a time when they were used for communication. They were called homing pigeons."

"No kidding!" says Ryan who has heard about this and finds it fascinating.

"Yep. Goes all the way back to Ancient Egypt from what I understand."

"No way!" continues Ryan. "So have you trained your pigeons to do all of that?"

"I think so; although, I haven't actually put them to the test yet, that is with carrying messages and all. Back in their day they were also referred to as carrier pigeons."

"Wow!" and turning to Mimi, Ryan says, "What do you think about that, honey?"

"I'm thinking that this is all very interesting", she says touching Metatron in her pocket. Mimi is thinking about her last conversation with the Major about not using Metatron for communication, and the possibilities these pigeons might present.

* * *

High Lord Yakov is sitting in front of his terminal at his workstation. His royal palace is located in a small town, just outside the old, deserted city formerly known as Moscow, in the Continental Territory of Euroslavica. He is working on his day's tracking assignment when the screen next to him activates with an incoming message. It is Yakov's High Overlord Contact and he accepts the incoming message. The transmission begins.

They speak in Russian:

"Good morning, My Lord, Yakov. How are you today?" asks the HOC.

"I'm fine, sir. And how are you?"

"Very well, very well, indeed!" says the contact.

"Yes, yes, indeed, sir. Yes, indeed."

"My Lord, we have a problem," says the contact.

"A problem, sir?" asks Yakov.

"Yes, yes, indeed. It seems that there is a rogue element somewhere in the UC."

"Really, sir? Are you sure?"

"Yes, My Lord. It seems that there is some kind of unregistered technology being used for a treasonous purpose. Do you understand me, My Lord Yakov?"

"Yes, sir. I do understand you. I do indeed!"

"We of the Council do believe that it is coming from Panamerica. However, we could be mistaken about that."

There is a pause and then the HOC continues:

"My Lord Yakov, you remember what you learned in your basic training about what to do in the event of such a situation?"

"Yes sir, I do indeed."

"Then we are assigning you to use *any and all means necessary* to find out who these traitors are, what device they have in their possession, and to bring them down. Do you understand me, My Lord?"

"Yes sir, yes indeed. Yes, indeed I do."

Chapter 12 – Homing

AFTER THEIR MEAL, MIMI IS READY to divulge a few things to the group, as well as find out what Lisa and Kenny know. Their hosts reveal that for the past few days there has been an increase in harassment from the Overseer Border Crossing Guards, especially to unknown travelers. This of course involves many people since a large portion of the population is trying to connect with their loved ones. There are stop-and-search points set up throughout the region, and no one knows how extensive these search points are.

The scariest part, though, is that there hasn't been one word mentioned about all of this on My Buddy, which is causing people, for the first time ever to have suspicions about the UC. Although the people have never especially cared for the UC, the people have trusted and respected them nonetheless. Folks have always believed that the UC needs them for their servitude, and if for no other reason, that is why they truly have the people's welfare at heart.

Mimi has been holding onto Metatron in her pocket the whole time, beginning to realize the implications of what might happen to any one of them if they are discovered, but especially to the Major and Kookie. She also believes that they must all coordinate their efforts and act in sync with each other if they are ever going to help anyone. Mimi looks around the table and says:

"The time for secrecy and suppression of the people is over."

Silence falls upon the table and they all turn toward her.

"We are *not* the children of the Council!" she bellows. "We have been lied to and basically treated like idiots for decades. We have been led to believe and to feel that we cannot take care of ourselves without the management of our so-called "loving parents" of the UC, who are anything *but* loving. They are murdering us! They are picking us off like flies because that is all we are to them. Expendable pests."

"Are you sure about all this, Mimi?" asks Lisa.

"I'm afraid so," she replies.

Everyone is lost in their own thoughts considering what Mimi has just said, when there is a knock on the front door. Lisa answers the door, and Mimi hears a familiar voice saying, "Hi there, ma'am. I'm a friend of Mimi and her companions and--"

"*HEY MAJOR!*" yells Mimi. "You found us! Woo Hoo!"

"Hey, woman!" the Major yells back, followed by a chorus of joyous "Heys!" going around the table.

"Lisa, this is the Major," Mimi says, and with much gratitude she adds, "And if it weren't for this incredible soul standing here before you, I would probably not be alive today."

"So very pleased to meet you, sir!" says Lisa.

"Likewise," says Kenny, and they both give the Major a big hug.

Ryan walks over to the Major and stands in front of him, looking down at the floor and searching for the right words to say. The words do not come. Seeing this, Mimi comes over to her beloved and puts her arms around him. "This is Ryan," she says to the Major.

Still looking down at the floor, Ryan says, "Thank you. Thank you, sir."

"You are quite welcome, my good man." The Major says to Ryan with a warm smile and pat on the back.

"You have come just in time to break bread with us, Major," Lisa says. "Won't you have a seat at our table and join us?"

"It would be an honor, ma'am," the Major replies as he sits down next to the one person he has not been introduced to yet. "And who are you?"

"My name is Vi," she says, rather interested in hearing what the Major has come to tell them.

"Well, hello Vi!" he continues, "I am so happy to see you all here and grateful that you were able to make it safely across the border. I've been hearing some bad things going on over there. Kookie and I have both been worried about all of you."

"Kookie?!" Angie perks up.

"Yes ma'am. In fact, he is also expected to join us, if that is all right with you two," he says, looking at Lisa and Kenny.

"Kookie? HERE?" howls Angie with great enthusiasm.

"Why yes. I do expect him shortly."

"WOO HOO! I get to meet Kookie! I get to meet Kookie!" Angie's enthusiasm is infectious and everyone starts to laugh, except for the Major.

He just rolls his eyes, shakes his head and thinks to himself, *Oh Lord!* and as an afterthought adds, *No, Kookie, not you!*

* * *

Kookie is just around the corner from Bear River Farm when he hears the pulsation of his Lord's Communication Device. He is expecting to hear from his High Overlord Contact by now since their last conversation.

Kookie accepts the incoming message as his HOC begins, "Well, My Lord Kenneth, what have you found out so far?"

Kookie has been preparing for this moment, "Well sir, according to my testing there seems to be some kind of systemic equipment malfunction. In other words, I think there is a nasty virus in the system, which has somehow managed to evade detection."

"Somehow, My Lord?"

"Yes sir. It *is* possible that we could be dealing with an AI virus that is so pernicious that it has probably invaded the system on more than one level. It will take time to get at it, but I'm confident that it can be rooted out. And once we expose the malfunction, it will be easier to set everything right after that."

"So, you don't think that someone in the UC is deliberately doing some form of sabotage, then?"

"Oh, no, sir. What makes you think it might be something like that?" Kookie is fishing for whatever his HOC may have stumbled upon.

"Apparently, my Lord Kenneth, there have been reports coming in of people at the Shelters being given the orange-labeled Ebola and living through it."

"You're kidding!" Kookie says, feigning surprise.

"No, I am not. In fact, when the last shipment was tested, three times before being sent to the Shelters, they all tested positive for Snake Bite. And yet there was not one death reported. *Not one,* Kookie! Out of three and a half million injections that were administered as of today, not one person has shown any symptoms of Ebola. Now how is that possible?"

Kookie has rehearsed his response to this moment for a long time, ever since he first hatched the idea. "Hmm," he says. Then continues in his best geek double-talk. "You know, it could be something to do with the duality of the polarity."

"*WHAT?*"

"Oh yes! It is very possible . . . very possible, *indeed,* sir. I can see how the virus is causing a swift swing shift in the poles of the matrix sequencing, thereby creating a pendulum effect of ripples that switch the sequencing and the magnetic fields on and off and back and forth, if you catch my meaning, sir.

"Huh?" The HOC is quite confused.

"Well yes, it's all very simple, sir. If a virus creates a duality of the polarity effect it could easily re-sequence DNA structure to change a thing into its opposition. Which means very simply put that an Ebola bioweapon could turn into a neutralizer and vice versa. I have not seen this before, sir, but know that in theory it *is* possible, and if this turns out to be the case, we can get this fixed."

"You mean to tell me that it's also possible for the Ebola bioweapon to become a neutralizer under this condition?!"

"Well, sir, theoretically yes. And, also, for the neutralizer to become a live Ebola virus, no matter how many times they have been tested. But not to worry; I'll have the other Lords on it right away. Meanwhile, I am checking a few things out at the source, to see if we can avoid such a thing happening again in the future."

"Okay, my Lord Kenneth. You stay in touch with me and do let me know when you come up with anything concrete."

"Yes sir, I will."

Although Kookie is confident about the runaround that he has just set in motion with the UC, he knows gibberish double-talk and deception can only go so far and for so long.

* * *

The Major is finishing up his meal. While all eyes are upon him for answers, he has told everyone that he really wants to wait for Kookie to arrive.

"There is just too much to go into without all of us being present," he explains, knowing that they are all trying to be just as patient as they can.

At that moment there is another knock on the front door, and Angie jumps up first and beats Lisa to it. As she slowly opens the door, Angie finds herself face to face with a man who appears to be about 40-something with raven hair, dressed in black from head to toe and smiling down at her. She notices that his eyes are the color of gold.

Wow, Angie thinks to herself, *this guy is a super genius Lord who cares about people enough to risk his life for us. AND he has golden eyes! Wow!*

"Hi there! Who might you be?" inquires Golden Eyes.

Angie's big brown eyes light up as she replies, "Hi! I'm Angie."

"Hi Angie. I'm Kookie."

"Hi Kookie! We've been expecting you. Won't you come in and join us?" she beams.

Kookie's smile broadens, "Thank you kindly, Angie."

"Hey, Bro!" yells the Major from the dining room table. "Come on over and meet everyone."

As they introduce themselves around the table, Lisa asks Kookie, "Would you care for some of our food sir?"

"Oh, that's all right, thank you ma'am, but I've already eaten."

"Okay," says Lisa, stepping into the kitchen. "We were just about to have dessert," she continues when she comes back to the table carrying homemade chocolate cake and a plate full of homemade chocolate chip cookies.

"There is also lots of coffee for anyone who wants it," Lisa offers as she goes to get the coffee flasks.

Golden Eyes eyeballs the plate of homemade chocolate chip cookies. "Uh, hmm, actually, there is always room for dessert!"

Angie giggles and passes the plate to him. "Help yourself!"

Now they must get down to the business at hand.

The Major begins: "I would like to begin by saying—" he pauses, lowers his head and clears his throat, "that I would like to offer my deepest apologies to all present . . ." the words come with difficulty "for . . . the sins of my father. May we have a moment of silence for all who have lost their lives, and all of you who continuously endure the hardships caused by the greed and corruption of the Upper Crust."

All heads bow in sad silence around the table.

After a few moments, the Major begins to speak again. "I would like to tell each and every one of you that the inhumanity expressed and dealt out by my people is *not* the way we all feel, that there are those of us who want very much to speak out and to change things. We have been too afraid of the Council and the far-reaching arm of control that they have to destroy us all.

"I am here to tell you good people that I am no longer willing or able to live with things as they are, and I vow to all of you to do what I can to—" he looks at Kookie, who nods at the Major as if to say, *continue* to him. So the Major continues, "To do whatever is within my power, and whatever my *true* Father in Heaven would have me do . . . to take the whole system down."

While they all quietly absorb what the Major has just told them, Kookie begins to speak. "Dearest people, it is my hope and wish that one day, with our most heartfelt efforts of redemption for the horrors and atrocities perpetrated against all of humanity by our people, that we will have somehow, most graciously earned your forgiveness."

Angie and the others are touched by Kookie's words of humility and shame.

He looks at the Major and continues, "For this the Major and I both vow to do whatever we can to remove the bondage of oppression from you and return that which was never the right of my people to take: the control of your minds, your lives, so many of your basic human rights, and worst of all your freewill."

Wracked with guilt, Kookie forces himself to hold his head up and glance around the table, looking everyone in the eye. "And I promise to you all that the Major and I will do whatever we can with whatever time is given to us, to return all of those things to you. I am ready and willing to give my life for this."

"And I am also ready and willing to give my life for this," repeats the Major.

He puts his hands out and they all join hands around the table as the Major and Kookie bow their heads one more time, in silent meditation.

After a while, a few chocolate chip cookies and coffee have restored much of everyone's emotions to harmony.

The Major and Kookie bring the others up to date about some of what Metatron can do, especially as a communication device. They mention the fact that this is unfortunately causing the Council to be aware that something is going on. Mimi and her companions share their experience at the border crossing using self-cloaking and the 7.83hz energy enhancement provided by Metatron, as well as the Monarchs and the "dancing guards."

Kookie and the Major are impressed with all that they are hearing and are especially amused by the dancing guards. One thing that neither one of them has mentioned is the bio-weaponization of the Ebola virus and how it has been administered, as well as the transformation of the live virus done by the 369 Program on Metatron.

Mimi had previously told the Major that Vi was already so grief stricken with guilt over all those people's deaths, that if she were to find out that she actually administered the fatal virus to so many people, including little Suzie, it would be too much for her to handle. The Major agreed with Mimi that she would let him and Kookie know when the time seemed right to reveal everything else to the whole group. This means that the Major must wait to tell them all the good news of what he was able to do with Metatron and the 369 Program to restructure the DNA of the bio-weapons on the factory floor of Howard Pharmaceuticals.

"So, it sounds to me like you are possibly in need of some other form of communication, eh Kookie?" says Kenny.

"Yes," Kookie responds, "I'm actually working on that one. Why? Have you got any ideas?"

"Well, as a matter of fact, yes!" Kenny replies cheerfully. "Why don't you all join me out back in my garden, and I'll show you."

While the others already have some idea of what Kenny is about to show them, Kookie and the Major are thoroughly intrigued. They all go outside and Kenny leads the way.

"Here it is!" announces Kenny cheerfully.

"Here *what* is?" says the Major. He sees a small building with what seems to be *pigeons?* Looking at Kookie, they stare at each other, baffled.

Kookie blurts out, "You don't mean to tell us that these are *homing pigeons,* do you?"

"Yes, sir, that is exactly what they are!" says Kenny proudly. "It is a hobby of mine. Been raising them for years."

"Wow!" exclaims the Major.

"What can you tell us about these birds, then?" Kookie inquires.

"Do they really deliver messages?" asks the Major in wonder.

"Oh yes. Their use as messengers, or carrier pigeons, which is their other name, goes back over 5000 years to ancient Egypt."

"No way!" says Vi, astounded.

Kenny continues, "They were also used during World War II as messengers, and in other wars as well in our past."

The small crowd of friends is in awe hearing how far back in history these birds have been used.

Kookie asks Kenny, "So just how far can they go?"

"Well, they typically go about 600 miles from one loft to the other; although, it has been said that they can travel up to 1000 miles or so. And that is using mobile lofts as well."

Kookie is excited as he asks Kenny, "Can *your* birds do all of that?"

"Well, I have only clocked them at a distance of about 30 miles or so, but I'm fairly certain that they can go a lot farther."

"How is this accomplished?" asks Vi.

"Homing is part of their nature, so all you have to do is train them to go from one loft to the other and learn how to work with them and care for them."

"Can you teach us to do that, and would you let us use your pigeons?" asks the Major.

"It would be an honor sir, for me to do both," says Kenny who is deeply humbled to be able to contribute. "It will require a day or so of basic training if you would all like to do this tomorrow."

Mimi looks around at everyone and says, "Sounds like a plan. What do you all think?"

"I think it's incredible," says Angie, "that a low-tech device like a pigeon can have such a profound effect on the Council who is using high-tech devices to harm us."

"Yes," says Kookie, pointing his index finger in the air "not everything powerful is high-tech, is it?"

Turning to the Major he says, "Like the time I blew my tuba mouthpiece at you and the joyful effect it had on everyone, and how we became best friends after that."

The two men chuckle for a moment over their fond memory and Angie suddenly blurts out, "Oh Kookie! *You play the TUBA?!*"

"'Good Lord!" says the Major, shaking his head and quickly adding in Kookie's direction, "Don't even *think* about saying it!"

"Wasn't going to," says Kookie with a sideways grin, rolling his eyes and tapping the tips of his fingers together.

Everyone responds to the pigeon idea with great enthusiasm. Kookie and the Major are blown away with the prospect that they will be able to take a serious stab at outsmarting the Council and the entire Upper Crust all over One World with 24 pigeons.

* * *

"Rise and shine, Little One. Today we will be at a place called Bear River Farm where I will offer my services as a farmhand. For that we will get three meals a day as well as a warm, dry roof over our heads."

Little One giggles and seems quite pleased with it all as Phil is preparing to leave their campsite.

He is thinking about what the man at the Center Coffeehouse said about the disturbances at the California/Oregon border. He says to Little One, "I understand that we will have to be extra careful at the border and be compliant with the Overseers' demands. That means that we basically say *Yes sir* and follow orders."

Little One smiles at Phil as he chatters away at her, but he is more than just a little bit apprehensive. "You know, young lady, I think that I will carry you on my chest instead of the sidecar as we cross the border. I mean, how dangerous can a guy be with a little Wakanjeja strapped to him?"

What Phil does *not* expect though when he gets to the crossing, is the strange looking van parked there with Slavic writing on the sides. Several men, wearing an unusual uniform are inspecting and interrogating people who are coming through on both sides, with guns drawn and much tension in the air. They are all speaking Russian to each other and Phil hears them calling the one who seems to be in command, Yakov.

As Phil approaches, he is aware of a local Panamerican Overseer Guard who appears to be taking orders from the Slavs.

Phil's turn is next as he watches the family in front of him being thoroughly searched with metal detectors and full electronic body scanning. Everyone's Buddy devices are scanned with a Lord's Communication Device.

It all feels so inexplicably bizarre to Phil, watching this whole weird scene unfold.

"Now what in the blazes it *this* all about, Little One?" he says looking down at his traveling companion strapped to his chest.

The family in front of him is finished and told to move along as the guy points to Phil and motions for him to step forward. Phil is tempted to ask questions but knows better and keeps his mouth shut.

The Slavic man gestures to Phil that he must remove Little One and hand her over. Phil gets a sudden bad feeling and refuses to let her go. The Slav calls Yakov over and they speak in Russian to each other.

Yakov turns to Phil and says in English, "It's all right. You can hold baby. But you must take her off you."

As Yakov is speaking, the Slavic man points a gun at Phil. Shaking, Phil does not hesitate and is grateful that they are letting him hold onto Little One while they search him.

When they are finished, Yakov says to him, "It's good. You and baby can go now," and Phil is almost sure that he detects a little smile from the Russian Commandant.

Passing through security, Phil gets back on his autobike. Though he is badly shaken and his legs feel like rubber, he takes off like the devil is chasing him.

* * *

The Pigeon Platoon over at Bear River Farm has been working all morning with Kenny and his birds. They are all enjoying getting to know their new "Communication Device"; the birds are not only intelligent and easy to work with, but they are loaded with charm and personality.

Kenny explains to everyone that as they increase the distance between the lofts, the pigeons will still be able to "home" to them.

"In fact," he says, "There is even a way to increase their speed, should that ever become necessary."

Vi is curious. "Really? So how is that done?" she asks.

"I have never actually tried it myself, but apparently if you introduce a second male into a small coop with a female who has already bonded with another guy, then releasing her sweetie as a carrier is a sure-fire way of getting him to hurry home!"

Everyone has a good laugh over that one.

Lisa calls from the kitchen to let the basic training Pigeon Platoon know that their meal is almost ready. They all come in from the garden and get washed up before helping out with the meal preparations, when there is an unexpected knock on the door.

"Are you guys expecting anyone else?" Lisa asks.

They look around at each other inquisitively and shake their heads.

"Not that I am aware of," says the Major.

"Well then I wonder who that can be," says Lisa as she goes to open the door. To her surprise, standing before her is an elderly Native American gentleman wearing a papoose on his chest with a baby in it.

"Hello, ma'am. I heard you and your Man are in need of some help on your farm? I would be more than glad to help out if you would have me and my Little One here." And extending his hand to her he says, "My name is Phil. I'm from Arbor Vista, California."

"PHIL!" screams Doc, Angie and Mimi in unison, as all three of them hear his voice and start rushing towards the front door. "PHIL!"

He recognizes them at once and is completely dumbfounded yet thrilled at the most unexpected reunion.

"Hello there, my Sisters! Hello, Hello!"

"It's so good to see you again," Doc says. "What a pleasant and unexpected surprise! Please come in and join us; we are just about to sit down to our meal."

Everyone receives Phil with warm greetings as he introduces himself and Little One. She is most happy to be passed around amongst all the new people at this gathering when everyone takes turns greeting her too. They are especially touched when Phil tells them that he met her at the Shelter where he was helping out and that her mama is no longer with us.

Saddened by that thought as the friends sit down to break bread together, they first say a prayer for those who are gone, including Little One's mother.

After their meal, Phil and the others relate their trials to each other since their last meeting beginning with their experiences at the border. Although the Major and Kookie are not generally subject to any kind of search and detainment at a checkpoint, they also remarked at how they did not see any Slavic patrol when they came through the day before.

"I guess they must have gotten there either late last night or early this morning," Kookie ponders, lost in thought.

Taking Metatron out of his pouch and showing it to Phil he tells everyone, "This is what they are after. They seem to be right on our tail."

"But how? So quickly, I mean," asks the Major.

Kookie does not want to get into a whole conversation about moles and how the Lords are all taught and trained to spy on each other, not yet anyway, so he just shrugs his shoulders.

The sharing continues about the flowers, and butterflies, and Arbor Vista and finally they talk about what is weighing most heavily on their hearts; the massacre at the Emmonsville Center. When Phil tells them that he was working at the Emmonsville Shelter after the vans came in with the survivors from the massacre and how one of the survivors handed Little One to him saying that her mama was there, Mimi suddenly puts two and two together.

In a horrible moment of recollection, she begins to cry, "Oh My Lord! I witnessed the murder of this baby's mother!"

She breaks down in tears and Ryan wraps his arms around her, holding her tight.

Then comes the moment that none of them were quite prepared for but knew that they would have to face sooner or later. Sparing Vi the truth about the orange-labeled bottles and the creation of Ebola as a bioweapon, her companions have all, with much compassion, kept that information from her for as long as possible.

Phil shares with everyone the grizzly bloodbath of death that he witnessed as his family died in his arms; and how he was helpless to stop them from receiving, what he did not want to really believe, was the orange-labeled injections filled with live Ebola.

Everyone cringes as they all look at Vi. She has turned white and looks as if she is about to pass out. Searching the faces of all her friends around the table, Vi knows it to be true; that these kind and loving people have been sparing her from the unbearable truth of what she herself has done. She was misled! She was lied to! Vi did not know that the hypodermic needles she put into the arms of hundreds upon hundreds of people were actually *causing* them to die in this horrific, violent manner with great suffering beyond anything she can imagine, including *little Suzie*!

Vi breaks down and starts screaming. *"NOOOOOO! OH GOD! NOOOOOO! I KILLED THEM!! I KILLED THEM ALL!! I KILLED A PRECIOUS LITTLE CHILD!! OH GOD!! KILL ME TOO!!"*

Vi lunges for a knife on the table, but the Major jumps up and grabs it away from her. He throws his whole body around Vi, and he speaks to her softly through her hysteria. "No, Vi. You didn't kill them. You thought you were giving them life. Vi.

"Vi, it was my father who killed them. He gave you and many other innocent, well-meaning folks in your shoes, totally unknown to you all, a loaded gun which he himself did not even have the guts to use himself, and witness the consequences of his own greed and hatred of humankind. You did nothing wrong Vi. You are a terrible victim of the avarice and lust for power of a few on top, who have taken over this world; and who **WE** are now going to take down!!"

Vi is sobbing so heavily that she cannot hear a word of what the Major is trying to tell her. She is beyond consoling.

* * *

Speaking in Russian: "Are you sure that it's here?" Yakov asks his second in command, Dimitri.

"Yes, sir. I got the information straight from our mole. I am sure it is somewhere in the vicinity, along with the traitor himself."

"Very well then, Dimitri, organize the men. We will do a house-to-house search until we locate him. Then we will put a stop to him and *all* of those who would dare to harm any of our beloved Council and Upper Crust."

"And our way of life, sir. Death by torture is the only way to let it be a lesson to others."

"Indeed, Dimitri. Indeed, it is," says Yakov.

"Yes indeed, sir. Yes, indeed," reiterates Dimitri.

"Let's begin with the outer perimeter of the coordinates from the Lord's Communication Device." Yakov says, turning on the device. "There is a place called Bear River, Oregon where we are picking up all these tracking signals.

"Let's go Dimitri! Lock and load!"

PART 3: OPERATION MONARCH

Chapter 13 – Fealty

EVERYONE IS SITTING AROUND THE TABLE in mournful silence, feeling brokenhearted for Vi and wishing there was a way to ease her emotional pain. The Major has not left her side; he holds her hand and gently rubs her back. He and Kookie realize this is the time to tell the group the whole story, including genocide and bioweapons, ongoing mind control methods, and the capabilities of Metatron and the 369 Program to alter DNA.

The Major finally shares the incident at Howard Pharmaceuticals and how he was able to restructure the DNA of the live Ebola virus into a genetically altered neutralizer.

"And thanks to Kookie," he says, "there is no trace of evidence to show what happened or how it happened."

Vi looks at them both for a moment and then whispers softly through her tears, "Thank you. You are both good men. Thank you."

Doc and Mimi come out of the kitchen with a pot of tea containing an herbal mixture they have brewed. They explain that the tea is a special blend that will help them all relieve the trauma they have experienced. "It is a concoction of Rose Petals, Baby Blue Eyes and Sequoia Twigs," Mimi says. Doc here made enough for all of us."

They pour out a small cup for each person, and as they sip their herbal tea a peaceful stillness fills the room. Vi falls asleep from emotional exhaustion.

Angie goes over to Kookie who is saddened by the trauma Vi is suffering. His own heart is filled with guilt and shame. She sees the anguish in his face as he looks down at the floor and is unable to speak. "You are not responsible for this either, Kookie, no more than Vi."

"Aren't I though?" he asks Angie, still looking at the floor.

"No, Kookie. Like Vi said, you and the Major are both good men, very good men. And I for one, am very grateful that you are here for us."

"Me too," says Doc, with Mimi, Ryan, Phil, Lisa and Kenny all nodding in agreement.

Kookie and the Major look at each other and decide that it is time to lay out the plans with their companions.

"Kookie and I have come up with a plan," says the Major. "We are not asking any of you to be a part of this, but if you want to you are welcome to do so. However, I think we should give Vi the opportunity to hear it all at the same time as the rest of you, so let's wait until she wakes up. Besides, it would probably be a good idea if we were all to have a break and take a rest for a while."

The others instantly agree. Angie continues working on her drawings; Lisa and Doc clean up in the kitchen; Kenny goes outside to do some gardening; Phil stretches out to take a nap with Little One; Ryan lies down and closes his eyes for a moment; Kookie goes back to staring at the floor; the Major checks in with the pigeons; and Mimi takes out her journal.

Not one person in the cohort of new friends is aware that just around the corner from Bear River Farm, a van with Slavic writing on the side is pulling up near their driveway.

Mimi opens her journal and begins to write:

Please help us, Lord, help us to help each other, to do the right thing in the times ahead; to think of your people all over One World and do what is right for them. Please help us honor and serve one another with loyalty, strength, and most of all with love. Thank you for bringing all of us here together and may we move forward in whatever way you would have us do. Please protect us Lord, that we may better serve you with every ounce of courage that we have.

Your faithful servant, Mimi.

* * *

"We are here My Lord Commandant," Dimitri says to Yakov as they pull up around the corner from Bear River Farm. The commando unit of seven is ready to go and waiting for their orders from High Lord Commandant Yakov.

"Okay," he says taking out his Lord's Communication Device and pulling up a screen of the few residences in the immediate area. He then assigns each commando to a dwelling that he is to investigate.

"Here are your assignments. We are going to interrogate the occupants of these dwellings and search for the presence of any sort of illegal device. You have all been equipped with a detector which you will use for two of its functions: as a metal detector and as a lie detector. The metal detector has been specifically programmed to detect the presence of unfamiliar electronic equipment. It has a radius of 12 feet, so you will have to go through the dwelling slowly, as well as the immediate surrounding area.

"The lie detector is to determine whether or not they have been approached by any strangers within the last 72 hours, and especially if they are harboring any of them in their homes. If they have been in contact with strangers who have since moved on, find out exactly what they know about them and where they have gone. According to our mole, I am almost certain that the strangers are still in the area and that they are the traitors we are looking for.

"Remember who these vermin are. They are treacherous liars and cunning enemies of the state. If you encounter any resistance *whatsoever* during your search and interrogation, do not hesitate to shoot and kill. Once you kill one member of a household you must kill them all; not a living soul is to be left alive who can spread more lies about us, the heroes of One World!"

The commandos all raise their fists and shout:

"ONE WORLD,
UNDER THE COUNCIL.
THE HIGHEST,
FOREVER!"

They all jump out of the van, fully armed and making tracks to their assigned dwellings. Yakov heads straight down the driveway of Bear River Farm.

* * *

Lisa is just about finished cleaning up in the kitchen when she looks out the window and sees a stranger coming down the driveway.

Hmm, must be another one of their companions, she thinks without giving it much of a second thought. She starts heading for the front door just as the stranger knocks. Kookie suddenly takes his eyes off the floor and looks up. Opening the door Lisa sees a handsome man dressed in an unfamiliar uniform. He appears to be about the same age as Kookie and the Major.

"Hello there, may I help you?" she asks the man.

With his hand holding onto something in his pocket, Yakov says, "Yes, please. You see strangers here today?"

Kookie knows that voice and is at the door in two seconds.

"Why, as a matter of fact, yes!" Lisa replies as she turns to Kookie who is already upon her, motioning quickly for her to back away.

Just as quickly, Yakov pulls out of his pocket what he has been holding onto as the two men come face to face with each other and lock eyes. Yakov thrusts his detector in Kookie's face and the lights are flashing red; Kookie grabs the device from him and does an instant reprogram. With the lights now slowly pulsating green, Kookie hands it back to Yakov.

He lowers his eyes and nods, "*Spasiba*[3], Yakov."

With a sad trace of a smile on his face, Yakov responds, "Thank you Kookie, my Brother."

As Yakov turns to walk back down the driveway he remembers something and calls out to Kookie:

"Brother?"

"Yes?"

"God be with you."

"God be with you, too *Bratan*[4]."

The two men smile at each other knowing they have chosen a road which may lead to their ultimate doom.

Lisa did not see or hear much of what just happened as she dutifully went back to the kitchen after Kookie motioned for her to back off. But seeing the look on his face as he closes the door, she cannot help asking him, "What was *that* all about?"

"It's a long story," he says, "but basically it is about fealty."

Lisa looks at Kookie quizzically. He holds his hand out to her and says, "Come on, it's time to gather the others together and discuss the plan."

Kookie sees most of the others in the living room and asks if they would all gather around the table. "Something has just come to my attention," he explains, "And it is time for us to move into action."

The Major and Kenny are coming in from the garden; Vi wakes up and comes to the table with the others as she watches Little One chew quite happily on a cookie that Lisa has made just for her.

---

[3] *Spasiba: Russian for "thank you."*
[4] *Bratan: Russian slang for "brother" or "bro'."*

A thought occurs to Vi about what she must do. She walks over to Phil and Little One, gets down on her knees, takes little Suzie's seashell necklace out of her pocket and holds it out to Phil. "Would you please see to it that Little One gets this necklace when she is old enough to handle it. Please let her know that it is a special gift from a little girl named Suzie, who died of Ebola.

Phil is moved. "It is an honor for me to carry this gift for the Wakanjeja and the message that goes with it. Thank you, Vi. I will see to it that she honors and remembers all those little ones who have died in this way, by keeping this necklace and by taking the name of the one whom it is honoring."

Phil holds out the seashell necklace before Little One and says, "Great Spirit, to honor you and the lives of all the children you have brought into this world and have now taken home to be with you, I name this sacred child *Suzie of the Seashells*. May she wear it and cherish it always, in little Suzie's name and in your name, Great Spirit."

Everyone is touched, and Vi becomes tearful once more. "Thank you," she whispers softly, "Thank you."

As the Major watches the beautiful scene unfold before him, hope begins to fill his heart, and he thinks of Master Howard.

"Okay," says the Major turning to Kookie. "So, what is it that has just come to your attention?"

"I cannot go into details about it but suffice to say that the Council was aware of our presence here. However, they have now been diverted and will be hunting for us someplace else."

"*What?*" howls the Major.

The others are equally shocked.

"It's okay," continues Kookie, "We are safe from them for the moment, but the sooner we all get on with the plan, the better."

"But what happened?" wails Mimi, all flustered.

"There is something that none of you know about me. Even the Major did not know this until I divulged it to him only recently. Out of the Lords, there are three who have been chosen according to our highly advanced intellectual and intuitive skills. The Council has chosen one of us from each of the three Continental Territories. Having been taken away from our families at a young age, we were raised by people from the Council to be the highest in command among our people. I guess you know where I am going with this, but I am one of the three High Lords, as we are called."

There is a collective "*WHOA!*" around the table.

"Although we were each raised in our native Continental Territories, we spent a great deal of time with each other as well, in various locations around One World. But the Council's intention was to keep us suspicious of each other by using various mind control techniques, similar to the ones that have been perpetrated on all of you your whole lives."

"Good grief! Heavens! Shame on them!" mutter the friends around the table.

"Yes, well, but what the Council never discovered is that they actually failed."

"How so?" asks the Major.

"They failed to recognize something important about humanity; that the Light is stronger than the darkness; hope is greater than fear; and love is more powerful than hate. A bond of love grew between us, which they never suspected would happen, and the three of us were smart enough to realize that we had to keep it as our secret."

Pausing for a moment, Kookie sees everyone smiling and nodding at him and at each other.

"The Council highly suspects that there is a rogue element among the Lords of the UC, and they sent my Slavic High Lord brother, Yakov, here to discover his or her identity, and to kill the treasonous one, which of course happens to be me. But the three of us have always had a plan should things ever come to this.

"My friends, you may choose to be a part of this or not, whatever you feel called to do. But as the Major and I have already told you, we are in this to take the *whole* system down and return all human life to the freedom that we once had. The overall plan is to use various methods, including Metatron here (holding it up for all to see) to help us bring down the evil of the corrupt Council and others of the Upper Crust who are enabling and perpetrating the greed. Hopefully one day, we will be able to help those who are willing to turn back to the Light!"

The group is stunned into silence until Mimi breaks the quiet with her question. "Kookie, can you guys really do that?" she asks.

"I guess we'll just have to find that one out, won't we," he says with a twinkle in his golden eyes. "So, for now let's talk about what work needs to be done and where to begin."

Vi has been considering all that has been said. She comes up with an idea and says to her companions, "I would like to propose that we give our mission a name."

"Yes!" the Major perks up, anxious to hear what Vi has to say.

"In honor of the Monarch Butterflies who are helping us out in such amazing ways, showing us how love is more powerful than even brute force, I would like to call our mission, Operation Monarch."

The Major smiles at Vi as he says to her, "I would like to second that."

Everyone else says, *"Amen!"*

* * *

The commandos are regrouped in the van awaiting each other's reports and further instructions from their High Lord Commandant Yakov.

Yakov asks his men to report. "What have you all discovered?"

Dimitri speaks up, "Nothing, Lord Commandant. Every house we searched was clean, and it seems that no one has seen or heard of any strangers in the vicinity."

"Hmm," Yakov says pensively stroking his chin.

Another commando speaks up, "What about you, Lord Commandant. Did you find out anything?"

"Could be," he says with a puzzled look on his face. "The house I checked and the woman whom I interrogated said that she saw a group of people on autobikes riding through here yesterday. They apparently stopped to fill their water bottles at the well over there," Yakov points to a well at the end of the property, "which is when the woman noticed them. She went out and asked them if they needed anything and they struck up a bit of a conversation with each other. They said that they were from California on their way to find relatives whom they haven't been able to contact since Ebola."

"Did you ask her which direction they were headed in?" asks Dimitri.

"Of course," smirks Yakov, as if it was a dumb question to even ask him. "She said that they were heading east to Wyoming."

"Oh, that's weird," says Dimitri. "Didn't the mole say something about a small town called Salena in Oregon?"

"Yes, indeed," says Yakov, "And I will most certainly have to check it out."

Yakov takes out his Lord's Communication Device and contacts the mole.

"While I am waiting for his report, we will not be wasting any time. So, let's find out where this Wyoming is and get going."

The men are all anxious to catch up with the traitors and mete out their punishment; with much haste the commandos get rolling . . . to Wyoming.

* * *

The Major is the first to speak regarding his assignment. "I will be going back to Howard Pharmaceuticals to ensure that the Ebola Neutralizers are just that, neutralizers, and not bioweapons. But I will also remain available for anything else you all might need from me."

"Please Major," implores Vi, "let me go with you. Let me be of service to you on our mission. You can say that I am a new servant at the plant, with experience administering the neutralizer at a Shelter. If I am ever to find real forgiveness within my heart for what I have done, then helping in whatever way I can to destroy this terrible weapon is perhaps the best way I can find true, inner peace.

"I understand," says the Major, ever so gently, "I will be honored to have you there helping me."

Lisa and Kenny speak up next.

"We can offer a safehouse for any who needs it as you and others pass through," says Lisa.

"And I can help set up and run a Pigeons Communication System, breeding and training more homing pigeons," says Kenny, "for as far as you need them to go, across the entire Continental Territory if necessary. Possibly, the pigeons can even go further depending on how many people are involved and where they are all located."

Doc is next. "First, I will need to go back to Judy's farm and get her hooked up with us and the pigeons. I'm sure she will want to be involved in our plan, including using her place as a safehouse. If it's alright with you Lisa, if you would have me come back and stay here with you guys, there is so much we can do to make herbal teas and other healing products right here on the farm. We can create and distribute all of our medicinals to so many people who are in need. Judy can also contact her network of farmers and create a chain of safehouses for those who also want to help."

"Which is probably *everyone!*" exclaims Phil. "Hoping you all will let me help too, ladies, with medicinal healing herbs. I think we will make a great team!"

"Yes Phil, and thank you for suggesting it, Doc." says Lisa. "I think there is a lot that the three of us can do if we put our heads together and share our knowledge of the natural world."

"Amen, Sisters!" Phil says to Doc and Lisa with a smile.

Looking at Suzie of the Seashells, Doc smiles to herself thinking how much she has always wanted a child to take care of, especially a little girl.

Mimi looks at the others. "I will go wherever you guys need me to serve and whatever I am called to do by the Good Lord."

Smiling at Kookie she adds, "That includes *this* good Lord right here, too!

The Major rolls his eyes, furrows his brow, and wants to barf.

"Just ask me, Kookie," continues Mimi," whatever you would have me do. But first I must continue to Salena and find my daughter's family. I just need to know that they are all okay, especially my little granddaughter Elli."

"That is totally understood, Mimi," says Kookie. "And please do not feel that you have to do anything other than that. Your family needs you too."

"And I need you too," says Ryan, as he puts his arms around Mimi. "I do not ever want to be away from you again."

"Nor I you," Mimi says, snuggling in close to Ryan.

Angie beams at Kookie. "Hey there partner, I guess that leaves you and me!" she says.

"I guess it does." Kookie replies. "That was some good work you did with Metatron when you figured out how to program it for a 7.83 hertz meditation."

"Thank you, Kookie."

"Maybe you can help me figure out some other things that Metatron can do, you know, for healing and the greater good, and, well, you know, for . . . um, me."

"Oh Kookie, I would just love that!" says Angie.

She sparkles at him.

He twinkles at her.

"So, um. . . you play the tuba, then!" Angie says enthusiastically.

"Well, I used to a long time ago."

"Do you think maybe you could play something on your tuba for me, sometime?" Angie asks him with a great big grin.

The Major imagines Kookie serenading this charming young lady with his tuba.

Oh, for crying out loud! he thinks to himself, shaking his head and rolling his eyes at the thought.

* * *

Master Howard is beside himself with anxiety. His Overlord has seen all the evidence that there has been no wrongdoing at the Howard Pharmaceutical plant. There must be some kind of technical malfunction going on. No matter how many investigations they launch using AI and all the latest technology, no one can come up with any explanation as to why their bioweapons are not killing or harming the people in any way. In fact, there has been a steady increase in recovery from Ebola, which is causing all hell to break loose in every stratum of the UC and the Council.

The Lords and Masters and their moles have not come up with anything concrete either, and suspicions are abounding on all sides and all fronts of everyone at the top. The Overseers who broadcast on My Buddy are continuing to report the same news and instructions to the people regarding neutralizers. They've even been lying to the people saying the death toll is increasing, when in fact it is significantly and rapidly *de*creasing. With all of the latest techniques of mind control, the Council simply does not know how much longer it can continue with the charade of falsifying the truth of the world's rapid recovery from Ebola. Master Howard is expecting his son to return momentarily hoping that he has some good news to report after being gone for several days and spending time with his Overlord.

Master Howard summons the Major the second he hears his son has arrived.

"Hello, sir," says the Major to his father upon entering his executive suite. "Any news regarding Operation Snake Bite?"

"No, son! I was hoping that you had some news for *me!*" Master Howard replies.

"Well, I think maybe I just might have some news for you, father. Since we have not been able to find anything wrong with Snake Bite, that left us only two possibilities that we could think of. One of them I already mentioned to you, which is a major malfunction somewhere in the equipment.

Master Howard quips, "I had the place turned upside down trying to find anything wrong with our machinery down to every last detail of the AI, as well as human factors of production. We tested everything and everybody from top to bottom and not one malfunction was to be found anywhere.

"So," the Major proceeds cautiously offering Master Howard the other idea that, allegedly, he and his Overlord Kookie came up with. In truth, it is an idea that he and Vi hatched on their ride down from Bear River Farm.

"My Overlord Kookie and I met with a group of Master and Lord experts who have scientific training in all the latest knowledge of epidemiology and immunology as well as the world of natural medicine. After brainstorming with them for a few days we have come up with a theory. In fact, we even brought in a woman who was an Overseer in a nearby Shelter Hut and has seen the effects first-hand of what I am about to describe to you. I have brought her back with me to serve in our plant and test out our theory."

"Excellent son, excellent! So, what is the theory?"

"Well, due to various health factors such as the stress-free life the people are living, you know since we take such good care of them and all of their needs, keeping them fed, sheltered and happy, and considering all the healthy fruits and vegetables that they are always eating, it is quite possible that many of them have developed a natural immunity to Ebola."

"WHAT?" Master Howard shrieks.

"We are going to conduct tests on them to see if this theory is true. And if it is, then we will have to come up with some other way of well, you know, dealing with the overpopulation problem."

"WHAT?" Master Howard is furious at the idea that the people could be immune to the deadly virus.

"It's all right father. Mankind has been coming up with inventive ways of killing people since the dawn of civilization. I'm sure you all can come up with something new. Just think, if it is *your* idea and invention, then the Council will be sure to reward you big time for your ingenuity and your fealty to them."

"What? Uh, hmm . . ." Master Howard considers the possibility.

"Yes sir. You just keep on thinking about that, and I will take our new helper down to the factory floor so she can get started immediately. I am having some survivors of Snake Bite brought over from the local Shelter Hut so the woman can begin her testing. Who knows, maybe even *she* will come up with a way of stopping all of this once and for all."

"Hmm," wonders Master Howard.

"Anyway, I've got to get the woman situated in the servants dwelling as well as set her up in the factory. So why don't I just catch up with you later."

The Major leaves Master Howard thinking about what new and improved form of genocide he can come with. Meanwhile, he is off to get Vi all settled in. He wants to be sure that she is assigned to a downstairs unit with a back door that leads to the communal garden. This will be the perfect spot for the other new arrivals that the Major and Vi have brought with them from Bear River Farm: #5 and #6; male and female pigeons.

* * *

At the safehouse farm, Judy has just come in from working in the garden. She is tired from all the hard work she has to do mostly by herself since so many people have either died of Ebola, left to find their loved ones, or simply disappeared. Every now and then someone will come through, stay for a while and help out, but then they too disappear unexpectedly. Suspicions have been growing amongst the people about what is really going on with Ebola, except that recently things seem to have changed. Now there are reports of people surviving, which is renewing everyone's hope, and Judy is encouraged that she will soon have regular helpers again.

Going into the front yard to pick some tomatoes for her afternoon salad, Judy stops in her tracks when she sees her friend Doc emerging from an Autovan. She unloads her autobike, the sidecar and another small crate from the Autovan which the Major arranged for her trip down to Judy's farm. As the Autovan takes off, Doc comes down the path.

"Hey, lady!" Judy calls out to her while frantically waving her arms in the air. "Hey, hey! It's so good to see you again Doc, and so soon! Come on in!"

Doc is thrilled to see Judy, too, given all that has happened since they only just saw each other recently. Doc is carrying a load of paraphernalia from the sidecar of her autobike into the house.

"Here, let me help you with that," Judy says as she grabs a couple of Doc's bags.

"Wow! Well, my goodness!" Judy exclaims, when she sees what else Doc has arrived with. Her two traveling companions #9 and #10 are looking very cozy in their little traveling coop.

"Hey Judy, how's everything been going with you?" Doc asks as she plops down on the nearest chair, in need of a little break and some good fellowship. "It's really great to see you again. And I sure do have news for you, my friend!"

"I'm sure you do." says Judy. "I saw that Autovan you arrived in. Wow, woman!"

"Yes, well, it's a long story, so why don't you go first."

"Well, okay," Judy begins as she plants herself on the chair next to Doc, also grateful to have a break. "The main thing is that there has been very little help for me on the farm lately, with Ebola taking so many lives and taking so many others *away* to look for surviving loved ones. So, I have had to do a lot of the work here by myself. Although business *has* been much slower than usual as you might expect."

"I'm sorry to hear all of that, Judy. However, have you heard the news that things are beginning to turn around with Ebola?"

"Yes! As a matter of fact, there have been rumors to that effect, although we haven't been hearing anything about it on My Buddy. Just the same-old-same-old with that one," Judy smirks, rolling her eyes. "I don't really listen to it as often as we are supposed to anyway," she snorts.

Doc laughs, "Yes, I haven't been able to listen to any of that stuff lately, myself."

"I know, and I wouldn't either except it's the only *news* that I get, if you can call it that. I'm pretty isolated here you know. Which is another reason why I am so grateful whenever you come for a visit," Judy says with a smile.

"Well then," says Doc in a more serious tone, "What you have just said about *news* brings me to the reason for my visit."

"Oh?" says Judy intrigued, when suddenly it begins to dawn on her, "I don't suppose this has something to do with your little traveling companions over there, which was going to be *my* next question. What's the story with *those* two guys?"

Bringing over the traveling coop containing #9 and #10, Doc replies, "Actually they are not two guys, well except for this one, that is." She takes #9 out and shows him to Judy, "This is a male homing pigeon and his name is #9."

"#9, this is Judy," and turning to Judy, Doc says, "Judy, this is # 9."

"Pleased to meet you, #9," Judy says with a giggle as she puts her hand out to shake the bird's foot, and to her delight, #9 extends his foot to welcome Judy's handshake.

"The other one is his sweetie, a female. Her name is #10," Doc says. She goes through the same introductions with the other pigeon. "Let me tell you why I have brought them here."

Doc brings Judy up to date with all that has happened since she, Mimi, Angie and the Major were last there, including all that was arranged at Bear River Farm regarding Operation Monarch.

"What would you think about being a part of our Pigeons Communication System and Operation Monarch as we have named them, respectively?" asks Doc.

"Oh, my goodness!" gasps Judy. "It would be an honor to be a part of Operation Monarch and the Pigeons Communication System in whatever way I can. In addition to these charming little winged creatures, I would also love to volunteer my farm to be a safehouse for all in need. And if some of the people have the time and wouldn't mind, it would sure be helpful if they could stay here for a few days and help out with the harvest, and whatever other work needs to be done."

"I'm sure that can be arranged," Doc beams with much gratitude, "And I will get the word out to that effect. In fact, I happen to have some time to give you now, my friend, over the next few days. I will show you how to work with the pigeons and also give you a hand with the farm."

"Oh, thank you, thank you!" Judy says. "First things first though, Doc. How about breaking bread together?"

"You got *that* right!" Doc laughs as both women make their way to the kitchen.

* * *

It is early in the morning in a quiet suburb of what was once another great city, now deserted. The city was called Shanghai, and a few of the small outer communities are still remaining. Liling is going out into her garden of wildflowers, which she tends to every morning with much love and care. Her favorite flower that she cultivates with special affection is the White Jasmine, her namesake in Chinese. Liling is speaking softly to her flowers, stroking their petals and holding her hands up to the sun asking Kuan Yin to bless them today with female wisdom and love, when she is presently interrupted.

Feeling her Lord's Communication Device pulsating in her pocket pouch, Liling takes out the device and sees a message; *"High Lady Liling of the Council; please accept message."*

Liling accepts the message from her HOC.

Speaking in Chinese:

"Lady Liling, we have an emergency! You will be hearing from your Brother, Lord Kenneth who will be filling you in on travel instructions. Be ready when he contacts you to leave very soon."

"Yes," she says, "I will wait to hear from my Brother, Lord Kenneth, and make preparations for travel. Is there anything else you would have me do, sir?"

"You will hear everything from Lord Kenneth, My Lady. Just know that we at the Council appreciate you, your honor, and your fealty to us."

"Thank you, sir," Liling says as they disconnect from each other.

Liling turns to her flowers, especially the White Jasmines, and tells them in a sorrowful voice that she hopes to return to them safely real soon. For Lady Liling knows that their time has come; the day which she, Kookie, and Yakov have been preparing for their entire lives has arrived.

Chapter 14 – Vows

MIMI AND RYAN CONTINUE THEIR JOURNEY TOGETHER heading north to Salena, Oregon. So much has happened that they need to take some time to be together in peace and quiet. Their first night after leaving everyone at Bear River Farm, Mimi and Ryan find a beautiful, secluded spot near a lake where they can rest and take comfort in each other's presence. There is a sadness about them because they wonder if they will ever have a simple, peaceful life together, which is their greatest desire.

"I'm so happy to be here with you, my darling Ryan," Mimi says with a somewhat somber tone in her voice.

"Yes," he replies tenderly as he looks deep into her eyes. "Mimi, there is something I would like to ask you."

"What is it, sweetie?"

"Well . . ." he hesitates, and then continues, "It is something I had given up on a long time ago but now, well I guess I have changed."

"Okay."

"Mimi . . ."

"Yes?"

"Mimi . . ."

"Uh . . . yes Ryan."

He picks a few wildflowers from the ground and holding them out to Mimi, Ryan takes a deep breath and finally comes out with it:

"Mimi, I love you, and I never want to be away from you again. Will you take vows with me?"

"Oh my!" Mimi begins to cry. "Oh, my darling sweetheart! Yes! I will take vows with you."

There used to be a time when they would have been able to get married, but that privilege is now reserved only for the Upper Crust. For the people, marriage is against the law. It is the Council that "owns" them. They are not allowed to be legally bound to anyone else.

The two lovers get on their knees and face each other to proclaim their life-long love through the vows of the people. Ryan begins.

"My dearest Mimi, I offer myself to you completely."

And Mimi follows, "My dearest Ryan, I offer myself to you completely."

"To be the best Man I can be,"

"To be the best Woman I can be,"

"With all the love that is in my heart, for you only,"

"With all the love that is in my heart, for you only,"

"In the sight of our Creator, this I promise,"

"In the sight of our Lord, this I promise,"

"To be your lover and best friend,"

"To be your lover and best friend,"

"Today, tomorrow and for all of eternity,"

"Today, tomorrow and for all of eternity,"

"Bless you Mimi, my beloved Woman."

"Bless you Ryan, my beloved Man."

Ryan leans over and kisses his Woman, Mimi.

That night, as Mimi and Ryan are wrapped in each other's arms they listen to the night sounds of the forest. Mimi and her Man feel the beauty of the love songs being sung to them by all of the sacred creations of life surrounding them. Drifting off to sleep, Mimi thinks of little Elli and hopes to be with her soon.

Mimi dreams that Elli is with her mom Lydia, and her dad Sam, laughing and playing in a beautiful garden. She is chasing butterflies while Lydia is picking flowers and Sam is snoozing in the sunlight. The colors of the flowers are radiating with the glittering light of the sun which softly spreads its gentle rays to the nearby trees.

Mimi is thoroughly enjoying the sound of Elli giggling with delight as the Monarchs perch on her shoulders and in her hair, kissing her little soul. Then the scene changes and the sky darkens as Sam, Lydia and Elli are standing on line in front of a Shelter Hut. Lydia is holding Elli in her arms and they all descend the steps to the dark hole below. Mimi is instantly horrified when she sees the orange-labeled bottles laid out on the table before them. It is their turn to receive the bioweapon and they all roll up their sleeves.

Elli turns to Mimi and says, "Don't cry Gramma, everything is gonna be okay. Elli loves you, Elli is just fine! Don't cry Gramma . . ." and the dream fades as Mimi wakes up in tears.

Ryan is fast asleep, and she snuggles up against him trying to take comfort in his warm side and steady breathing. Mimi's thoughts immediately turn to the Major's account of the DNA restructuring of the Ebola bioweapon, and she hopes and prays that however it played out for them, her family was spared the horror of the terrible effects of the virus, and that they are all safe and alive. Of course, she realizes that very soon now she should find out, one way or the other what has happened to them.

* * *

Kookie's Kastle is full of countless rooms, suites and accommodating areas of all kinds. He has a small staff of servants who maintain the grounds and all aspects of the property, interior and exterior. Therefore, it is easy for him to bring on board another "helper" from the outside to fulfill whatever role that he, the High Lord of his Kastle, deems necessary.

There is one very cozy suite in particular that is close to Kookie's own private living quarters that he feels would be comfortable for Angie. It also has a veranda that overlooks a lovely garden. Upon their arrival

Kookie gets Angie set up in her new suite, along with his other new residents, #3 and #4. Of course, the birds get the veranda.

"Let me show you around my workstation," Kookie says to Angie, as he brings her into the room with the large monitors and massive console.

Angie looks around, amazed. "Wow! This is fantastic!" she says to her host.

"Thanks! Allow me to show you how this one in particular works," he says.

"What is it?" Angie asks.

"I call it a Holographic Imager. What that means is I can create whatever image I want of anything whatsoever going on here in this room."

"*Whoa!*" Angie chuckles thinking of the possibilities of *that* one.

"Yep!" Kookie beams, "In fact, let's have some fun with it. What would you like to pretend is going on here, right now?"

Thinking about it for a moment Angie smiles gleefully and says, "I would like to pretend that I'm sitting here in a comfy, overstuffed chair being serenaded by someone I know who just happens to play the tuba!"

Kookie roars with delight, tapping the tips of his fingers together. "Now let me see if I can think of anyone who fits that description!"

He enters the description on the keyboard of a debonair tuba player serenading a lovely young lady; Kookie uploads it onto the Holographic Imager. Angie is enthralled and asks him what piece of music he is playing.

"It is called, Tuba Concerto in F Minor." Kookie finger-taps, fully pleased with his creation. And he hits the SAVE button thinking to himself *I better keep this one. Never know when it might come in handy.*

He takes out one of the Metatron devices that he was hoping to be able to give the others. But he changed his mind after Yakov showed up, realizing it would be too risky right now to have any more of them out there.

"This is for you, Angie. Although we dare not use them for communication right now, there are other things that we can still work on with Metatron. It seems that you have quite the intuitive skills that we need to delve deeper into the capabilities of Metatron. So here you go," he says handing Angie her very own Metatron device. "But for the time being, be sure to only use it in this room, okay?"

"Absolutely," Angie says as she holds out her hands to receive Metatron from Kookie. She takes it into her hands as if it were the most precious thing anyone has ever handed her.

Turning it on, Kookie shows her how to activate the 369 Program as she holds the device against her chest.

Angie asks Metatron to "speak" to her with whatever message she is supposed to receive at the moment. Almost immediately, Angie feels great tension in her chest as if fear were gripping her heart. She looks at Metatron and sees the golden pyramid has appeared and is spinning rapidly; in her mind's eye she also sees a red heart flashing behind it.

Kookie sees the spinning golden pyramid and is flabbergasted. "What are you feeling Angie?" he asks her.

Suddenly, she feels gloomy and a bit fearful. "There is a woman . . . she is very sad, somewhat frightened. I believe she is somewhere in Sinopacifica, something about . . . your Sister?"

At this Kookie blanches; dropping his head and nodding, "Yes. I understand."

"Who is she Kookie?"

"Remember when I told all of you that I am one of the three High Lords?"

"Yes."

"And that one of the other High Lord's, my Slavic Brother Yakov was sent here to uncover the identity of the traitor, which of course is me, and then to kill the traitor?"

"*Yes!*" Angie is becoming agitated.

"Well," Kookie says with some hesitation and sadness, "The woman you are referring to is the third one. Technically, she is of course a Lady, not a Lord. She is my Sino High Lady Sister, Lady Liling."

"What does it all mean?" asks Angie. "Why is she so sad?"

Kookie closes his eyes and takes a deep breath. "When the three of us were younger we saw what was happening in the world, how people were being used by the Upper Crust for their greedy and selfish agenda for power. We saw how people became little more than mere objects to the Council and how they would do anything to diminish the natural powers that people are born with in order to control their freewill and every aspect of their lives. We also realized that we were being groomed as the loyal servants of the Council because of our intellectual abilities. But the Council did not realize that we never really believed as they do, that we are somehow better than or above all other people of the world; that if we told our High Overlord Contacts anything other than what they wanted to hear we would be in big trouble with them.

"Angie, we always felt that one day their world would implode, and they would fight back tooth and nail to stop the inevitable from happening. So, we made a promise to each other. We vowed that when it became apparent to us that their time had come and that their world was beginning to crumble, that no matter what, we would somehow manage to fight together for the truth and for all that is fair and just. But most of all, we vowed to fight for the people, knowing that it would probably be the end of our lives as we knew it."

Feeling much sadness and compassion in her heart for the three of them Angie says, "Do you believe that their time has come, Kookie? And do you think that Yakov and Liling also believe that?"

"Yes, to both questions," Kookie says to Angie, feeling a tenderness growing in his heart for her.

At that moment, there is a transmission coming in on one of the screens. Kookie turns on the Holographic Imager and "removes" Angie's presence from the area as he proceeds to accept the incoming message from his HOC.

"Good evening My Lord; I am afraid that I have more bad news for you."

"What is it, sir?"

"To begin with, so far we have been unsuccessful at locating the traitor. I sent your Brother, High Lord Yakov along with a team of commandos to the region where the traitor was expected to be according to one of our moles. Lord Yakov and his men almost caught up with the treacherous one, but somehow he managed to elude them."

"Gracious!"

"Yes, and our mole has made it quite clear that the guilty party is still at large, and his identity is unknown."

"I am sorry to hear that, sir."

"Yes, well, that's not even the worst part. Howard Pharmaceuticals and its regional plants throughout the three Continental Territories of One World have not been able to ascertain what has gone wrong with Operation Snake Bite. My Lord, there are even reports coming in from all over One World that people who have received the bioweapon are actually *better* in some strange way than they were before! This means that as of now we have no choice but to abandon our mission of massive, global slave extermination using the Ebola bioweapon!"

"*Whoa--*" Kookie just came dangerously close to revealing a gleeful sound in his voice. "*Woe is me!*" He jumps in with a quick recovery.

"So, we are calling for a Gathering of the High Lords of the Council, to convene at our polar location by this time tomorrow. We will discuss, organize and put into action another plan of operation. Be prepared to be picked up by the Council Cloudtransporter, tomorrow morning. Oh, and you are to pass along all of this information to Yakov and Liling who will also be picked up and brought to our polar location."

"Yes, sir."

"Until tomorrow, then."

The HOC disconnects.

"Oh, my goodness!" says Angie who has heard everything. "What will happen now, Kookie?"

"I am afraid that I must leave you for a little while as I am being summoned to this gathering. Angie, I will need you to help me keep everything running at the Kastle, especially here at my workstation. I will show you how to program the Holographic Imager and make it look as though everything is functioning in my absence as the Council would expect, even though you will be doing 'other work' for me here. It might be dangerous for you though, and I really hate to ask you to do it."

"Kookie, it is my honor to do it for you. Just show me what to do with all this stuff and I promise you that I will not let you down."

"Thank you, Angie, thank you," Kookie says graciously and proceeds to open the programs that Angie will need to learn to work with. He knows that she will have to give the appearance that Kookie has her doing what the Council expects of someone in his servitude to do in his absence, not only for himself but also for her own safety.

Later that evening, the Groundskeeper Overseer is finishing up his day's service in the garden near the veranda of Angie's living quarters. It suddenly strikes him that he is hearing a forgotten but somewhat familiar sound coming from the direction of her veranda. He stops what he is doing and listens to it musing for a moment. *Is it possible? Could it be? Sounds like I'm hearing a . . . tuba?"*

* * *

Doc is preparing to leave Judy's cottage and return to Bear River Farm. Having completed her training with #9 and #10, Doc has Judy send her first message via homing pigeon to Kenny and Lisa that all is well and they should expect Big Deal (Doc's code name) in a few days. As part of Judy's training Doc explains to her that they all chose code names at Bear River and that she needs to choose one too. The best kind of code name is one that does not sound like a name but reminds you of the person in some way. Judy thinks of how much she enjoys life and especially the things that make her laugh, thus giving herself the code name, Laughs Alot.

"Okay, Laughs Alot," says her buddy Big Deal, "It seems like we are all ready to go. I'm sorry to have to leave you; it is always such a pleasure to spend time with you my friend, but we will stay in touch with the help of our new friends, #9 and #10.

"Yes," Judy replies, "We certainly will. And you take care of yourself out there, Doc. Be safe my friend, and please let me know what else I can *ever* do for you, and for Operation Monarch."

"Thank you, Judy." Doc says, leaving her friend and heading north back to Lisa, Kenny, Phil and little Suzie of the Seashells.

Doc is well stocked with provisions for her trip and feels confident that there will probably be no need to stop at a Center. She is now well familiar with the backroads and best ways to avoid people; keeping herself protected, out of sight, and out of trouble.

Later in the day Doc stops for a rest and a meal. She takes out her Sequoia Twigs and assorted flowers, all of which are well dried by now and looks at all the other wildflowers growing in the nearby field.

My goodness, she thinks. *How much there is to learn from all of you; so much healing, so much life, so many wonderful messages, and so much love. Teach me my Sisters and Brothers of the earth, please teach me. Show me how to use your powers to help heal our people around the world. And that includes those who are doing us harm. Please help us to fulfill Kookie's vision, and our mission of Operation Monarch. May we somehow, someday, and with your help, turn as many as we can back to the Light, back to Love, and back to the humanity that I DO believe, with all of my heart exists in all of us.*

As daylight fades and the stars come out, Doc takes out her writing tablet and night light and records all that she is hearing from the flowers and the trees as they are calling out to her soul. She can hear their messages and feel their promise to work with her and all who seek their wisdom and love.

They whisper, *have hope, Lady of Nature; know that all the things you seek are possible, and that Love is the most powerful force there is. Stay faithful to your mission, to each other and to the world, and many good things will come to pass.*

With those comforting words floating through her heart, Doc falls into a deep and peaceful sleep.

The next morning Doc awakens refreshed and feeling hopeful as she begins her journey back up the coast to Bear River. She is even feeling safe enough to stop at a Center around midday to get some news from people at the Coffeehouse regarding Ebola. Much to her joyous surprise, there are reports coming in from all three Continental Territories that people are getting well, in spite of the daily warnings and admonitions to the contrary that are still being dispelled on My Buddy.

Riding along, Doc passes fields and meadows filled with Indian Paintbrush, California Poppies and Baby Blue Eyes, as well as magnificent trees and streams, and quaint little cottages. Most of the people all over One World live in small dwellings and in towns or suburban communities, but those who live out in the more rural areas such as Judy are either groundskeepers, or farmers of some sort. They are what remain of the stewards of the Land. Among the people themselves, they are very honored, loved and respected. However, to the Council, they are looked upon with disdain and mistrust since they are not as easily manipulated with mind control techniques. They are the people who live closest to any semblance of freedom among the world's population, and for this reason they are actually feared and despised by the more manipulative and controlling elements of the UC. Riding along through this region of stewards Doc is experiencing a little bit of what it must feel like to be free.

Later in the afternoon, Doc sees what appears to be a town Center up ahead. She is feeling hungry and ready to take a break from traveling, but her hunger is not so much for food or even for news and information. She is hoping to meet some of the people in this rural community of stewards at the Coffeehouse and experience some good fellowship with them.

Pulling up to the main entryway of the Center Doc is distracted thinking about the pleasures of meeting new people, possibly even making a few new friends. She does not notice that a van is pulling up right behind her.

Once inside Doc heads straight to the Coffeehouse. She gets herself a coffee and tea cake and finds a table next to a young man.

"Howdy stranger!" says the man, smiling at her.

"Well, howdy to you, sir!" she smiles back. "I was wondering if there was news of any kind in these parts?"

Sure is," says the friendly young man. "In fact, you've come on just the right day for that. There's a whole bevy of good folks out back," he says pointing to the rear exit. "They all arrived this morning from the local Shelter."

Suddenly, Doc's inner radar perks up. "Really?"

"Said they had to spend all day yesterday and most of the night there 'cause they were not doing very well. You know, thought they were going to die of Ebola. But as it turned out, every one of them got better by the morning!"

"Is that so?!"

"Yes ma'am! In fact, not only did they get better but they swears that now they are even *better* than better, if you catch my meaning."

"Wow! I'm not sure that I do catch your meaning, but it sounds incredible!" says Doc.

"I know. Just go on out there and see for yourself."

Doc heads out to the back garden area of the Center and sees a most heartwarming sight. A few hundred people or so are picnicking on the grass together: eating, laughing, little ones playing games, and everyone having a wonderful time. The truly magical part is what she feels in her heart just from being in their presence. There is a feeling of love and compassion that is sweeping through every person on the grass, which Doc has never before experienced in the presence of another human being, let alone a few hundred of them all at once.

She can see it in their shining faces, sparkling eyes and sweet soft smiles; in their gentle touches of one another and the loving arms held out when a little one takes a tumble. There is an innocence and inner peace about them as of those who have never known trials or tribulations and have always lived in the Garden of Eden. Doc can also see and feel a radiant beam of light coming from each and every person as if they have *always* lived in the presence of the Heavenly Father, and in His Garden. Any cares they may have once experienced are now and forever gone, and Sacred Love is all that remains.

Doc remembers what the Major said about Metatron, and what he did to the Ebola bioweapons at his father's pharmaceutical factory. But before she can think of anything else Doc realizes that something is going on behind her inside the Coffeehouse. Turning around she sees through the glass doors about 12 commandos rounding up the people inside and lining them all up against the wall. Sensing trouble, Doc implements her internal self-cloaking meditation.

Then she hears shooting coming from inside.

Doc is hiding behind the door against the building as she hears one of the commandos say, "I can see the slaves from here. They are all outside in the back,"

They burst through the doors and rush outside. All the people stop what they are doing when they see the commandos standing with guns aimed straight at them. Once again Doc witnesses something completely inexplicable that breaks her heart in half.

Those who are seated get on their knees and those who are on their feet stand perfectly still. Gazing into the eyes of the commandos, they offer a gentle smile, unflinching, unhesitating, and without fear. They look up, holding their hands up to the sky, and then nod to the men standing before them with weapons drawn. And with one last peaceful smile from these beautiful People of Light that says, *it's alright my Brothers, we forgive you*, the gunmen open fire.

Within minutes the massacre is all over.

The commandos go back into the Coffeehouse and Doc hears one of them saying, "Send for the clean-up crew; tell them they've got a big mess here to clean up. Let's just get the hell out of here."

They all mutter in agreement and take off, leaving Doc standing there all alone in the brutal aftermath of a mass murder. Not a soul is left alive; not inside, outside nor anywhere in the center. Not one witness has been left to tell the truth of what has happened here on this day. Not one, except Doc. She collapses on the ground.

After a few moments when she is able to catch her breath, Doc holds her hands up to the sky; tears pouring down her face in total horror. In deep anguish she cries out, "Oh Lord, what would you have me do now?"

Doc looks at all the bodies before her, all of whom were but moments ago the living embodiment of love and compassion. She whispers softly to the souls who are just a little way above her head now and says:

"People of Light, loving stewards of the Land, bless you all for letting me see you in all your glory, and showing me the true depths of love that human beings are capable of. Thank you and bless you.

I vow to you all that on this day, I will open my heart to understand and receive this Higher Love which you have all been given, so that I may pass it on to others."

A great rush of wind passes through Doc's heart as she feels the voices of all those above her saying, *AMEN!*

* * *

Lady Liling's Lord's Communication Device is pulsating in her pouch. She sees that it is an incoming message from Kookie. Accepting the incoming message, she says, "Hello, my Brother. HOC said you would call me with instructions."

"Hello, my Sister. Yes, you will be picked up shortly and taken to the polar location for an emergency Gathering of the High Lords of the Council."

Kookie is aware that this is not a secure line so he must speak cautiously to Liling as he continues, "Something has gone wrong with Ebola, and the Council has had to cancel the mission."

"I see, my Brother. Any special instructions?"

"Yes, Liling." Kookie continues with words that he knows the Council expects to hear, camouflaging another message to his High Lady Sister. "We are dealing with dangerous elements amongst the populace, so be sure to bring along the latest man-hunt programs and related devices which I have sent you. You and I and our Brother Lord Yakov will have to put our heads together with our best efforts to root out the treacherous ones. And remember our *promise* my Sister Liling, to always help each other as best as we can when carrying out the will of our esteemed fathers of the Council."

"Yes Kookie, I remember our promise!"

"See you soon then, at the polar location."

Kookie and Liling disconnect and all during their conversation he has been monitoring another incoming signal. It is a secret warning system that Kookie has created for his official Lord's Communication Device, which the Council does not know about. Its function is to detect and display all incoming signals, reporting who they are and where they are coming from. This particular signal that is being tracked has Kookie confused because the data analysis says that it is unidentified and coming from an unknown source. This means that somebody or some*thing* has been tracking Kookie unbeknownst to him; possibly putting all of his security systems at risk, as well as all those who are involved with him.

Fear begins to sink into Kookie's gut as he wonders, *who has the capability of doing this, and if they are onto me, why have they not said or done anything?*

Then it hits him, with a darkening fear growing in his heart. The Council has a mole on his tail.

Chapter 15 – Moles

THE LORDS ARE BEGINNING TO ARRIVE at the polar location. It is a hidden subterranean palace that was built as a refuge for the Council members, the Lords and their families to "ensure the survival of the human race" as they claim, in the event of a global catastrophic event. The Council has had a number of these palatial estates built around the world with several Lords assigned to each of them. The existence of these subterranean palaces is kept hidden from everyone else, including the Masters, as they are not deemed necessary to perpetuate the human species.

The Council considers it to be a good precaution to pamper their Lords whenever propriety dictates, in order to insure continued fealty. So as the Lords arrive, they are escorted to their luxurious suites where they can settle in, get comfortable, and get ready for the evening's dinner followed by the gathering. The three High Lords have the most opulent suites of all, including a private sauna, hot tub, swimming pool, game room with a floor-to-ceiling screen, and a life-size, human-looking AI droid to serve their every need.

When Kookie arrives at his suite, he unpacks, freshens up and heads to the game room. Switching on the control panel, he programs it to an orchestra playing the background instrumentation for the Tuba Concerto in F Minor. Kookie takes out his tuba and plays with the orchestra.

Later that day the Lords gather in the Great Dining Hall. As they arrive, they greet each other in a friendly manner making every effort to be pleasant and gracious to one another. Although things seem friendly on the surface, there is great tension in the air. Apart from the fact that this is an emergency gathering, they have had plenty of those over the years, this seems different somehow.

One thing weighing heavily on Kookie's heart is the "unidentified tracking" that he detected on his Lord's Communication Device. He knows that he must communicate this to Yakov and Liling and warn them that they are being watched. He sees his High Lord Brother and High Lady Sister already seated at their table and walks over to receive a warm welcome from both of them. Without saying a word, they all have the same sad expression in their eyes, though they are grateful for being with each other again. They do their usual three-way greeting; joining hands in a circle, raising their hands high and saying, "Ni Hao[5], Privyet[6], Hey!" altogether.

Even now, in what they know is a sad moment, their childhood greeting still makes them smile.

After a sumptuous dinner the lights are dimmed, and the Lords' and Ladies' attention is turned to the front of the room. There is a giant monitor on the wall that activates with the signal of an incoming message. One of the Lords seated up front is acting as the evening's host and hits a button on the control panel in front of him to accept the incoming message. The Lords and Ladies make sure that their Universal Translator earpieces are all activated as the large blank screen opens. The voice of PA begins to speak:

"Welcome My Lords and My Ladies with a very warm greeting from the Highest."
The Lords and Ladies all respond in unison, "Welcome, Your Highest."
PA continues. "I have summoned you all here today because something serious is happening all over One World. As you know, our plans for population control have shifted over the years as the slaves have continued to breed beyond our control, no matter what we have tried. Of course, it was for the greater good of all that we finally decided the only way to curb the massive global population expansion

---

[5] *Ni Hao: Chinese for "hello."*
[6] *Privyet: Russian for "hello."*

was to *eliminate* much of the populace, bringing it down to a sustainable number. However, as there are still way too many of them, it is a threat and a danger to our very existence to allow this problem to remain unchecked."

There is a stone-cold silence around the Great Dining Hall with expressionless faces on many of the Lords and Ladies as they listen to PA the Highest continue.

"I know that you are all aware of the efforts we recently made at using bioweaponry to fix our slave problem. It was working just fine, initially. But for some reason it stopped working. However, what you may not be aware of is that it appears to have done worse than just *stop working*. It seems as though the slaves who received the most recent batch of live Ebola, not only did *not* get sick, they actually changed in ways that we do not understand."

The Lords and Ladies look around at each other confused.

"We sent a squad of commandos to northern California to exterminate an entire lot of over two hundred slaves who had survived the bioweapon and were celebrating together at a Center."

Kookie's eyes widen and he goes pale.

"And according to the Master Commander who reported the incident, the slaves all stood there with guns pointed straight at them, looking into the eyes of the commando's, smiling, *without fear*, as the men opened fire on them."

Kookie, Yakov and Liling can barely contain themselves, but they know that if they show any signs of emotion, they will jeopardize the lives of all whom they are so desperately trying to save. Kookie is also painfully aware that the three of them are being watched. With a fire burning inside of him, he looks around the room wondering who the mole can be, feeling the very presence of eyes upon him.

"We do not understand what is happening My Lords and My Ladies of the Council, but one thing is for certain: *THEY MUST BE STOPPED!* The greatest threat of insurrection against all of us by these worthless creatures is if they become fearless. If our mind control techniques somehow cease to work on them, then based on their numbers alone, they will have the ability to take us down. Of course, they must *never ever* realize their strength in numbers, and that is why you are all here right now.

"It is up to all of you to come up with a plan to deal effectively with the vermin. I am charging you to come up with a course of action to once and for all eliminate the lives of those who are unworthy of life. Talk about it amongst yourselves and put your best ideas forward to each other. We shall reconvene here this time tomorrow. And now, I shall take my leave of you."

As PA the Highest disconnects, there is dead silence in the Great Dining Hall. The Lords and Ladies look around at each other astonished as none of them ever imagined that their mind control methods would fail. The thought of fearless slaves is too terrifying a prospect for them to even consider.

Kookie, Yakov, and Liling are experiencing a different apprehension from that of the others. For *their* agenda they must find a way of being in a secure and private location to talk about it.

A thought occurs to Kookie. "Well, I think I may have a few good ideas. Why don't we get together later in my hot tub and talk it over."

Yakov and Liling look at him strangely but trust that he is onto something. They agree to get together later for a private meeting . . . in Kookie's hot tub.

* * *

"Oh Ryan, look! We're almost there!" Mimi exclaims as she points to a road sign indicating that the Salena Center is only 10 miles away. "My daughter and her family are not far from the Center at all! Oh honey!"

Mimi is suddenly filled with the same dread that has been haunting her for most of the journey. As excited as she is to see Elli, Lydia and Sam, she is also worried about whether or not they are okay, especially in light of the last dream that she had.

As they get closer to Salena, Mimi's fears grow. The sight of the Center sign has suddenly increased her anxiety, causing her to suspect that the worst may have happened.

Ryan sees his Woman's panic and tries to calm her by saying ever so gently, "I'm sure they're okay, sweetheart."

But Mimi is beside herself with anxiety as they approach their destination.

Rounding the corner to the small compound where Elli, Lydia and Sam live, Mimi suddenly stops dead in her tracks. Ryan sees it too.

Her heart is pounding in her chest as she looks at the compound, *"Dear Lord!"* she says.

The entire property of the fruit pickers and their 22-unit dwelling is boarded up and shut down. Mimi sits on her autobike unable to move. Putting her hands over her mouth she begins to cry, "Good Lord! What happened? Where is everyone?"

Ryan is also beside himself with worry, but he musters up his courage for Mimi, "Honey, this doesn't mean that they are not *okay*. It means that they are not *here.*"

Taking Mimi into his arms he holds her while she continues to sob, releasing so much pent-up emotion that she has been carrying with her since this whole Ebola ordeal started. "We'll find them. We'll find them. It's okay, Mimi. I'm here. And we're going to find them."

Mimi stops crying for a moment and looks at her sweet Man, grateful that she does not have to go through this alone. "Thank you, my darling. Thank you."

Then Ryan has an idea. "Why don't we start with the Salena Center. If anyone has any information, someone there might be able to fill us in."

"You're right," says Mimi brushing away her tears. "Let's go right back there."

When they arrive at the Salena Center, Mimi and Ryan notice that it is practically deserted. There are just a few autobikes parked outside and at least one of them has to belong to the Center Overseer. Before going inside, Mimi looks at Metatron to check the safety level, which is, thankfully, pulsating green.

"I guess it's okay to go inside," she whispers to Ryan. However, something in her gut is telling her to remain cautious.

They enter the Center Market, look around and no one is there. They check out the Freshen-Up area and see three people camped out on the ground, listening intently to My Buddy with the day's news, instructions and programming.

Then they move on to check out the Center Coffeehouse, hoping to discover the whereabouts of the fruit-pickers, including Elli, Lydia and Sam. There is only one person there; the Center Overseer who is seated, having coffee and looking rather bored. Looking up at Mimi and Ryan he actually seems happy to see some new faces, or *any* faces for that matter.

"Hello friends!" the Center Overseer says, taking the two by surprise with his cheerful manner. "Where you folks from?"

Mimi and Ryan proceed with caution as she answers, "We are from Amber Beach, California, sir."

"Well, that *is* a far piece from here now, isn't it though?" he says, still smiling. "What brings you good folks all the way here?"

Hesitating for a moment and looking at Ryan, Mimi continues, "Not much doing down there now, sir. After getting our Ebola Neutralizers we thought it might be a good idea to travel up the coast and see if there might be any place for us where we can be of service."

"Ah, yes! How right you are ma'am. Good thing it is to have a dwelling with a place to be of service, a very good thing. What kind of ways are you all looking to serve the Master, then?"

Ryan speaks up, "Dunno. What kinds of ways to serve the Master *are* there around here?"

The Center Overseer looks at them both while rubbing his chin, appearing to be lost in thought. "You know," he says, "There is something for motivated folks such as yourselves which y'all might be interested in."

Mimi and Ryan both perk up.

"Really? What is it?" Mimi inquires.

"Well, something strange happened here just a couple of days ago."

Now he *really* has their full attention.

"Folks came back from the local Shelter after they were neutralized, only they didn't seem, well, you know . . . quite right."

"In what way?" Mimi asks trying to appear as casual as she can.

"It's hard to explain," he continues with a puzzled expression, "But they were *happy*. I mean *really* happy. I guess we all figured it was from the feeling that you get, you know, like when you hear the news that you are going to be okay after having been very sick for a long time."

"*Yes?*" Mimi is bursting inside.

"Yeah, only it was more than that. I got a look at some of them when they came in here right after they got back. They weren't just happy; they were beaming. I mean, they were like *glowing* or something, almost unnatural, superhuman-like."

Mimi has to turn away to hide her agonizing expression. Ryan picks up the conversation with the Center Overseer and asks, "Uh, so what happened?"

"Well, the next thing you know these commandos came here. Said they were here to pick up folks from the fruit pickers dwelling just down yonder. Um, that's where they all came from, those who were neutralized and turned into *beaming weirdos*. Said they picked up most of the people there but were told that the rest of them might be here. Well, sure enough they were, so I pointed them out to the guy. And when he took them outside, I saw them all being loaded into a van."

Mimi turns around to look at the Center Overseer with the best poker face she has ever had to put on in her entire life. She clears her throat and asks him, just as calmly as she possibly can, "So, where did they all go?"

"Funny you should ask that question ma'am, 'cause that's exactly what I asked the commando. I asked him where they were taking these folks, and he said that it wasn't clear if they were really okay or not. So, they were being taken for further testing. But the *really* weird part is *where* they were being taken. He said that orders were for them to be taken to the local Howard Pharmaceuticals plant. He then told me that if I knew of any others who had received the Ebola neutralizer recently and who appeared to be strange in any way, I was to report them to him immediately and a squad would come and pick them up. He gave me his contact information and then told me that they were also looking for some people to help out over there. It appears that they are short-handed. Well, now that was the first thing that *didn't* surprise me about all of this, considering everyone is short-handed these days what with so many Ebola deaths and all."

Mimi and Ryan now see where all of this is leading, and they are both ready to jump into action. "So that is the work you mentioned?" asks Mimi.

"Yes, ma'am. You all seem like good folks and I thought this might be a fine opportunity for you, as well as keep me in good with the Masters, if you follow my drift."

"Yes sir, we do, um, follow your drift, that is," says Ryan.

"Here's the contact information the commando gave me, and I will also give you a referral which you can give them at the Howard Pharmaceutical plant. Now that's what I call a win/win situation for both of us!" the Center Overseer says, beaming with delight at his ingenuity. "Yes?"

"Oh yes, yes, indeed!" says Ryan.

Mimi is hardly able to contain herself.

"It's at Silver Beach, and I'll give you all directions on how to get there. It's not too far from here, you know."

"Thank you, sir," says Mimi, "Thank you *so* much! We really do appreciate all of your help."

"Not at all," says the Center Overseer. "Glad I could be of some help."

Mimi and Ryan leave quickly without looking back, jumping on their autobikes and riding away as fast as they can. Once they are sure to be out of sight from the Salena Center they stop, pull over, and fall into each other's arms.

* * *

Kookie is ready and waiting in his hot tub for Yakov and Liling to arrive. He knows that the most important thing the three of them must figure out as soon as possible is who the mole is, or at least how to protect themselves from him or her. Otherwise, the consequences for all of them, as well as Operation Monarch will be disastrous. Sitting in the hot tub with his Lord's Communication Device lying next to him on a towel, there is a distant memory gnawing away at his brain of something he can't fully remember.

It has been one of the jobs of the Lords to keep the people under full psychological control so that they will be forever following the word and will of the Council. Over the years, Kookie and the other Lords have developed and been privy to a variety of techniques which serve that end. It has always pained Kookie that he was obligated to be a part of this and now he is sensing something familiar with those methods and the mole who is stalking them. It has to do with body temperature.

Putting his ideas to the test just before the other two arrive, Kookie turns on his Lord's Communication Device and checks the secret warning system. There is no sign of anything unknown tracking him at the moment. He climbs out of the hot tub and jumps in the nearby swimming pool; when he comes back to check the secret warning system on his device, lo and behold, there is an incoming signal of an unknown source on the screen. As Kookie gets back in the hot tub, the signal disappears.

Now he is remembering, and with one last test, Kookie takes the device and puts it on the other side of the room, positioning it so he can see the unknown incoming signal. The signal is back and he watches it carefully as he backs away several feet towards the hot tub. As soon as he gets about 12 feet away from the device the signal disappears. Repeating the experiment several times at different distances, near and far from his Lord's Communication Device and in and out of the hot tub, Kookie has deduced that the signal can only track him within a distance of 12 feet or less and as long as he is *not* overheated. At that moment, Yakov and Liling show up together.

They speak to each other in a combination of English, Russian and Chinese:

"Hey there, you guys! Come on in, the water is fine!"

"Hey there yourself!" Yakov says, "What's the idea of having us show up here half naked and exhausted from the day to take a dip in a hot tub with you?"

Kookie looks at them both with a certain look in his eyes that only they recognize. Tapping the tips of his fingers together he says, "Well why don't you both come on in and join me and you'll see what I'm talking about."

Yakov and Liling know well enough to just shut up and get in the tub.

Kookie's tone changes and looks directly into their eyes. "Let me have your Lord's Communication Devices," he says in a low, serious voice.

Looking confused but knowing when not to ask any questions, Yakov and Liling get their devices from where they set them down nearby and hand them over to Kookie. He puts them all down for a moment, gets out of the hot tub, fans himself down with a towel and holds up his own device in front of them saying, "Okay, now both of you look at this and tell me what you see."

"Looks okay to me," Yakov shrugs.

"Me too," Liling reiterates.

"Okay, now watch this, and be quiet. Don't say anything; just look." Kookie says, climbing back into the hot tub. He points all three of their devices in their direction so that Yakov and Liling can see them and turns on the secret warning system. The unknown signal begins to flash across the screen and without thinking Yakov says, "What the—"

"*YES!*" exclaims Kookie bright and loud, effectively cutting off Yakov. "But it *was* a lovely dinner wasn't it, though?!"

For a second, they both look at him like he has lost his mind, but they quickly catch on and say, "Oh yes, it was. Very nice, very nice *INDEED!*"

Kookie then gets out of the tub and sets the three devices just beyond 12 feet away, again positioned so that Yakov and Liling can see the signal. Then he gets back in the hot tub and says, "Okay, now look at it," and they both see that the signal has disappeared. Looking at the expression on both of their faces Kookie says to them, "Okay, it is safe. *Now* you can say it."

Staring at Kookie in shock and disbelief, Yakov and Liling say to Kookie each in their own languages,

"What the hell was that?!"

Kookie says to them both with a whimsical smile and tapping the tips of his fingers together, *"THAT,* my dears is our mole!"

Yakov and Liling look at each other understanding what has happened. "WHOA! Kookie! You are a genius!" says Yakov.

"Yes well, aren't we all though?" Kookie says with a chuckle.

"Do we each have one of those things implanted in us?" asks Liling.

"Let's find out" Kookie proceeds to run the same test on the two of them that he just did on himself. Sure enough, Yakov and Liling are also *infected.* Kookie takes both of their Lord's Communication Devices and programs them with his secret warning system.

"Now you will know when you are tracked and when, if ever, they are unable to track you, apart from over 12 feet distance from the communication device and an overheated body temperature. My guess is that there are probably other blind spots in their tracking program. I also think that this has only recently been implanted in us, or we would have been in big trouble by now."

"So, what do you think we should do about it?" asks Yakov.

"Nothing," Kookie remarks. "It is actually to our advantage to know that they are spying on the three of us and that they do not know that *WE* know they are spying on the three of us."

"Yes, that does make sense," Liling nods, thinking about the possibilities this opens up for them.

"Okay, so let's talk about the business at hand then, now that our communication is secure."

Kookie proceeds to fill them in on all that has happened with Mimi, Ryan, Doc, Angie, Vi, the Major, and the rest of them. He also tells them about the Metatron device and the 369 Program and what it can do including the DNA restructuring of the Ebola bioweapon.

Yakov interrupts briefly to fill Liling in on the close call that he and Kookie had at Bear River Farm.

Kookie continues to tell them the name he came up with for the device and how it is based on the properties of Metatron's Cube. Last but not least, Kookie tells them that since Metatron cannot be used right now for communication purposes without being tracked, they have come up with another form of getting messages back and forth to each other. With great pleasure, and lots of fingertip tapping, Kookie tells Yakov and Liling all about the homing pigeons.

They are both delighted with the idea and declare that they look forward to learning more about them.

"That can most definitely be arranged," says Kookie, as he fills them in on the rest of the plans of Operation Monarch.

The three High Lords talk well into the night of all that they have witnessed and experienced, the grief that it is causing each one of them, and what the Council is now expecting of them. They believe that they are not the only Lords or Ladies who feel the way they do about the injustice and inhumanity of servitude, and especially of taking away the freewill of the people and their ability to think for themselves.

Most important is that they come up with an idea of what role they will play as they move forward in Operation Monarch. They also agree to meet on a regular basis, giving the impression that they are being loyal to the Council.

"We must be very careful about keeping up all appearances that we are helping the Council," says Kookie. "Never for one second are they to suspect otherwise or we will be endangering our mission."

"Yes." Liling smiles, "And thank you Kookie for being the wonderful human being that you are, someone who cares about life and is willing to die for it! You too, Yakov!"

As they are about to retire for the night, they all hold hands and promise to be true to one another and to all people everywhere.

* * *

Mimi and Ryan have just arrived at Silver Beach. The sky has darkened and a full moon is rising with the first stars of the night. They decide to set up camp on a cliff overlooking the Pacific Ocean. The cliff is also overlooking the Howard Pharmaceutical plant in this charming little beach village.

Looking at the stark, gray factory building reflecting a somber hue in the moonlight, Mimi is saddened by the thought, *my sweet little Elli is in there?!"* Off in the distance they can see and hear the waves crashing against the shore. Combined with the familiar salty breeze, a feeling of peace and calm comes over both Mimi and Ryan's troubled hearts.

"It almost feels like we are back home, doesn't it?" Ryan sighs.

Smiling sweetly at her beloved, Mimi says to him, "I guess this *will* be our new home, at least for now. I suppose I can at least be grateful that we are back on the beach, the home of our heart."

Ryan kisses her gently.

Mimi adds, "Actually my darling, wherever you are *that* is my heart's home."

And for a moment she forgets her sorrows as the two lovers settle down for the night. Eventually Mimi falls into a restless sleep. She fitfully tosses and turns with several dark and frightening dreams, as one dream begins:

Mimi is inside the Howard Pharmaceutical plant. A bone-chilling fear settles into her heart as she walks down endless aisles of the factory floor. There are no people anywhere to be seen; only androids and small drones transporting mechanical parts back and forth on conveyor belts. Mimi is searching desperately for signs of life in this lifeless place with an aching feeling deep in her soul and a terrible foreboding that all human life has ceased to exist. She enters a dark hallway with a very long tunnel ahead. Fear grips Mimi as she begins to run down the endless dark tunnel until she makes out a faint gray light glowing up ahead. Approaching the gray light source, Mimi suddenly has a terrible feeling of helplessness and despair. Coming to a small room, she can barely make out prison bars with bodies moving about behind them. She sees Elli with her little arms reaching out to Gramma through the prison bars.

Mimi bursts into tears as Elli says to her, "Don't cry Gramma, everything is gonna be okay. Eve Elli loves you. Eve Elli will see you very soon! Don't cry Gramma . . ."

Mimi wakes up sobbing heavily and holds Ryan closely against her. It is early in the morning and he is just beginning to stir. Thinking about the day that they are about to face, she wastes no time in preparing their morning meal and getting ready for what lies ahead.

As Ryan wakes up and gets ready for whatever awaits him at Howard Pharmaceuticals, Mimi shares a thought with him.

"You know honey, once you start working for them, we will be living in one of their dwellings. It will give me an opportunity to snoop around, ask questions, and find out whatever I can. I think that with you on the inside and me on the outside we can do some good spying."

"You mean, like moles?" Ryan says, somewhat whimsically.

"Well, I guess so!" chuckles Mimi.

"I like the sound of that," beams Ryan, proud that he can be of service to Operation Monarch in such a manner.

"Me, too." Mimi nods in agreement.

The two of them get ready, pack up their gear and head on down to the Howard Pharmaceutical plant.

* * *

"That was Master Howard himself on the incoming message," says the Managing Overseer of the plant floor of Howard Pharmaceuticals at Silver Beach. Speaking to one of the servants, the Managing Overseer continues, "Sounds really weird. He is actually sending his son, you know, the Major, over here to investigate. Got something to do with all those people who arrived here the other day."

"Like what?" asks the servant.

"Like the Super Ebola Neutralizer has given them some sort of mental problem or other . . . weird! We are to give the Major our full cooperation, as usual."

"You bet," says the servant, puzzled about what problem these folks might have.

"Sure wish we had some more help though. I mean you can't exactly expect top performance from us without enough people to get the job done."

"Ain't *that* the truth!" the servant says.

The Managing Overseer goes to a room down the hall and takes an inquisitive look inside. What he sees leaves him feeling completely flabbergasted: all alone and behind bars is a small child who appears to be about three years old. She is on her knees smiling at the ceiling with her hands held out and palms turned upwards. Her face has a serene look as if she were in a kind of paradise. The child is sitting in filth, covered in her own excrement, yet seemingly disconnected from the reality of her physical circumstances.

When she notices the Managing Overseer looking at her, she smiles brightly, waves at him and says cheerfully, "Hi! I'm Eve Elli!"

Chapter 16 – Rescue

VI HAS BEEN ASSIGNED TO SERVE in a small testing area of the factory floor at the Howard Pharmaceuticals main plant in California. She is in close proximity to the lab, which allows her easy access to all of the materials used in the creation of the Ebola bioweapon. Of course, she is not told that by the Managing Overseer who is not aware of the bioweapon himself. The Managing Overseer thinks Vi is studying the correlation between a strong immune system and the survival from Ebola.

Those who are involved in production do not have any idea of what it is they are actually producing except that it is an Ebola Neutralizer. Only the Council, the Lords, Master Howard and a handful of his trusted lab servants know the truth about the bioweapon. Although the Masters are trusted as faithful to the UC, they are also suspected of having a hand at whatever went wrong. So, they are being monitored by the moles along with everyone else in a so-called position of trust. The Council does not really trust anyone.

The survivors have been rounded up and brought to the main facility for Vi to examine. Every location of Howard Pharmaceuticals throughout One World is doing its own investigation and testing to see what might be causing the terrible crisis of people surviving Ebola. Vi is allegedly doing the same, so she has to be cautious about making her work look convincing. The people who are brought here are kept in a detention center until they are ready to be tested and observed.

Arriving at her post, the first person is waiting to see Vi.

"Welcome, and come on in," Vi says in a cheerful voice. "Please sit down and make yourself comfortable. I have some questions to ask you and this will not take very long at all."

The gentleman walks slowly over to the chair with his head slightly bowed, eyes lowered and a trace of a smile. As he sits down, he clasps his hands together with everything in his manner suggesting humility and a heart that is at peace. He even seems to be glowing in an inexplicable sort of way.

Vi makes a mental note of all this and is rather taken in by it.

"Are you feeling alright, sir?" she says to the man, feeling an unusual sense of tranquility coming over herself as well.

"Why yes, ma'am," he replies, "I am feeling just fine."

"Yes, you certainly are, aren't you!' she says, pleasantly surprised at how much better *she* is suddenly feeling in his presence. The man appears to be in about his mid-forties. "How old are you, sir?" asks Vi.

"I am 75-years-old," the man says in a jovial manner, "And most happy to be here."

Vi is taken aback when he says that he is 75-years-old, but even more shocking is his claim to be *most happy to be here*. Vi has seen the squalid conditions of the containment area for the people who are brought to the plant and it is anything *but* a most-happy-to-be-here kind of place.

She continues with her examination. "You say you are happy to be here, sir? May I ask you to elaborate on that a little?"

"Why certainly! Don't rightly know how to put it into words, though, but I shall try my best for you, ma'am" he says looking straight at her with kindness and love glowing from what appears to be the very center of his being.

The man's gentle demeanor touches an emotional nerve in Vi. "Okay, take your time," she says.

"I know what has happened to us, what is happening now and what *may* happen in days to come. Being here in this place and talking to you now is all a part of that. It is wonderful ma'am, truly wonderful."

Lowering his eyes again he says, "And I am honored to be amongst those who have survived and can now help others."

"So—" Vi is hesitant to ask the next question, "So, you don't feel the *discomfort* of being detained against your will in a dimly lit cage with little food or water, no bathing facilities, no other human contact, and for an indefinite period of time?"

Gazing deeply into her eyes, radiating a kind of inner-harmony that Vi has never experienced, he says, "My spirit is rejoicing knowing that all of those things you mention are at the very heart of what it will take to free our people. It is really very simple, ma'am, though not easy for all to do. That I am able to experience it without suffering and serve you in this way is my honor, my pleasure and my blessing."

Awestruck, Vi realizes she has forgotten to ask the man his name. Glancing down at the form in front of her she asks him, "What is your name sir?"

"Adam Steve," the man replies.

"Well, I guess that is all I need from you right now. Please let me know if there is anything I can do to make things more comfortable during your stay here with us. At the very least, I will see if I can get you more food and water. I'm so sorry, Mr. Steve, I shall try my best."

Adam Steve is beaming with happiness as he says to Vi, "Why thank you *very* kindly ma'am. You are truly most gracious. Just one correction though, for your paperwork so to speak. My first name is Adam Steve. I do not have a last name, not anymore."

"Oh, I see." She does not see at all. "Well, then, Mr., um, that is, Adam Steve, thank you for your help. You may go now."

Adam Steve stands up, bows his head to Vi and departs from her office to the custody of the Security Guard Overseer waiting outside to escort him back to his cage.

Staring off into space for a moment trying to digest what she has just experienced, Vi looks at the questions on the paperwork in front of her. Apparently, she is supposed to ask these people; *Do you listen to My Buddy every morning? Do you eat your fruit and veggies every day? Do you follow your daily instructions given to you by the Buddy Overseer?* and other assorted nonsense.

She reads down the questionnaire and thinking of Adam Steve, says to herself *I shall do my best for you.* Vi writes fictional answers to all the questions that she figures will satisfy the UC.

The rest of Vi's astonishing day continues with one person after another giving an almost identical account of their joy in spite of their abusive captivity. The weirdest thing of all in her estimation is what they all call themselves. They all have two first names and no last name; the men being called Adam Steve, Adam Joe, Adam Henry and Adam Mike, respectively, and the women being called Eve Beth, Eve Felicity, Eve Jennie, Eve Susan and Eve Marie.

Vi *knows* that this will cause a red flag to go up with the UC, so she adds to the already fictitious answers on the questionnaires, Steve Smith, Joe Davis, etc. giving everyone whatever last name comes into her head. She also writes down the age that they *appear* to be so as not to draw any further attention to whatever it is that has happened to them.

One thing Vi does realize, however, by the end of the day, is that these extraordinary human beings who have miraculously been transformed into something the likes of which she has never seen, have got to get out of their deplorable captivity.

She knows that her next conversation with the Major will be about devising a rescue plan.

* * *

Mimi and Ryan walk into the Howard Pharmaceutical plant at Silver Beach and are greeted by a Security Guard Overseer. "Is there something I can do for you?" he inquires.

"Yes sir," says Ryan producing the letter from the Overseer at the Salena Center. "The Center Overseer there says you all are short-handed and could use some help."

Reading the letter, the Security Guard Overseer says, "Well ain't *you* just a sight for sore eyes, buddy. We sure can use some help around here. Just follow me and I'll get you all set up.

"Howdy ma'am. Nice to meet you. You his Woman?"

"Yes sir, that I am. Um, we sure do appreciate this."

Mimi and Ryan enter the factory floor and are handed over to the Shop Overseer. "Got these two here for you. Our friend at the Salena Center sent them. Sure was a good idea of the Center Overseer letting folks know that we are short-handed."

"It certainly was! Well, great! I can get you both started right away!" says the Shop Overseer. Turning to Mimi and Ryan he says, "Why don't you all come this way and roll up your sleeves. There's a major project we got going on here. Don't know if you've served in a place like this before, but typically we try you out for a week before deciding whether or not we want to keep you. And if you serve us well without causing any trouble then we'll let you stay.

"When you are both finished serving for the day, I will take you over to your dwelling unit. Of course, meals are provided by the Master."

"That sounds most wonderful sir," says Mimi, and Ryan nods in agreement.

"Very well then, come on over here and I'll show you what needs doing first."

Mimi of course, was not expecting any of this and realizes that she now will have to do her "spying" after the plant shuts down for the day. They both follow the Shop Overseer to an area on the factory floor that is piled high with what looks like hundreds of boxes. There is one lone servant taking them apart and emptying the contents into a large metal bin which is lined on the inside with soft padding.

"Okay," he says to them, "So here's the deal. Only just this morning before you got here, we got these totally bizarre orders from above to destroy every single one of the Super Ebola Neutralizers in these here boxes. Can you imagine? No one seems to know why or what happened, but Master Howard's son, you know, John, or as he likes to call himself, the Major, is coming here himself to oversee the project. Rumors are it was a Council decision, but no one really knows for sure, or why it has been ordered. I guess we'll find out when the Major gets here."

Mimi and Ryan stare at each other stunned and straining every ounce of self-control to not show any outward reaction to the Overseer's news regarding the neutralizers.

"Oh my," exclaims Mimi. "It sounds like you really do need our help then. Sounds like we got here just in time. Yes, indeed!"

"Yes, yes, indeed! You said a mouthful there, Woman! So, you just follow what the servant over there is doing and maybe we can have them all destroyed by the time the Major gets here. I'm sure that will please our Master."

The Shop Overseer leaves them to it.

Mimi and Ryan introduce themselves to the servant.

"Hi there," says Ryan. "I'm Ryan, and this here is my Woman, Mimi."

"Hello," says Mimi and they both extend their hands out to him.

"I guess you folks ain't never served in a Howard factory before, have you?" he says to both of them.

"Why, no," says Mimi.

"They don't like us to know each other's names here. Not the Overseers neither. They say this ain't no place for nothin' personal like, and bein' on a first name basis with anyone is too personal."

"Oh, I see. I'm sorry," says Ryan.

"Me too," says Mimi. "So, what *do* we call you then . . . that is, if we need to communicate with each other?"

"We don't," the servant answers. "But if needs be, we just says *hey* one to the other."

"Okay then, um, *hey,* can you show us what to do and then we'll get started and mind our own business?" Mimi says.

"Sure. Oh, and for a woman we calls her, *woman.* We don't see much of any kinda woman around here, but *hey* is for him," he says pointing to Ryan, "and *woman* is for you."

"Okay. Well then, me *woman* and *hey* him would like to thank *hey you* for showing us the ropes. So now what do we do with these here boxes? *Hey?*"

* * *

The Lords are gathered once more in the Great Dining Hall but the atmosphere is more somber than it was the other evening. They look around at each other searching for any indication that someone has come up with a good proposal for the Highest; an idea for a plan that will wipe out the rest of the populace while keeping them stupefied in the process.

The lights dim and an incoming message on the giant blank screen is activated. The voice of PA the Highest addresses the gathering:

"My Lords and My Ladies of the High Council, welcome again to our Gathering and may we have a successful evening together."
The Lords and Ladies all respond, "Welcome, Your Highest."
"We have confirmed the news about those who have recovered from the effects of the Ebola bioweapon, including reports of an uncanny fearlessness and total resistance to our mind control methods. This is completely untenable and for that reason we have decided that the weapons which were developed at Howard Pharmaceuticals have to be destroyed. This is happening as we speak in every one of their plants around One World. There must not be a trace of anything left which

could infect the slaves further with courage and resistance to our methods. And though we *have* managed to get rid of quite a few of them this time around, it is nowhere near enough for us to be safe from the vermin.

My gentle Lords and Ladies it is time for us to implement another plan of execution."

The crowd mumbles to one another around the Great Dining Hall. It is hard to tell how many voices are consensual with the Highest compared to how many are doubtful of starting another crisis at this time. They all know that the mind control methods are less effective if people get too suspicious and start to awaken. Tampering with the freewill of the human spirit is a delicate business, and the Council knows this all too well.

"So, I am asking you all, what ideas have you come up with to help us resolve this problem?"

There is a deafening silence throughout the Great Dining Hall, which is broken only by the sound of uneasy shuffling. Finally, someone raises a hand to be recognized by the Highest. All eyes turn towards the one brave Lord among them as the Highest says:

"Yes, My Lord Kenneth! What ideas have you come up with?"

"Well, Your Highest, last night as I was sitting there in the comfortable suite which you have provided for all of us, partaking of all the pleasantries which you have so graciously afforded to us, your esteemed High Lords. . ."

Kookie is deliberately taking his time, tapping his fingers together and casting sideways glances at Yakov and Liling, who look at him like he has completely lost his mind.

"Something came to me which I think can fix this whole situation rather simply."

Kookie pauses and the whole Great Hall holds their breath, transfixed upon Kookie and what his idea might be. With an impish little grin and a twinkle in his golden eye he taps his fingertips some more, strokes his chin, and continues, "Well, it's really quite simple, My Lords and My Ladies. We have these luxurious places to stay here underground, which the Council has built for us with a global catastrophic event in mind. So, what I propose is that we all lock ourselves down in our appointed subterranean palace for oh, shall we say, five years or so, and unleash a global catastrophic event which is, well, you know, one great big Bon Voyage to everyone else left on the surface."

With a little-boy grin, Kookie turns to everyone, with a trace of a wink at Yakov and Liling which only they pick up on as he says, "Your thoughts?"

* * *

The Major and Vi are in his Autocar racing towards Silver Beach. After Vi gave him her actual reports of what she observed of the survivors, he knew there was no time to waste, and that if he didn't do something immediately, they would all be selected for extermination. Later that evening he heard that the detainees at the Silver Beach plant were from Salena, Oregon, and that Mimi's three-year-old granddaughter Elli was on the manifest to be exterminated. He left orders for the detainees right there at his father's main plant to remain in custody until he got back. With his AI autodriver at the helm the Major and Vi can sleep in the Autocar and reach Silver Beach before dawn. They will hopefully arrive before the plant opens and before the commandos arrive with their vans.

* * *

Mimi and Ryan are fast asleep when something causes Mimi to awaken in the small hours. She has a gut feeling which is filling her with a sense of foreboding and fear. A nagging voice inside of her head tells her to get up and look around, and the voice gradually grows louder and louder as she tosses and turns, trying to ignore it and get some more sleep.

With a sudden jolt in her gut the voice screams, *get up woman!*

"Okay, okay, I'm up!" she says out loud to herself.

Mimi gets dressed quietly, not wanting to disturb Ryan and get him all worried, and she slips out the door of the dwelling. It is dead quiet outside in the wee hours before dawn, but the security night lights have the place well lit. Mimi does not want to be caught lurking about on any security camera, so she is careful to stay hidden in the shadows. Nothing seems particularly out of the ordinary and she is beginning to feel ridiculous out there until something strange grabs her attention.

Coming from a window not too far from where she is standing there seems to be a faint eerie glow. Proceeding with caution and watching out for security cameras Mimi moves slowly towards the glow. It's coming from a small, high window with bars on it, and as she reaches the window, Mimi is barely able to stand on tip toe and peer inside. What she sees almost causes her heart to stop beating.

Mimi stifles a scream inside of her chest seeing her little Elli asleep on the floor, covered in filth. Whispering in a barely audible voice she says, "Oh my darling sweet baby! Elli! Elli! My precious Elli! Oh Lord, what have they done to you, my little angel?!"

* * *

Just before the Major left for the Silver Beach plant, he sent out pigeon #5 to Kenny and Lisa with the following message:

Attempting rescue of about 100 units; to deliver cargo soon. Nasty Stuff

When Kenny receives the message, he tells Lisa about it right away. "This is it, honey! The Major (code name, *Nasty Stuff*) is on his way!"

"Oh, my goodness!" exclaims Lisa, all excited. "Do we have enough food? Are the farmhands' living quarters all in order? Does he say how *many* are coming, sweetie?"

"He says about 100!"

"Woo Hoo! Oh, Kenny! We must get ready quickly and be prepared with enough of everything for everyone!"

As an afterthought Lisa adds, "And we must pray, pray very hard, that they are all brought through safely."

"Amen," Kenny nods.

* * *

Master Commandant Dimitri is receiving an incoming message on his Master's Communication Device. Accepting the message, his Overlord is giving him new and urgent orders.

Speaking in Russian:

"Hello, Dimitri."

"Hello, My Overlord."

"I have an assignment which needs to be carried out as soon as possible. It is regarding the slaves you and your men transported the other day from Salena to the Howard Pharmaceutical plant in Silver Beach."

"Yes, sir," replies Dimitri.

"You are to go in there and round up all the slaves, making sure that you get every last one of them."

"Sir, yes, sir!" says Dimitri. "We are not a full unit right now, sir. I have had to send some of the men to respond to a call at a nearby Shelter

Hut. Would you have me wait for them or do you want me to go in with the three of us who are available right now."

"My orders from on High are to take care of the situation *immediately*, Dimitri! Do you understand the word *immediately*, Dimitri?!"

"Sir, yes, sir! I understand the word *immediately*, sir!"

"Once you have them all rounded up you are to take them down to the beach and march them just a few minutes north up the shoreline. There you will see a large, motorized shipping crate on wheels with a side ramp. Your orders are to march the slaves into the shipping crate, gun them down, close the ramp and drive the crate into the ocean. It has been programmed to travel to the bottom of the ocean floor."

"Sir, yes, sir."

"Dimitri."

"Sir."

"This must all be accomplished before the sun comes up."

"Yes sir."

"I cannot stress to you how important this is to the Council."

"It will be done, sir, before sunrise."

"Good man, Master Commandant."

"Thank you, sir."

The Overlord signs off and Dimitri jostles his two sleeping commandos.

"Wake up! We have just been sent back to the Howard Pharmaceutical plant at Silver Beach. And we need to get moving, *NOW!*"

* * *

Mimi is shaken to the very depths of her soul when she sees her precious little Elli lying in the prison cell. She puts her hands to her mouth unable to stem the tidal wave of tears that are flooding down her cheeks. There is no time to think or process what is happening when, at the very next moment, Mimi hears hushed voices coming from around the side of the building. From what little she can make out they appear to be speaking Russian.

"No!" she says and steps into the shadows.

Seeing three men in uniform entering the building, Mimi goes into self-cloaking mode. She strains to hear scuffles and other muffled sounds when people begin to emerge from the entrance. One of the men is escorting the prisoners and telling them to line up and be quiet. The prisoners do as they are told while more emerge to line up.

Mimi sees little Elli with Lydia and Sam, all holding hands, and smiling at each other! In fact, she notices that all of the people gathered there together do not seem to be at all afraid. They are smiling at one another and appear to be in a state of total peace and joy, including Elli. Mimi cannot comprehend what she is observing but she *does* know that there is no peace or joy for *her*. As the group of people are led up the coast in the darkness of the pre-dawn hour, Mimi follows close behind them in her state of self-cloaked concealment.

By the light of the moon, Mimi can make out something on the beach looming up ahead. It is large and rectangular, like a huge box of some sort and it definitely looks out of place on the beach. Mimi's heart is racing. She is terrified and angry at the thought of Elli being taken here. As the crowd approaches the large box, Mimi can hear one of the men yelling at the people:

"You go in box now! Move! Fast! Fast!"

The people do as they are told, filing into the crate together, holding hands, arm in arm, glowing with a pale, heavenly light.

The three men in uniform draw their weapons.

Mimi realizes what is about to happen, and she starts screaming. *"NOOO!! NOOO!! NOOOOOO!!!"*

Dimitri and his men turn around in a flash, not knowing who or what is behind them, when all of a sudden the moonlight goes out as a dark shadow is cast in the sky. The armed gunmen look up, shaking with fear as a swarm of thousands of Monarch Butterflies come screaming down upon them.

* * *

Ryan runs out of the dwelling frantically searching for Mimi, fearing the worst. *Oh No! We've been discovered! They've taken her!* When out of nowhere the Major and Vi appear running towards him.

"Where is she?" yells the Major.

"I don't know!" Ryan howls back frantically. "I don't know! *I DON'T KNOW!!*"

At that very moment, they hear Mimi screaming, and Vi yells, *"THAT WAY!"*

Ryan, the Major and Vi take off running wildly towards the sound of Mimi's screams when all at once the moon goes dark. Moments later they all hear gun shots firing away in the darkness.

"OVER THERE!!" yells Vi when the moonlight returns.

Ryan, the Major and Vi see the large shipping crate straight ahead. They stop short when they see Mimi.

She is running on the sand towards a small child whose arms are reaching out to her. As she reaches Elli, Mimi falls on her knees and embraces her precious granddaughter while all the people around them are holding each other, smiling at grandmother and grandchild in adoration.

Ryan, the Major and Vi see something else which they cannot explain. Nearby there are three commandos lying face down, motionless in the sand.

The three of them come closer to this sacred scene, where Mimi is sitting on the sand, holding her little angel close, rocking Elli and crying her heart out.

Smiling ever so sweetly, Elli says to her: "Don't cry Gramma. Everything is gonna be okay. Eve Elli loves you. Everything is just fine!"

"Come on you guys," the Major says softly to everyone gathered around. "It's not over yet. We've got to get you all out of here right now!"

Turning to Vi he says with a wink and a sheepish grin, "Wait 'til you see what *this* thing can do!"

Taking out his Master's Communication Device he says, "Well, in all fairness not all of our devices can do what this one can. Kookie did a little extra programming on it for me," he says rather proud of the little gadget. Speaking into it he says, "This is the Major calling autodriver. Come and pick me up at my present location and summon four large vans to come here as well. Make it snappy my AI friend!"

Vi looks at him and rolls her eyes saying, "Oh, good grief!"

"Ha ha!" the Major says and almost finds himself tapping the tips of his fingers together.

While they wait for the auto vehicles to arrive, Ryan turns to Mimi and asks her, "My love, what happened here?"

"It all just happened so fast. I started to scream and suddenly the Monarchs were here."

"The *Monarchs?*" says Vi, getting excited.

"Yes! It was the strangest thing! They charged at the gunmen who got really scared and started to swat at them. In the turmoil, I guess one of them dropped his weapon. I was self-cloaking, so they didn't see me, but the Monarchs sure had them going crazy. When I saw the gun laying on the sand, though, I thought I had better pick it up. I guess they must have heard me or something because the next thing I knew the Monarchs left and the others started shooting in my direction. I don't think they could see me since I was self-cloaking, but I had to defend myself, so I started shooting back. And, well, there they are."

Ryan, the Major and Vi are speechless as Mimi tells her story of the last of Master Commandant Dimitri and his commandos. Although Mimi expresses sadness over what she has done to them, she is reassured by one and all that it was self-defense, the right thing to do, and that she saved the lives of all the people there including her daughter, son-in-law, and little Elli.

"You are amazing, Mom!" says Lydia, as Sam and the others all nod in agreement.

"Yep! That's my Gramma!" squeals Elli with delight.

"Well," says the Major, "it seems that your transport has arrived. I am having you all taken to Bear River Farm where the owners Kenny and Lisa are awaiting your arrival.

"As for you two," he says, turning to Mimi and Ryan, "Let's go get your things and take you in my Autocar. I will let the management here know that I had to leave with the two of you immediately and will talk to them later on my device regarding their new orders from my father."

"Oh Major, don't you think that Elli can come with us in your Autocar?"

"Well, I suppose that's up to her mom and dad," he says.

"Sure!" Lydia and Sam agree.

The Major says, "We'll meet up with you all at the farm."

"Oh boy oh boy! *Yippee!*" laughs Elli. "That's a nice Autocar, Gramma! Let's go!"

"Okay sweetie," Mimi says tenderly, but let's take a few moments first just to give you a quick rinse in the water."

Elli giggles, "Okay Gramma, just a quick splash in the waves."

They all get into their respective vehicles and are on their way to a life of freedom that they have never known, filled with love that they are ready to share with one and all.

Chapter 17 – Chrysalenes

PA THE HIGHEST IS IMPRESSED with Kookie's idea of the Masters, the Lords and the Council going underground while creating an atmosphere on the surface that is inhospitable to humans.

> "That is certainly a good idea, My Lord Kenneth," his Highest says, "and we are going to take a serious look at that one. There are many things to consider, but it most certainly is worth entertaining. Anyone else have any good ideas?" he says to the other Lords and Ladies of the Gathering at the Great Dining Hall.

Another hand goes up and the Highest recognizes a Lady from the Continental Territory of Euroslavica. Kookie is listening to her intently as she begins:

> "Your Highest, Lords and Ladies of the Council, and High Lords of the Council, it is with honor that I am recognized by you to offer my ideas on this grave situation that we have before us. I think that the idea put forward to us by the High Lord Kenneth is a fine one, but it is missing one element which will guarantee its success."

Kookie is leery as he listens to her continue.

> "Since the slaves have managed to survive many things that we have thrown at them in the past, including the current Ebola pandemic, I am concerned that to truly eradicate them through environmental means might involve something so toxic as to make the surface completely inhospitable to *us,* even five years later when we will want to return to our lives here."

All heads nod in agreement throughout the Great Dining Hall and murmurs of "Yes," "that's true," "the vermin *are* quite tough," and the like resound through the hall.

The Highest interrupts everyone and says to the Lady from Europacifica:

"Yes, yes, *do* continue My Lady Bella."

"Okay, so here is my idea. We take our current mind-control methods to the next level. That is, instead of merely sedating and hypnotizing the slaves into submission as we are currently doing, we add a toxic element to their food and water. This way we can exterminate them at a faster rate, and they won't even know what is happening to them, until it is too late."

"I see," says the Highest. "This is all very interesting Lady Bella. Very interesting, *indeed!*"

"Yes, yes, *INDEED!*" proclaims a loud voice of Lords and Ladies in unison. They repeat themselves, chanting into a frenzy:

"YES, YES, INDEED!

YES, YES, INDEED!

YES, INDEED!

YES, INDEED!

YES, YES, INDEED!"

Kookie, Yakov and Liling are saying the words along with everyone else, but in a subdued tone. Kookie looks around and notices there are a few others who also seem unenthusiastic and even a few more who are not chanting at all. Kookie nudges Yakov and Liling who are seated on either side of him and just as nonchalant as they can the three of them shoot an eyeball glance between themselves and the ones who are not chanting.

They give each other a knowing nod and a barely imperceptible grin as Kookie says, "I sure do look forward to relaxing later in the hot tub with you guys."

Yakov says, "Sounds like a great idea to me."

Liling reiterates, "Sure does relieve that muscle soreness though, doesn't it?"

"These are all wonderful ideas so far," says the Highest. "Does anyone else have anything further to add before we all retire for the evening?"

Another hand goes up and the Highest recognizes a Lord from Sinopacifica.

"Yes, My Lord Ekene, you have another suggestion?"

"With deepest respect, Highest One, I do *indeed* have another suggestion. In addition to emitting the 440 hertz frequency through My Buddy to the populace as we are already doing, I suggest that we might amp that up a bit by adding a low level of static. It must not be within hearing range, but it will have a great subliminal effect of irritation and distraction, especially when combined with 440 hertz pulsating during the broadcast of the Buddy message and programming. The slaves will be put into an even greater state of, shall we say, suggestibility, and I daresay this might even intensify the addiction that we have already created in them for My Buddy. Then perhaps they will be *completely* in our control where we can create what we have always dreamed of: the implementation of Operation Pied Piper. That is, the total annihilation of the populace by mass suicide.

"EXCELLENT, EKENE! EXCELLENT!" PA, the Highest cries out, and the Gathering at the Great Dining Hall is roused into an intense hysteria:

"EXCELLENT! EXCELLENT! YES, INDEED! EXCELLENT!
EXCELLENT! EXCELLENT! YES, INDEED! EXCELLENT!
EXCELLENT! EXCELLENT! YES, INDEED! EXCELLENT!
EXCELLENT! EXCELLENT! YES, INDEED! EXCELLENT!"

When the excitement calms down, the Highest exclaims with great enthusiasm:

"Well, My Lords and My Ladies, I would say that you all have given us plenty to consider. We shall now adjourn this Gathering as well as our time here at the polar location. You may all leave first thing in the morning, and we shall be getting back to you when we have reached a decision regarding our plans for extermination of the vermin and how we wish for it to be implemented.

Thank you, one and all. You may all retire to your suites and enjoy the rest of your evening."

As they all begin to file out of the Great Dining Hall, Kookie, Yakov and Liling look at each other and say, "To the tub!"

* * *

It is early in the morning in the sleepy little town of Bear River. The sun has just peeped over the horizon, and Kenny and Lisa are waking up to a new day on the farm. All is peaceful and quiet in their little cottage as Lisa goes into the kitchen to prepare the morning meal for her Man and the few remaining farmhands that they still have.

Suddenly the calm, country ambience is disturbed by something happening outside. Peering out the kitchen window Lisa sees five large vehicles coming down the driveway.

"LORD HAVE MERCY!" she shrieks and starts howling for her Man at the top her lungs, *"KENNY! KENNY! THEY'RE HERE!! THEY'RE HERE!"*

Lisa holds her hands up to the heavens saying, "Thank you, thank you Father in Heaven! Thank you for bringing them safely through!"

She rushes out the front door with Kenny right behind her. The first ones to step out of the front vehicle are the Major and Vi, followed by Ryan and Mimi, who is carrying a very precious child in her arms.

Lisa runs to greet them, "Praise the Lord!" as the Major and Vi warmly embrace both her and Kenny. Lisa looks at Mimi in a questioning manner because Mimi seems to be holding back her greeting, and the other passengers have not yet gotten out of the vans either.

"Is everything okay?" Lisa calls out to her, somewhat concerned at Mimi's hesitation to come closer.

"Yes, Lisa, everything is just fine." Mimi looks at Vi who explains the situation to Lisa and Kenny.

"Little Elli and all the survivors who are in those vans, are not the same," Vi explains.

"What do you mean?" asks Lisa.

"It is hard to explain, but they have suffered neglect and psychological torture while in captivity, and they were held at gunpoint and almost executed, but, well . . ."

"*Yes?*" Lisa and Kenny say at the same time. They are both concerned.

"They do not register *any* signs of trauma considering what they have just gone through. In fact, they are radiant with love, even glowing ever so slightly in the dark, if you can imagine. It is as if their souls have been to Heaven and are still there. I know that sounds outrageous and hard to understand but—"

"No, it doesn't honey. It doesn't sound outrageous at all." Lisa says cutting, Vi off and smiling with great joy.

Lisa looks at Elli with devotion as if she is seeing an angel.

"In fact," continues Vi, "there is a special kind of healing power that they seem to have. I mean, just being in their presence is like, well, magical!"

Looking whimsically at Lisa and Kenny she says, "It's as if they have been affected in some way by the DNA restructuring of the live Ebola virus. Like *they* have also been genetically restructured and transformed to, well, to the next level of human consciousness, like a metamorphosis of the human soul. I have come up with a name for them, if they don't mind that is. Maybe you can ask them, Mimi, after we leave."

"Sure thing," says Mimi. "What name have you come up with?"

"It's a cross between chrysalis and Essenes, you know the folks from biblical times who were supposed to be healers? And of course, chrysalis is the pupa stage of the transition of a caterpillar to a butterfly. The name is Chrysalenes," says Vi.

"Wow! That's beautiful! Awesome, Vi!" everyone agrees.

"Oh, my goodness," says Mimi, looking at Elli in her arms. "Did you hear that sweetheart? You are a Chrysalene! Do you like that honey?"

"I *LOOOVE* that Gramma! Eve Elli is a *Chrysalene!*" she says with a great big smile on her face.

Mimi is happy but a bit puzzled. "*Eve* Elli?"

"Yes Gramma, my name is Eve Elli."

Vi interjects, "It is the same with all the others. The women are all Eve, plus their first name, and the men are all Adam, plus *their* first name. They also claim to have no last name anymore. Chrysalenes . . . I'm sure we will be learning many new things about them and from them in the days ahead."

"Wow!" says Lisa. "What do the Chrysalenes need from us right now?" she asks Vi.

"They badly need to get bathed and hydrated. Then they will need some food. After that, I guess they will have to tell you themselves," Vi says smiling at everyone.

"Well then," says Kenny. "Perhaps you can bring them in the vans directly to the dwellings in the back. There are quite a few empty ones since we lost so many folks to the Ebola outbreak, either directly or indirectly. That is, many have gone looking for family, just like Mimi here. Only, not so many have reported finding their kin, unfortunately. Still, we have plenty of vacancies as well as large comfortable tents so we hope they will be okay."

"I'm sure they will be," says the Major. "Now, if you good people will excuse us. I wish we could stay and visit for a while, but Vi and I have urgent business to get back to at my father's main plant."

"Thank you, Major, "Mimi calls out, "thank you for all you are doing and all you have done. Once again, I can hardly thank you enough."

Before anyone can say another word, the doors of the vans open and the Chrysalenes slowly emerge. One by one they bow their heads to Lisa and Kenny, who introduce themselves saying, "My new friends, welcome to Bear River Farm. We are honored with your presence and hope you will want to make your home with us. I understand that you are in need of washing up and sustenance. Please come along to the dwellings in the back so we can get you all settled in and comfortable."

One of the Chrysalenes says to Lisa and Kenny, "Thank you both for all of your kindness. It is our pleasure to serve you in whatever ways we can. Thank you, thank you. My name is Adam Nelson. We all heard what you said Miss Vi about calling us Chrysalenes. Speaking on behalf of everyone else, we are all touched and honored to be given such a sacred name. We shall wear it with love and respect for all people of the world and hope that we may be of great service to everyone."

"Thank you," says Vi as she bows low before all of them. "Thank you, Brother and Sister Chrysalenes."

As the Major and Vi bring Mimi and Ryan's things to the dwellings in the back, they find Phil and Suzie of the Seashells just starting their day. They are just being introduced to the Chrysalenes while Kenny and Lisa help them settle into their new dwellings.

"Hello, hello, Brothers and Sisters!" Phil says, greeting them with great honor.

Suzie of the Seashells is excited when she sees Eve Elli and reaches out to her. "Ooo! Ooo!" Suzie exclaims with glee as Eve Elli comes skipping over to her.

"Hi there! I'm Eve Elli," she says to Suzie of the Seashells, gently touching her hands. They share a moment of squeals and giggles together, warming Phil's heart.

"Hello there, Brother Major and Sister Vi!" exclaims Phil with joy. "We are all so happy to see you!"

"Thank you, Phil," says Vi. "I wish we could stay longer but we are on another rescue mission and must be leaving immediately."

"I understand," says Phil, "I shall be sending prayers to the Great Spirit on your behalf."

"Thank *you*," says the Major.

On his way back to the Autovans, he programs three of the vans to leave while telling Lisa and Kenny that they can keep one for emergencies. "Just be sure to keep it well hidden and out of sight," he explains, "You know in case anyone comes around and starts to get suspicious."

Kenny says to him, "We sure do understand that one, Major, and thank you very much!"

The Major and Vi jump into his Autocar and take off.

Lisa, Kenny and Phil all show the Chrysalenes to their new homes. There are several picnic tables set up and Lisa announces that there will be plenty of food brought out to them shortly.

"We shall be along soon to help with the food preparations, ma'am. Bless you and bless the food that you grow on this land. May we be of service to you and to the land, and may we all rejoice in a most abundant harvest!"

* * *

The Major and Vi are just returning to the main headquarters of Howard Pharmaceuticals, arriving not a moment too soon. A unit of commandos with several transport vans arrived only an hour or so ahead of them, and the commandos are pressing forward with a mission that has just been handed down to them from the UC.

The Major asks who is in charge of the operation and is referred to a Slavic Commandant who is barking orders at everyone. He seems to be angrier than the Major would expect, even for a Master Commandant. Trying not to appear too anxious, the Major approaches him.

"Excuse me Master Commandant, I am the Major, son of Master Howard. Do tell me what this is all about, sir, and show me your orders."

"Son of Master Howard! You?"

"Yes sir, that would be me."

"Son of Master Howard, early this morning these dirty slaves, they kill my brother!"

"What are you talking about sir? These people have been here in our custody for the past several days."

"*NYET[7]!*" he yells in a raging fury. "My brother is die! Now *THEY* die!"

"Did that happen here at this plant, Master Commandant?"

The Major is beginning to catch on.

"*NO, IS NOT HERE! Is Silver Beach, Oregon! Why you ask so many questions?!*"

"Oh my! Oh dear, oh dear! I was just up there this morning. Yes! Yes! You are absolutely right sir! I was sent there on a mission to deal with the slaves and when I got there, I discovered their murderous treachery. No sir, we cannot have that! Absolutely not!" the Major says, playing along.

"*You was there? You see Dimitri?*"

"Uh, yes sir, yes. I was there, I see, that is, I saw Dimitri."

Lowering his voice and leaning into the Commandant like he is sharing top secret information, the Major says to him, "I took the

---

[7] *Nyet: Russian for "no."*

treacherous murderers out to a secluded area nearby and shot them all. I have a secret weapon you know. I can order the vans to do whatever I tell them to do and they will do it automatically. So, I had the vans drive out into the ocean with all the bodies. The treacherous ones should all be at the bottom of the ocean floor by now."

The Master Commandant has gone quiet now, listening to the Major spin his yarn.

Seeing that he is on a roll with this, the Major continues, "So I came rushing back here to take care of this lot in the same way. Leave it to me, sir."

Looking square into the eyes of Dimitri's brother, whom Mimi gunned down just before dawn, the Major says to him passionately, "I swear to you on MY LIFE that I will personally deal with these slaves just EXACTLY as I dealt with the slaves in Silver Beach! You have my promise and my word of honor. On your brother's grave, you have my word, Master Commandant!"

He is still and quiet, staring at the Major.

"Oh, there's one more thing, sir. I also heard of a group of treacherous ones in Wyoming who are wreaking havoc. Something about an illegal, contraband hand-held device that is being used for treasonous purposes. The UC just came down with orders for our commandos to shoot and kill on sight when they catch up with the ones who are wielding this evil device. There is even mention about a promotion to becoming a Lord, for the one who retrieves the device and kills the traitors!"

The Master Commandant finally speaks, "Is true? Become a . . . *Lord?*"

"Why yes sir! You just leave these here deceitful ones to me. I'll take care of them just as I've promised you, while you can get going on the *real* prize."

The Master Commandant pauses for a moment, looks around, and then starts barking at his men in Russian.

One of them comes running over to him and shouts, "Alexei!" followed by something in Russian.

As they are about to leave, "Alexei" turns to the Major one more time, "You good man, son of Master Howard."

The Major nods and the commandos take off.

"VIIIIIEEE!" the Major shouts.

She comes running out of her office, *"Whaaat?"*

"GET MOVING, WOMAN!"

"What?"

"Now! I'll tell you in the Autocar!"

"Okay! Okay! Sheesh!"

The Major finds the Managing Overseer and tells him that there has been a change of plans. "The Master Commandant has been called to another assignment and left me in charge of finishing the task at hand with the detainees," says the Major.

"Well, that's a good thing Major," the Managing Overseer says, "'cause these here people are already loaded into the vans and ready to go."

"Most excellent my man, you've done a great job."

"Thank you, sir, thank you."

As the Major and Vi are about to get into his Autocar, he pulls her aside and asks if she can send a message to Judy, through #5, letting her know that they are all on their way with the Chrysalenes.

"Sure thing!" Vi says with a grin. "I'll do that immediately."

"Good," he says, grinning back. "Go get the bird, and then let's get these people and ourselves the heck out of here!"

* * *

Judy is just coming in from her gardening. Her knees are aching and her back is sore, but just as she is about to go inside, she sees another pigeon in the flock.

"Oh my, this is exciting!" she exclaims, "My first message from Operation Monarch! Woo Hoo!" Seeing the new guy with the #5 band and a message attached to it, she reads it immediately:

NEW FRIENDS – INBOUND – BUTTERFLY

Chattering excitedly to the pigeons Judy says, "Oh my! We've got to get ready you guys! Who knows how far away they are! Thank you #5, thank you! And thank you too, Miss Butterfly Vi!" she laughs.

Judy forgets all about her achy knees and sore back and heads straight to the pantry to pull out enough food to feed an army. Since Doc left, for the past several days Judy has been taking out and organizing all of the old tents and supplies that were once used by the farmhands. She never quite got around to getting rid of them and is grateful she still has them. The small dwellings are also still there, although they have not been inhabited much over the years. Just the occasional folks looking for some temporary lodging in exchange for help in the garden. They are a bit dusty but otherwise functional and cozy.

I will get the fruits and vegetables prepared and start baking some bread, Judy says to herself. *Cake and cookies wouldn't be such a bad idea either.*

As Judy is running back and forth from the garden to the kitchen, she sees another pigeon flying overhead, coming in for a landing.

"Oh, my goodness!" she cries heading straight for the loft to meet the new arrival. It is #1 and the message reads:

JUST RETURNED – NEW FRIENDS HERE – BIG DEAL!

"Ha ha! I love it, Doc! Just love your code name!" Judy says out loud, laughing as she reads Doc's message; and thinking to herself, *Thank you for letting me know that you and the new friends have arrived back in Bear River, and that you all are safe and sound.*

* * *

"Hello, hello Doc! Welcome back!"

"Hi there, Lisa. It's *so* good to be back," Doc says with a sigh of relief. "There is so much to tell you, as I'm sure you'll want to fill me in too."

"Absolutely!" Lisa exclaims, "But I'm sure you'll be wanting something to eat after your long journey."

"Oh, yes that *would* be wonderful! Thank you, Lisa! Actually, may I send a message to Judy first? Is #1 available?"

"Sure thing, Doc. Let me go and get him for you."

After Doc sends her message to Judy, the two women go into the kitchen. Lisa starts to fill her in on the miraculous rescue of the Chrysalenes, how happy they are, and how well and quickly they are adjusting to their new home here on the farm.

"Oh Doc!" Lisa declares, "You just wouldn't believe what these people are like! It's like they are above and beyond any kind of human the world has ever known. When Vi and the Major brought them here, Vi said that she was assigned at the Howard Pharmaceutical plant to run tests on them. According to her findings she claims that the genetically altered Ebola bioweapon somehow has changed the DNA structure of these people. I know that sounds completely weird Doc, but—"

"I know," Doc interrupts Lisa, and with a sadness suddenly falling upon her she says, "I have seen them too."

"Wait, *what?* What are you talking about Doc? Where? When?"

"On my way back here from Judy's a few days ago. I stopped in at a small town Center to pick up some supplies and maybe get a bit of news from someone there. Oh Lisa!" Doc begins to cry, "I don't feel like going into all the details right now, but it was horrible."

"That's okay honey, take your time."

Lisa and the others are already hearing rumors of massacres and it is something that no one really wants to believe. And of course, My Buddy gives a completely different story.

Doc catches her breath and continues:

"Lisa, there were about 200 or more of them who arrived from a local Shelter. They all had been neutralized with what *we* know as the Ebola bioweapon and they were well, alive and happy, and having a picnic out in the back garden behind the Center. The joy radiating from their spirit was the most beautiful human sight I have ever seen Lisa, like they were angels or something."

The words catch in Doc's throat as she begins to cry. "And then the commandos came," Doc continues tearfully, "and they drew their guns on the people. The people faced them without any fear, only love as their spirit shown forth with an energy of total compassion. *We forgive you,* they seemed to be saying with their eyes. The commandos opened fire, and they killed them, Lisa! They killed every last one of them! They gunned down the angelic souls!" With a heavy heart, Doc proclaims, "They may have forgiven them Lisa, but Lord help me I am no angel, and *I . . . DO . . . **NOT** . . . FORGIVE THEM!!*"

Doc breaks down in angry wails of sorrow and grief. Lisa comes over to her friend, putting her arms around Doc and comforting her.

After a few moments Lisa says, "My friend, you are now going to see some other beautiful angelic souls; ones who have survived. They are out in the fields."

The warm sun is shining down upon rows of seedlings of tomatoes, zucchini, cucumbers, eggplants, corn and bell peppers. To be sure, it is a beautiful sight for Doc bringing her back to her childhood and the fields of her parents' farm. The green of the seedlings mixed with the fragrances of the earth and the gentle rays of the sun are soothing for her body, mind and spirit.

In the distance she sees people walking slowly through the crops with their hands held out. She is not really sure what they are doing but feels compelled to get a closer look. She can sense that there is something holy going on and that she must tread lightly on this sacred ground. Getting close to one gentleman, Doc decides to ask him what he is doing, although she feels reluctant to disturb him.

Gingerly she speaks to the man, "Pardon me sir, my apologies for disturbing you. My name is Doc, and I was raised on a farm. I am intrigued by what you are doing, if you wouldn't mind telling me about it. Or perhaps you could tell me about it later if you would rather not be disturbed at the moment, um, it's okay," Doc says with a feeble attempt at an awkward smile.

The gentleman beams looking straight into Doc's eyes, holding his hands out to her and saying ever so softly, "Hello my friend Doc; my name is Adam Nelson. I am here to serve you and all of the Lord's bounty here before us. These tomatoes that you see are receiving much goodness from the healthy soil that they are rooted in, as well as the water and sunlight that is nourishing them. And we, their human Sisters and Brothers have our own special gift to give them."

"What *is* our special gift, Adam Nelson?" Doc asks him, already feeling a peace beginning to sooth her soul.

"It is the gift of love, gentle lady. All life on earth can survive with physical nutrients, but to truly thrive and do well, everything and everyone needs to become that which is called love."

"To *become* love?" Doc questions him.

"Yes ma'am. To *be* love. To be the radiance of all knowing, all giving, all flowing, with the Light of the Eternal. To *be* love, my good lady is to be fully in harmony with all that is; to be a mirror of the Light of God in the eyes of another; to know of the Light by coming out of the shadows; to know of life after coming close to death; and remembering that we are all made of pure love by forgetting the falsehood of fear. That, my kind friend is to *become* love, to *be* love, and *to* love. And when we are one with love, we simply *are* love."

Adam Nelson holds his hands out to the budding tomatoes in front of him and continues, "I humble myself before you, Brother Tomato. I sing praises to the purest form of love that you are, as you give your life to sustain the life of another. Thank you, my Brother. Thank you for the nourishment which you will give to the body, mind and soul of a human spirit."

Adam Nelson starts singing to the tomatoes in an angelic voice like Doc has never heard. There are no words, only sweet, enchanting, uplifting tones of joy and peace. Doc lifts her face towards the sun and listens to Adam Nelson sing.

The sunlight kisses her face as she sees the faces before her of those who died in the massacre and hears their gentle voices inside her head saying, *One day, good lady, you **will** learn to forgive them just as we have. Peace be with you, Sister.*

* * *

Angie is sitting out on the veranda of her suite at Kookie's Kastle. She is holding Metatron close to her chest, feeling the presence of Kookie and the struggle that he is going through.

I'm so sorry, she softly whispers to him. *It's okay, my sweet Kookie, we can figure this out together.*

* * *

During the time that Kookie has been away, there has not been much to do around the Kastle. In fact, the Overseer Groundskeeper has been wondering about this unusual feeling of solitude here, thinking that it has been perhaps more quiet than usual. He can't quite make it out, but he knows something is not altogether as it should be. Tending to the flower beds near Angie's veranda the Overseer Groundskeeper notices Angie relaxing on a chaise lounge. As he is watching her, he grins inwardly remembering Kookie's last night there and the tuba playing coming from the young lady's suite.

Well, well what do you know, he thinks to himself, with his grin growing wider. *So that's what My Lord has been playing with!* He begins to chuckle. *Imagine Lord Kookie finding himself a sweet, young thing like that to serenade! Ha Ha!*

Shaking his head, the Overseer Groundskeeper continues with his gardening. But a few minutes later the niggling feeling returns to his gut that something is not quite right here. As he looks up again and begins to scrutinize Angie a bit more carefully, he realizes that she is not in fact, relaxing. She is holding a strange looking black device against her chest and seems to be meditating or praying. Suddenly a red flag goes up inside of the Overseer Groundskeeper. He takes out his own communication device from his pocket and sends out a message, which is accepted almost instantly.

Speaking in Russian:

The incoming voice says, "Privyet, Nikolai!"
"Privyet, Alexei. Where are you?"
"On my way to a place called Wyoming. I just got a tip regarding the device we have been looking for."
"Me too," says Nikolai, "me too."
"What?!" mutters Alexei, surprised and confused.

"Da, da[8] that's right. We must meet now before Lord Kenneth gets back."

"Okay, Nikolai. I'm on my way. Will signal when I arrive at the Kabin."

The two men disconnect and the Overseer Groundskeeper Nikolai retreats quickly to his quarters.

He does not notice when Angie suddenly jumps up and says, "He's here, he's here, my Kookie is back! Be right there, sweetie!"

---

[8] *Da: Russian for "Yes."*

Chapter 18 – Indeed!

ANGIE ENTERS KOOKIE'S WORKSTATION. She looks around, checking all the monitors, consoles and assorted whistles and bells to make sure everything is ready for him. The door opens and Angie skips over to Kookie thoroughly delighted to see him. Kookie has deliberately left his Lord's Communication Device outside the door of his workstation so he feels he is safe from the mole.

"Hi Kookie! Hi! Hi! Hi!" sings Angie, opening her arms for a big bear hug. But when she sees Kookie's dark expression, she approaches him more gently. "Are you okay, sweetie?" she asks.

Kookie holds his arms out to her and pulls Angie snuggly into his chest. She can hear deep sadness in his voice. He whispers, "No. I'm not okay. I'm sorry . . . I'm so sorry."

Kookie begins to cry in Angie's arms.

"My goodness, was it that bad?" she whispers back to him.

Wiping away his tears Kookie says, "Come on over here, Angie. I want to show you something."

He takes her over to the main control panel and turns everything on.

"I tried to offer them a suggestion, one that I could control, you know, with my usual twists and tweaks. Something where no one would actually be harmed, and the Council wouldn't even know what was really happening. My plan was to have them all retreat to their underground Shangri-la thinking that everyone else left above ground was being annihilated in some sort of worldwide catastrophic event. I was going to use the Holographic Imager transmitting to them in their underground world, scenes of mass death and destruction going on above ground. Meanwhile, the people would be free to actually create a new world. By the time the UC came out several years later the people would have taken their own lives back. The UC would then be powerless to exert their mind control and influence anymore.

"It was a good plan, Angie, a very good plan. But I know now that they will never go for it."

"Why not, Kookie?"

"Because two others came up with better ideas than mine; and, Angie, I just don't know how to subvert what they are going to do."

"Maybe not yet, but I believe in you and know that you will think of something else. I also believe that there are others like us who are awakening to the truth."

The study that Kookie has pulled up on the main monitor is showing a series of charts and graphs and statistics that look like a whole lot of gobbledygook to Angie. "Okay, so what does all that mean?" she asks him.

"It means that the ideal form of genocide that was once proposed many, many years ago has never actually been tried; mainly because no one ever figured out a way of pulling it off. Two people proposed two different ideas at the Gathering, which, when combined, I fear might give them the effective genocide they want. And these charts and graphs that you are looking at are the studies to prove it. After the meeting, Yakov, Liling and I got together and did some research. This is what we came up with."

"So, what is this effective form of genocide then?" Angie inquires, while looking at the tangle of statistics. Before Kookie can give her an answer she sees the words, Operation Pied Piper. "Operation Pied Piper? Now *what* in the..." Angie stops herself cold.

"Yes, Angie," Kookie says sadly. "You remember the old fairy tale The Pied Piper of Hamlin?"

"You mean—?" she cannot even speak the words.

Kookie says the words *for* her, "Luring children to their own self-destruction."

"Angie," he continues, "Operation Pied Piper is about creating a pandemic of mass, global suicide."

Angie goes cold as she listens to Kookie describe this indescribable horror.

"They can do it, too. That's what these studies are all about. Yakov and Liling and I checked it out and for this," he says, lowering his voice in despair, "there is no human way on earth with all of our knowledge and technology combined that we would be able to stop them."

Angie is in shock, unable to process what she is seeing and hearing. But one thing she does know as she says shaking her head, "No, Kookie, my sweet friend. *No!* I do not believe they are as powerful as they think they are, or even as *you* seem to think they are. I do *not* believe that we were all put here on this earth to, you know, destroy each other, or ourselves, or that the bad guys are more powerful than the good guys.

"When I was a little girl, I was so afraid of the dark. My mother would always try to comfort me at night and say that there was nothing to be afraid of, that the dawn always came, and the sun would rise in the morning. But during the night it was not much comfort to me. Then, one night when she was trying to console me in my little-girl misery, she brought a candle over to my bedside. When my mother asked me what I saw, I answered her with a bit of sass that it was a lit candle, like she was being weird or something. *And how big is this candle,* she asked me. I showed her with my hands. Then she asked, *And how big is the darkness in this room?* And I can remember holding my outstretched arms wide open, to which she tenderly said to me, *Now then, do you see how the light of this tiny little candle, which is so much smaller than the huge darkness covering the room, is brighter and more powerful than the darkness? Yes mama!* I told her with great relief, and I was never afraid of the darkness again.

"My dear Kookie, the Council and the bad guys of the UC are nothing more than the darkness of night, fearful of their own shadows. Our light is more powerful than their darkness, and I don't give a hang for all the charts, graphs, statistics and fairy tales that you can throw at me. *We* are the ones with the real power, not them. I do believe they know that too, and that is why they are so afraid of us and need to control us or kill us, or both. I also believe in the candle that is lit inside each and every one of us and the power of truth and love which it holds."

Kookie is staring deeply into Angie's eyes and knows that she is right. A flame is growing inside of him too.

Finally, Angie looks at him and says, "Okay partner?"

Smiling softly, Kookie replies, "Okay, partner." As an afterthought, he says, "Angie, you're a smart woman."

"Wow! Thank you! Praise from a Master!"

"Actually, I'm, well, you know," he looks at her and smiles sweetly, "a Lord."

"Oh, give me a break!" She howls with laughter. Kookie chuckles and taps the tips of his fingers together. He is truly pleased with himself.

* * *

Three screens have been activated as PA messages ES and SPA. They accept the transmissions and begin speaking to each other through their Universal Translators.

PA: "Greetings, Brethren of the Highest."

SPA: "Greetings, Highest Brethren."

ES: "Greetings, all powerful Brethren of the most High."

PA: "We have urgent matters to discuss here today and a most serious decision to make."

SPA: "Yes, PA. I concur."

ES: "And I agree with you both, my Brethren."

PA: "As you both listened in on the Gathering that I conducted at the polar location, we need to decide immediately upon a plan of action."

SPA: "Yes, we do."

ES: "I concur."

PA: "What did you both think of the three ideas presented by the Lords and Lady of the Council?"

SPA: "Excellent."

ES: "Yes, truly excellent. However, it seems that there were two ideas presented that are *most* excellent."

SPA: "Yes, yes, I concur: the poisoning of the food and water as well as the frequency disturbance and subliminal programming."

PA: "We came up with a similar idea once before but have not tried it as of yet.

SPA: Yes; I do believe that it was called Operation Pied Piper."

PA: "It was, SPA, yes it was."

ES: "And was it not supposed to be directed at the younger slaves?"

SPA: "Yes, ES, I do believe that it was. In fact, there was some experimentation done to that effect in the past and it was quite effective from what studies have shown."

ES: "Well then, why not direct it at *everyone!*"

PA: "Yes! Excellent, ES! *Most* excellent!"

SPA: "I *thoroughly* concur! In fact, if we combine it with poisoning their food and water, or perhaps simply *drugging* the slaves through the food and water supplies, then we could manipulate them even *more* easily, could we not Brethren?"

ES: "Yes! Yes! We certainly could! Truly the most excellent idea of all, brother SPA!"

PA: "I fully concur! We must pass this down to all of the Lords and Ladies at once!"

SPA: "Yes! Immediately! You know, what I really like most about this idea is that the slaves will think there is something wrong with *them* or with each other, right up until the end. They will never suspect anything! And how convenient it will be for them to do all the killing themselves, or shall I say, *to* themselves."

ES: "Oh, absolutely, SPA! No need to go through all that time and trouble of developing another bioweapon. Especially since the current one has failed so miserably."

PA: "Yes, that is true. Speaking of which have we ever found out who or what is responsible for the failure of the Ebola bioweapon, my Brethren?"

There is a pause as all three of the Highest are thinking about this.

ES: "No, we have not. However, our Lords are still on it. In fact, one of our moles is presently on his way to a meeting to discuss recent findings in the matter."

PA: "Good, because insubordination is something we simply cannot tolerate."

ES: "Agreed, Brother PA."

SPA: "I concur."

PA: "So Brethren, let us adjourn for today and give the orders for Operation Pied Piper to commence."

SPA: "Agreed."

ES: "I concur."

The screens from the three Continental Territories disconnect.

* * *

It is 9:00 p.m. in California, 7:00 a.m. the next morning in the region of Moscow, and noon the next day in the region of Shanghai. In every Center, on every My Buddy Device, Master's Communication Device and Lord's Communication Device in all three Continental Territories throughout One World, the Universal Translators are activated on ALL communication devices of the Masters, Lords, and My Buddy, so that ALL people hear the following message broadcast in their own language:

"Greetings my Dear Ones! Greetings one and all! We have miraculous news for you! It is so wonderful that we are sharing it with all of our children all over the world at the same time. For those of you sleepy heads who are not fully awakened yet, WAKEY WAKEY! Ha ha! And for those of you bone loafers who are thinking of turning in for the night, think again! Ha ha! What is this wonderful, miraculous news? The Ebola outbreak is over my dears! Yes, indeed! Indeed, it is! Isn't that a miracle? Yes, indeed! Indeed, it is!

I want to hear every single one of you good little boys and girls all around the world saying, thank you Council, thank you Lords, and thank you Masters, for making us all safe and sound. Yes, indeed! Wherever you Dear Ones are right now, right in this very moment, stop whatever you are doing, stand up, place your right hand over your heart and say 'thank you my loving Council, thank you my loving Lords, and thank you my loving Masters. Yes, indeed! Thank you from your child--state your name. I promise to be your good and faithful servant, listening to the news and instructions every day and doing all that I am told, so that I may stay happy and healthy. This I promise, yes indeed! Yes, indeed! Yes, indeed!'"

Liling, Yakov and Kookie are listening along with the rest of the world and they bow their heads in shame, knowing what is coming next. Lifting their hearts to Heaven they ask for forgiveness and guidance in the days ahead and how they might somehow be able to stem the tide of the deadliest pandemic yet to come. They each go over the message in their hearts again and again, trying to come up with a way of stopping the terrible genocide that is creeping on all fours, inbound from hell towards the beloved people of One World.

The High Lord Kenneth feels a burdensome weight on his shoulders to come up with a plan. He knows there is no time to lose, but he also knows that a good idea sometimes just has to come in its own time. Lost in his thoughts, Kookie looks at Angie who is peacefully doing what she does best to relax; she is drawing. The thought occurs to him that he must also take a little time for himself and do what *he* does best to relax. He retrieves his tuba.

* * *

It is late in the evening and Judy is about ready to turn in for the night. She has gotten everything ready for her new friends who could arrive anytime. She is so excited by the thought of how special they must be; although, she has yet to learn the full extent of their uniqueness.

She notices My Buddy flashing red. Checking the time, it is 9 p.m., and she thinks to herself, *now what in the world do they want at this hour?* Being out in a remote location, Judy has always felt a certain degree of detachment from the UC and prefers to get her *real news* as she calls it, from the flora and fauna of the natural world around her, including her garden fruits and vegetables. So, it is quite normal for Judy to ignore the flashing red light of My Buddy and continue with her bedtime rituals of closing things down for the night. Just as she is about to climb into bed, there is a stream of light coming down her driveway.

"They're here! Woo Hoo!" Judy shouts out loud, jumping out of bed and rushing to the front door. She opens the door and sees the Major and Vi stepping out of his Autocar with a whole caravan of vans behind them. Judy is overcome with emotion as she dashes out to meet them.

"Oh, my goodness! Hello! I'm so happy to see you all! Welcome!" Judy bubbles with enthusiasm to the Major and Vi. But they appear to be somewhat somber and not as enthused as she is.

"Hi there Judy. Did you not just hear the news?" asks Vi.

"News? No! What news?" she asks a bit worried about the new arrivals. "Are they okay?"

"Oh yes," says the Major, "It's not them. I just heard it on my Master's Communication Device. Did you not get the message on My Buddy?"

"Oh, good heavens, no!" exclaims Judy. "I don't pay much attention to that thing. So, what's the news?"

"It can wait a bit," says Vi. "Let's get these good people settled in first. Shall we?"

"Absolutely!" says Judy.

"I'm sorry we are arriving at this hour. Please let us help you get everything organized so you all can get some rest," says the Major.

"Oh, that's quite alright. Thanks for your help. I think between the empty farmhands' units and all the camping equipment, which I have already prepared, there should be enough to make everyone comfortable. I'm much too excited for bed now, anyway!"

"Oh, and before you meet them," says Vi, "There is something you should know. They have been genetically altered in a very special way, which we will fill you in on later. You will see for yourself as they are not like any other human being. In fact, I came up with a name for them. It is a combination of chrysalis of a butterfly and Essenes. The name is Chrysalene."

"Wow!" exclaims Judy, looking at the vans. The doors open as the Chrysalenes emerge. Holding her arms out to greet them Judy says, "Welcome, dear people, my name is Judy. Welcome to my home."

"Hello Judy, my name is Adam Steve. You are most gracious to receive us at this late hour. Thank you very, very kindly."

"You are very, very welcome, Adam Steve, and *all* of you. Won't you come on around to the back and get settled in? I have prepared some food for you as I'm sure you must all be very hungry."

The Chrysalenes bow to Judy and nod in appreciation of her generosity.

"Most kind, dear lady, most kind," they all chant.

"Not at all, good people. Just follow me and come this way," Judy says as she shows them to their new home.

The Major and Vi are helping prepare the vegetable sandwiches, fruit and tea cakes. Judy asks them, "So what is this news about?"

"It was a message from a Communications Overseer," says Vi, "You know, one of those annoying, *Greetings my children,* things."

"Only this one was very eerie," the Major interjects, "Like when they are sugar-coating a mind control message. And this one definitely has a foreboding ring to it."

"Whatever did he say?" asks Judy.

"He said that the Ebola pandemic is over," continues the Major, "and how thankful we should all be to our great and wonderful UC. But it was the *way* he said it, Judy, that was so weird. He had everyone swear fealty to the UC in a way which I have never quite heard before. Honestly, it sounded more like a threat, or I don't know my kinsmen."

"Good grief!" exclaims Judy. "That does sound ominous!"

"Yes, it does," Vi sadly agrees. "I can feel it in my guts. Something is very, very wrong. And we must all keep alert and stay wide awake to whatever it is that is about to come down."

"Notice if anything happens out of the ordinary," says the Major. "Pay special attention to anything, you know, unexpected. Especially if it is something you are being asked or told to do."

"Okay. I sure will."

For a fleeting moment Judy considers what she heard today at the local Center Market, but her thoughts are interrupted when the Chrysalenes enter the cottage.

"If you please ma'am, may we help you serve the food?" asks the Chrysalene, Eve Jennie. "There are so many of us and it is far too much work for the three of you."

Before Judy has a chance to say anything there are several people crowding into the kitchen bringing the sandwiches, fruit and tea cakes out to the table. Most of the folks are comfortably seated on the floor, laughing and chattering amongst themselves as if they hadn't a care in the world. It warms Judy's heart, as well as Vi's and the Major's, to watch them interact with each other and experience their energy of joy, love and laughter. As they all break bread together, Judy addresses everyone:

"Thank you one and all for the honor you bestow upon this humble home. May we all enjoy a renewal of life here in the days to come, as we are now told that the Ebola outbreak is over. I certainly will need plenty of help on the farm, getting things going again!" Judy laughs, as everyone joins her joyous energy.

"Thank you, Sister Judy, thank you!" they respond.

"In fact, "Judy continues, "I was out getting supplies at the local Center Market today in preparation for your arrival," sounds of cheerful chatter permeate the cottage, "including lots and lots of seeds for us to plant together. And wouldn't you know it, they were all out! Now *that's* a new one on me. In all my years of living and being a farmer, I never saw *that* happen before!"

"Dear oh dear!" they all laugh.

"*'But not to worry,'* the Center Overseer told me, because I was shocked and asked him what was going on. *'We'll have a whole new batch of seeds in tomorrow. In fact, they will be better than anything else you folks have ever planted before. Something brand new! I'm sure looking forward to your harvest this year!'* he went on to say. And—"

But before Judy can finish her sentence, she is startled by the Center Overseer's words she has just repeated. She is thinking about what the Major just said about paying particular attention to something unexpected. Judy, The Major and Vi stare at each other with the same worried expression.

* * *

"Hello, hello, my children! Greetings to one an all in Panamerica, Euroslavica and Sinopacifica, on this wonderful, wonderful day! My, oh my, it certainly is a MOST wonderful day, isn't it dear ones! Yes indeed, it is! Yes indeed, yes, indeed. And I do have the most wonderful news for you all on this wonderful day. Yes indeed! On this very day, your local Center Market is going to start procuring brand new fruit and veggie seeds to you Dear Ones. The Council who cares for you so much has discovered that it was the old seeds which caused the Ebola outbreak! My goodness! Bad seeds! Naughty seeds! So, they are all gone now, and you will be able to obtain brand new, safe seeds which have been made even healthier than ever. Just for you, Dear Ones. That is how much the Council loves you! So be sure to say thank you today. Thank you, my Masters, thank you my Lords, and thank you my Council. Thank you for loving me and taking care of me. I am forever your child- - state your name."

The Communications Overseer has finished his day's message and turns to his Lord.

Speaking in Chinese, the Communications Overseer asks, "How was that, My Lord Ekene?"

"Excellent, Communications Overseer. Truly excellent," Lord Ekene replies. "Your fealty is duly noted and appreciated."

"Thank you, Lord Ekene. Thank you, sir. Is there anything else I can do for you?"

"Yes, there is. You can help me put the finishing touches on this program. I think I've got it, but a test run with you would be most helpful."

"Absolutely, My Lord Ekene. Anything to be of service to you, sir."

"Good man. Now just sit down on that chair over there by the open window. There is a little tea cake with some juice on the table that we are trying out as a new treat to serve up at the Coffeehouses. So do eat and drink that and let me know what you think."

"OOO! It is *very* yummy My Lord! Truly yummy!" the Communications Overseer exclaims as he scarfs down the tea cake and juice."

"Excellent, Overseer. Now put on those headphones on the table, sit back and relax."

Lord Ekene turns a couple of knobs on his console and makes a few minor adjustments to the inaudible level of subliminal static and 440 hertz pulsating under some soft music.

Okay, he thinks to himself, *now let's see what happens.*

The Communications Overseer hears the music playing, appearing to be comfortable and relaxed.

So far so good, Lord Ekene thinks to himself.

He turns up the static, just a trace, not quite within hearing range.

The Overseer looks around for a moment in a state of confusion, but after a few moments, closes his eyes and appears to be trying to relax to the music again. His face is showing slight signs of emotional strain, but nothing significant.

Gradually Lord Ekene turns the static up higher, a little bit at a time, *not* within the Communications Overseer's hearing range. The man's signs of emotional discomfort increase exponentially; his body tenses up, his face contorts, and he begins to tremble.

Yes, very good, Lord Ekene thinks.

Finally, he turns the static up to where the Overseer can actually hear the static.

The Overseer makes a face and just laughs, saying, "Well now, is that what you wanted me to listen to?" He appears to be more relaxed again, just showing minor discomfort at the audible static.

"We are not quite done yet," says Lord Ekene smiling at the Overseer.

The music has no static now and is still playing softly. Once again, the Communications Overseer sits back, closes his eyes and folds his arms across his chest, appearing to be very relaxed.

Lord Ekene reaches for another knob now and turns it up. It is the same music which has been playing a moment ago, but this is a different version which is tuned to a stronger pulsation of 440 hertz.

There are still no visible signs of change in the appearance and behavior of the Communications Overseer.

Good, and now for the grand finale, Lord Ekene thinks.

He turns up another knob with an inaudible, subliminal recording of a single word, combined with the music still playing. The word is, "INDEED." It is spoken as a continuous chant with a steady beat, followed by an intermittent beat, followed by a mixture of steady beat and intermittent beat: INDEED . . . INDEED . . . INDEED . . . and INDEED, INDEED . . . INDEED, INDEED, INDEED . . . INDEED . . . INDEED, INDEED, and so on.

Lord Ekene is watching for signs of discomfort coming from the Communications Overseer. To his delight the discomfort is beginning to vary greatly. Then, he adds a prerecorded subliminal message, and the effects are instantaneous and dramatic. Lord Ekene is now blasting the Communications Overseer with a high subliminal level of static and a steady beat of subliminal "INDEED" combined with a stronger pulse of 440 hertz and the pre-recorded message.

In addition to all that, the tea cake and juice which the Communications Overseer consumed have been laced with added toxic ingredients. The drugs are now kicking in. Low and behold, the Overseer is in tears.

"What's wrong Overseer?" asks Lord Ekene.

"I, I don't know sir."

"INDEED!" says Lord Ekene, in a sharp tone of voice.

Suddenly the Communications Overseer screams at Lord Ekene like a wild man, "MAKE IT STOP! MAKE IT STOP! WHAT IS HAPPENING? OH NO! MAKE IT STOP!"

Lord Ekene turns everything off and tells the Overseer to remove his headphones. "There you are, Communications Overseer. All better now?"

But he is still shaking with terror and sobbing heavily.

Lord Ekene says, "Well then my good man. What are we to do with you?"

"I don't know, My Lord, I just don't know."

"Are you feeling hopeless?"

"Yes," his sobbing is getting heavier.

"Are you feeling like you just want to end it all?"

"*YES! YES! Oh, please help me. HELP ME!*

Suddenly, Lord Ekene's demeanor changes. With an ice-cold stare and cold-blooded voice, he speaks out loud part of the pre-recorded message that the Communications Overseer has been listening to subliminally.

"Now you listen to me, you worthless piece of human trash. There *IS—NO—HOPE—FOR—YOU! DO YOU UNDERSTAND ME! NO HOPE. NO HOPE. NO HOPE!*"

The Communications Overseer starts to scream again throwing himself against the wall.

With one final blow, Lord Ekene turns his bloodlust against a fellow human being.

"See that open window over there? *THAT IS YOUR ONLY HOPE, SLAVE! JUMP!*"

The Overseer runs over to the open window and jumps out.

Lord Ekene activates his Lord's Communication Device and sends out a communication request. It is accepted. A blank screen is activated, and SPA's voice come on:

"Yes, my Lord Ekene. Do you have any news for me?"

"Yes, Your Highest. The Pied Piper weapon has just been successfully tested. It is fully functional and ready to go."

"Excellent my trusted and faithful Lord! Most excellent! Well done, my son, well done."

"Thank you, my father SPA, most High."

The communication is terminated.

$* * *$

Out in the sunny fields, the Monarchs are singing to the seedlings and the hearts of all human creatures, everywhere:

Wakanjeja, sacred child,
Be still and have no fear.
You may not see, or feel my arms,
But always I Am here.
You may not know or hear my voice,
But always I Am calling,
Softly whispering words of hope
Into your heart belonging.
Look deep within and you will see,
A Flame that's burning strong.
I Am the Light within your soul;
I Am your sacred song.

To be continued...

MONARCH RISING

Book 2

GATHER

Acknowledgements

So many thanks go out from my heart to all of you who have inspired the characters in this book. Though your names and true stories have been changed, your spirits are very much alive, breathing life into the *human creatures* of these pages.

Thank you, Leanne Sype, for your magnificent editing, constant support, and incredible patience. Thank you for your encouragement and your willingness to listen while I kvetch.

Thank you, Wendy C. Garfinkle, for your incredible gift of book interior design; and for sharing a few good laughs.

Thank you, Taylor Dawn at Sweet 15 Designs, for creating such a gorgeous design and final cover from my concept, and for your patience with my numerous tweaks and modifications.

Thank you, Glenda Nowakowski and Lea Olivares Raudes, for taking the time to read through the manuscript and come up with very wonderful tips and suggestions.

Thank you, Pooja Lama, of the UPS Store in Sherwood, OR, for your enthusiasm and support in helping me to print out those preliminary pages of my manuscript. It has been a joy working with you.

Last but not least, thanks to all of the gracious baristas at the Starbucks in Sherwood, Oregon. You guys always made me feel so welcome, treating me like a princess, as I pounded out this book in front of you day after day.

About the Author

Sylvana C. Candela, L.Ac. MATCM, licensed acupuncturist, Master of Acupuncture and Traditional Chinese Medicine, resides in Sherwood, Oregon. She has supervised in community acupuncture clinics in Los Angeles, California, including Samra University and Yo San University of Traditional Chinese Medicine.

She received her bachelor's degree in special education from Queens College of the City University of New York, and taught children with autism at the Sybil Elgar School in London, England.

Sylvana has five children and six grandchildren.

She is the author of *Gently Heal Thyself: Healing the Soul with Energy Medicine*.

Monarch Rising: Awaken is her first novel.

Printed in the USA
CPSIA information can be obtained
at www.ICGtesting.com
LVHW021114090923
757737LV00048B/832